QUARTER

ALSO BY JULIA GOLDING

The Darcie Lock novels
Ringmaster

The Cat Royal books
The Diamond of Drury Lane
Cat among the Pigeons
Den of Thieves
Cat O' Nine Tails
Black Heart of Jamaica

The Companions Quartet
Secret of the Sirens
The Gorgon's Gaze
Mines of the Minotaur
The Chimera's Curse

The Ship Between the Worlds

EMPTY QUARTER

JULIA GOLDING

EGMONT

EGMONT

We bring stories to life

First published 2008
by Egmont UK Ltd
239 Kensington High Street, London W8 6SA

Text copyright © 2008 Julia Golding
Cover illustration copyright © 2008 Symbolon

The moral rights of the author and cover illustrator have
been asserted

ISBN 978 1 4052 2819 0

1 3 5 7 9 10 8 6 4 2

www.egmont.co.uk
www.juliagolding.co.uk

A CIP catalogue record for this title is available from
the British Library

Typeset by Avon DataSet Ltd, Bidford on Avon, Warwickshire
Printed and bound in Great Britain by the CPI Group

For my sister, Jane

Michael Lock exited Vauxhall underground station with a strong desire to kill his father. He considered his options: bullet, bare hands, the rolled umbrella he carried at his side, but none seemed satisfactory. No commuters heading into London that morning would have guessed the sober-looking man they passed on the escalator was harbouring such murderous thoughts. But then, none of them had recently emerged from captivity to find that their daughter's life had been risked by MI6. How could they understand the anger that filled Michael when he discovered that the operation had all been sanctioned by his own father?

A grandfather should know better than to put his granddaughter into a highly volatile situation, Michael thought bitterly. It didn't matter that he had believed it was the only way to save his son – it was still

1

inexcusable. How dare he play games with Darcie's life!

In the draughty far reaches of the underpass, Michael walked by the beggar who made a living shuffle-dancing to music from a battered stereo, and threw him a coin. It had become an almost superstitious ritual with him – something he did every time he came to the headquarters of the Secret Services. He emerged on to the pavement. The home of MI6 looked as if it had been made out of huge cream-coloured Lego bricks. It made no attempt to appear either secret or at anyone's service: it squatted on the massive Vauxhall Cross junction, the front commanding a position on the Thames with a view of Westminster Palace and the Tate Britain art gallery; its rear looking down on queues of traffic, passing trains and distinctly dodgy pubs. Power and culture backed up by ugliness and brutality – not a bad summary of the job carried out by the spies.

Michael had followed his father into the family profession, thinking that spying was a necessary evil. He had been proud of the personal sacrifices he had made to protect British interests. That was until the sacrifice had been far too personal – his own daughter. He was no longer proud; he was angry.

'Good morning, Mr Lock,' said the security guard as Michael swiped his pass across the reader. Michael automatically surrendered his umbrella to be checked through the detector while he entered one of the glass cylinders. As soon as his foot touched the pressure pad, the door slid closed behind him, leaving him for a fraction of a second in the transparent tube while the sensors scanned him. Then a door opened in front and he stepped into the lobby, retrieving his umbrella.

'Not seen you for some time, sir,' said the guard, an old hand who knew all the faces.

'Not for a year or so, Derek,' Michael acknowledged.

The guard knew better than to ask what he had been doing. 'The old man's office is on the third floor now,' he said, gesturing towards the bank of lifts. 'Lovely view.'

'Thank you.'

Michael rehearsed all the speeches he had had time

to plan on the plane to London: largely, what had Christopher Lock been thinking when he had sent his only granddaughter into a nest of arms smugglers? The words in his head reached a crescendo as he knocked on the door – no title, just a number: 310.

'Come,' a deep voice barked from inside.

Michael opened the door, having an unwanted flashback to the days when he had to enter his father's study at home to own up to some misdemeanour or failure at school. Well, it was not him who was in trouble now.

'Ah, Michael, it is wonderful to see you alive and well!' Christopher Lock rose and held out his hand, his voice smooth and genial. Michael hesitated then shook it, noting that his father had lost none of his vigour and that his hair had reached a perfect shade of white. Trust Christopher Lock to draw the lucky straw in the ageing game. People no doubt now described him as 'a distinguished English gentleman', not knowing the cad within.

'Michael, you must be furious with me – I

completely and utterly understand. No doubt Ginnie is sticking pins into a wax image of me even now. You both have every reason to hate me.'

'We want to know –' Michael began, but his father cut across him.

'But I can put up with that because it is enough for me that you are alive. Hate me for saying it if you wish, but I'm proud of my granddaughter – proud she's carrying on the best traditions of the family.'

'We are very proud of Darcie too. But that doesn't change the fact that –'

'The operation has given a tremendous boost to the department – the prime minister was delighted, even the Palace was singing our praises for once – we are all in her debt. Please do take a seat. Of course, you're proud. You're the parents of the youngest ever spy to be recruited and already she's far more successful than many who are reaching the end of their careers.'

Michael saw a tiny gap in his father's flow of conversation and took it. 'That's just it: Darcie is not a spy. She's a fourteen-year-old girl who should be at school.

Instead, she's on the run, worried that an assassin might finally catch up with her.'

Christopher Lock tutted. 'Oh, she mustn't worry about that. All she need do is keep her head down for a few years. Madame Tsui's bound to be killed by a rival or caught by the police before long – it's only a matter of time.'

'You don't know Madame Tsui.' Michael had uncomfortably close knowledge of the Hong Kong woman's ruthlessness and intelligence. Her cover as a fashion designer had masked a far-reaching empire trafficking all illegal substances known to man.

'Michael, you mustn't worry – these criminal types are all the same, usually destroyed by their own minions once they get a hint of weakness; and Darcie certainly showed everyone how feeble Madame Tsui is.'

Michael knew his father wasn't going to get it. It was hopeless to try, but he had to anyway.

'Look, sir –'

'Are you here as my son or my employee?' asked Christopher sharply. Over the years, he had refined the habit of pulling the rug out from under people – regarding each conversation as a battle to take the upper hand. 'If the latter, then we should discuss events purely from the operational perspective and in the presence of your line-manager. If you wish to raise any other, shall we say, more personal matters, then perhaps you might like to remember that you normally address me as "Father". I like to maintain the distinction so that I am not guilty of partiality in work-related affairs.'

Michael wanted to yell with frustration. He restrained himself with difficulty. He also had been trained not to let emotion get the better of him.

'But that's just it, Father, you did let personal feelings influence your judgement. Would you have risked a teenager for any other field operative?'

Christopher stroked his chin, giving the question considered thought. 'Possibly not – but since it's been so successful, I might in future.'

'But Darcie is just a child! At least I had a choice when I left university as to whether or not I was going to follow in your footsteps; Darcie had no say – no choice. It might have made it easier for you that you've not seen her for years, but you know full well you nearly killed her. At one stage I honestly believed she *was* dead and I had survived: if that had been the case I really would have murdered you when I came in here this morning.'

'Michael, patricide is not recommended,' Christopher commented drily. 'The Greeks had a few things to say about the horrors of revenge for that crime.'

'Father, stop talking about the damned classics and listen to me! You're not to use Darcie ever again, you understand? She's to be allowed to salvage what little is left of a normal childhood in peace and quiet.'

Christopher poured two glasses of mineral water, offering one to his son. It was refused. 'So she won't be living with you then? That is, unless you also came to hand in your resignation today?'

Michael fell silent. He had considered doing just that until Ginnie reminded him that the bills would keep on coming and they had Darcie to support.

'So, are you resigning?'

'No.' Michael felt his position weaken as he made this admission. 'I'm discussing a new posting with personnel – somewhere no one will make a connection with Kenya.'

Christopher had known this already, of course. As Director of Regional Affairs, it was his job to keep tabs on all his operational agents.

'It'll be hard to find a place where both you and Ginnie can work. The CIA and MI6 do not usually cooperate as harmoniously as you two do in your marriage.'

This was a subtle reminder that Michael should not have married his CIA partner, let alone have a child together.

'We know.'

'Perhaps, while you are sorting out all this, it might be a good idea to give Darcie a little break – call it a reward for her hard work.'

'Oh?' Michael was instantly suspicious.

'We can't pay her, of course, but the PM was anxious

9

that her service to her country be recognised in some way. He suggested it actually, being very fond of the place himself.'

'Fond of what place?'

'The southern Mediterranean. He mentioned to me that a friend of his was sending his daughter on a very exclusive cruise aimed at young people – a modern version of the Grand Tour. A finishing school on water. We thought it would be a wonderful way to repay Darcie, and would have the added advantage of giving her time to recuperate while you and Ginnie sort out your future.'

Michael searched for the hitch. 'How long does it last?'

'A month. She can meet the boat in Naples at the beginning of August and she can be back with you wherever you are in September, ready for the new school year.'

'And it's just a holiday?'

'It's more than that: a life-changing cultural experience – pyramids, the Nile, tombs. I rather fancy it myself, but apparently I'm too old.'

'You can do it when you retire, Father – very soon now, thank goodness.'

Christopher chose to ignore the barb.

'So what do you think, Michael? Will it appeal to my granddaughter?'

'It might. I'll ask when I next speak to her.'

'In Paris now, isn't she?'

Michael nodded.

'Shopping with Mother?'

'Not if Darcie has a say in the matter, but she's still in a wheelchair after having been caught in the explosion in Nairobi – mending well but she still has a way to go. Sometimes I think Ginnie believes a little retail therapy cures anything.' Michael allowed himself a wry smile.

'So my little Darcie doesn't like shopping.' Christopher seemed very pleased to hear this.

Michael immediately regretted letting down the barrier he'd tried to erect between his family and Christopher. 'She's not yours, Father, and no, she doesn't like it. She's a tomboy. You didn't know that either, did you? Not surprising since you've not seen her since her christening.'

'And whose fault is that, Michael?' Christopher gazed out at the choppy water of the Thames. If Michael had not known him better, he would have said his father was wistful.

'I can't help it that Ginnie's never trusted you – and, to be frank, the events of the past weeks have proved her to be right.' Michael rose. 'I'll let you know about the holiday idea. It does sound like the kind of escape that Darcie needs right now.'

'Good. I hoped you'd think so.'

Michael Lock showed himself out. His father sat down at his desk with a contented smile. It had gone well. He had known exactly how to handle his son – he would hardly be where he was today if he hadn't been able to manipulate those around him. He drew Darcie Lock's personnel file from his desk drawer. Michael thought that his father knew very little about Darcie, but in fact he had made a careful study of her

12

over the past months. He had learned all about her love of sport, particularly football and fencing, her friendships, even her adoption as mascot by the SAS team who had so spectacularly failed in their attempt to rescue her – partly because she had rescued herself first. He now took an ink pen and noted in the margin: *dislikes* shopping. He rang his secretary for his morning coffee, well satisfied with the way things on this operation were progressing. It was wonderful how Darcie's reward – for he was convinced it would be first and foremost an interesting holiday – also served a second purpose of a little light spying on a very sensitive target. Two intelligence agencies happy; his granddaughter content; and a certain young person kept out of mischief. Yes, Darcie would be perfect. Just the right girl for the job.

'I'll have the sushi platter and my daughter will take the grill.' Ginnie Lock folded the menu decisively and handed it to the Japanese waitress. 'We'll both take the green tea.'

Darcie stared out over the rooftops of Paris from the restaurant at the top of Galeries Lafayette, a grand department store in the Opera Quarter. In the distance she could see the black spike of the Eiffel Tower in the rainy July skies. Pigeons circled looking for somewhere to rest but all the ledges were studded with long spikes to keep them away.

'You OK, darling?' asked Ginnie. Dressed in a chocolate brown trouser suit, she gave the impression of effortless elegance. Her shoulder-length black hair was slicked back behind her ears. 'Your neck not hurting you?'

Darcie shook her head. In some ways she looked very like her mother – same hair, same tall, slim build. But Darcie's hair was bunched back in a scruffy ponytail and she was wearing a Chelsea football shirt and tracksuit trousers – the antithesis of smart. 'My neck's fine. I could have ordered myself, you know.'

'Didn't you want the grill? I thought you disliked raw fish.'

'The grill's fine. It's just that you keep treating me like a baby.'

Ginnie bit her tongue. She was finding this so hard. To her, Darcie *was* her baby: one who had just been through a terrible ordeal, leaving her in a wheelchair for six weeks and with scars she would bear for life.

'Sorry, sweetheart. I'll remember next time.'

You won't, Darcie thought sullenly. Her mom knew she hated shopping but this morning, when Darcie had asked to go to the Louvre, Ginnie had taken one look at the queue and somehow they had ended up here instead. If Mom was going to put her through this trial, it was about time Darcie asked the difficult questions she had been saving up.

'Why did you do it, Mom?'

'I said I was sorry. You can order for me next time.'

'I don't mean the menu. I mean why did you decide to do what you do?'

Ginnie went quiet and instinctively glanced at the mirror behind Darcie's head, checking to see if they could be overheard.

'I joined because I am a patriot. Your dad is too, in his own way.'

'But why join the –?'

Ginnie held up her finger, preventing Darcie from saying 'CIA' – Central Intelligence Agency.

'Why not the army? Politics? I don't know – there must be hundreds of ways of serving your country.'

'Our country, Darcie. You're half-American too, don't you forget.'

The waitress appeared and poured them both a cup of pale, scented tea. They paused until she moved away.

'Why choose a life where everything is a lie?'

Ginnie raised her eyebrows in surprise. 'It's not all lies: it's about finding out the truth.'

'But you have to live a lie, lie to your friends, lie to your family.'

Ginnie sighed. 'I'm sorry, Darcie. Yes, we did lie to you. We're *both* sorry. But think, what *could* we tell you? You were too young to be trusted with the truth.'

'But you made my whole life false too!' Darcie could feel her anger rising. 'I've no idea where you really come from, what schools you went to, even what your real surname is. In Nairobi, you acted like an all-American desperate housewife; sitting here, you're chic and smart. Which is the real you?'

'Not so loud, please,' Ginnie said in a low voice. 'And you mustn't mention that place again.'

'What? Nairobi? Mustn't mention the city I grew up in, made friends, went to school? This is ridiculous!'

'No, you know you mustn't – for your own safety. This attitude is exactly why we didn't tell you anything.'

The waitress returned and placed the wooden boards bearing their meal in front of them, as well as two packets of chopsticks.

'My daughter will have a fork, please,' said Ginnie with a polite smile.

'No, she will not,' Darcie snapped. 'She will use the chopsticks, thank you.'

The waitress gave a puzzled nod and backed away. Ginnie sighed again.

'I was looking forward to spending some time with you, Darcie, getting to know each other properly.'

'Help yourself – here I am. But which "you" do you want me to get to know, Mom?'

Darcie knew she was being rude, but she couldn't help herself. She wanted to punish her parents for lying to her. Part of her understood why they had done so, but this didn't change the fact that she hated that they'd kept the truth from her all these years. What she wanted – what she couldn't have – were two *normal* parents with two *normal* jobs.

Ginnie ignored the dig. 'Look, darling, I know you

must still be shaken by what you went through. It'll take a long time to get over it.'

'Mom, why are you turning this into a problem about me? The problem is you and Dad leading the kind of lives you do.'

'This sushi's lovely. How's the grill?'

'Don't change the subject, Mom.'

Ginnie put down her chopsticks. Her grey-green eyes were steely. Darcie suddenly understood how her mother might be good at her job.

'OK, Darcie, you want to hear it straight? We are both proud to work for our governments. They pay us for doing so. We feed and clothe you with that money. You are angry because you've just had a confrontation with the unpleasant reality we are trying to protect others from. That should never have happened, but it has. You're also angry because you're fourteen and there are all sorts of hormones and teenage stuff happening to you that makes you despise your parents – that's natural.'

'I don't despise you,' Darcie muttered.

'I'm pleased to hear it. But this is how it is for our family. Part of it stinks, part of it is good – you can't have one without the other. Try and understand how your father and I see things, please. Don't be so selfish.'

Darcie had lost her appetite. She fiddled with her chopsticks, conscious that her left arm was itching in its cast. She couldn't wait for it to be taken off. Was she selfish? People had spent the last few weeks telling her how brave and selfless she had been to try and save her dad, now her mom was accusing her of being the opposite. She pushed her food around her plate, as if trying to rearrange it in a more pleasing pattern. Ginnie despatched her own meal with elegant precision, taking small sips of tea between bites. Finally, Darcie gave up on hers and put the chopsticks down.

'I'll try and see it your way, Mom, but do you ever see things from my point of view?'

'Of course I do, sweetheart.' Ginnie signalled for the bill. If she noted her daughter's uneaten meal, she said nothing about it.

'So why did you bring me shopping?'

Ginnie wheeled her daughter to the floor below.

'There's a couple of dresses I just want to have a quick look at,' she explained a little guiltily.

Darcie subsided into resentful silence as her mom held the clothes up against herself, frowning with concentration. Ginnie knew better than to ask her daughter's opinion. A shop assistant came over and engaged her in a rapid conversation in French. They both became increasingly animated as they searched the rails for the perfect outfit, completely at one in that all-important task.

Darcie hated feeling so helpless and bored. She rolled herself to the rail so she could admire the stained glass dome that arched over the central atrium of the store. The colours were wonderful – she may have missed out on the Mona Lisa, but at least she had this to appreciate.

'Out of my way, moron!' a loud American voice bellowed behind her. Darcie turned in her chair to see a spiky-haired girl on rollerblades heading straight towards her. The rollerblader was wearing a black T-shirt with 'Hell's Belle' written across the front and shorts made from cut-down jeans. Behind her ran a flock of people, led by two furious guys with ear-pieces and gun holsters showing under their flapping jackets.

Darcie had nowhere to go – she was hard up against the balcony rail – and if she backed up she'd collide with a display of swimming costumes. The girl was not slowing. The rollerblader was now close enough for Darcie to see that her eyebrow was pierced, as was her nose. She yelled at Darcie again, displaying a stud in her tongue. Putting her good arm protectively over her broken one, Darcie braced herself for the impact. At the last moment, the girl swerved behind the chair, knocking over the bikini-clad dummies, and continued round the balcony. The two security men bumped past Darcie, followed by a bunch of men with cameras. Last to arrive was Ginnie. She rescued the wheelchair and pulled it out of the gangway.

'You OK?'

Before Darcie could answer, there was a scream and a crash from the other side of the shop floor. Flash bulbs went off like flickering lightning.

'Let's get out of here before they ask you for an interview,' Ginnie said swiftly.

'What?'

'Didn't you recognise her?'

'That mad girl on rollerblades? I was too busy trying to stop more limbs being broken to think about it.'

'That was our president's beloved youngest daughter.' Ginnie stabbed the button for the lift. 'Shelly Morris. The press would love to interview the wheelchair victim she almost crushed, believe me. And the last place we want your face is in the international news.'

The lift doors slid open.

'Is she normally like that?' Darcie asked. She was intrigued: she hadn't expected presidential daughters to look and behave so outrageously. She'd only ever seen them in dinky suits standing respectfully behind their fathers on the podium as part of carefully stage-managed national events.

Ginnie selected the ground floor.

'Uh-huh, the original wild child. According to the *New York Times*, she's been sent to Europe to get her out of the way while her father faces re-election. She doesn't quite fit into his idea of the perfect family.'

Darcie grinned. 'Hey, Mom, you might be disappointed in having me as a daughter, but at least you didn't get one of those.'

Ginnie kissed her on the cheek. 'I'm not disappointed, darling; I have never been disappointed. Now, where was it we were going? The Louvre should be quieter in the afternoon. Let's go see if the Mona Lisa is worth the hype.'

3

'There we are – as good as new,' said the doctor, cutting off the last piece of cast.

Darcie flexed her leg experimentally. It looked very pale after being in plaster for six weeks. No more wheelchair; no more itchy cast: heaven.

'When I say new, I really meant that it will be once the muscle tone is restored. Keep exercising it gently.' The doctor got up to throw the remains of the cast away. 'No high-impact sports for a bit. Still, I don't suppose you play rugby like many of my other patients.' He turned to smile at the girl sitting in the consulting chair. The army didn't usually send him children to treat; his normal bill of fare was to patch up soldiers home from Iraq and Afghanistan. Everything to do with this patient was all very hush-hush, according to the CO, but he couldn't help wonder how she'd come by her injuries.

'Actually, I play football,' said Darcie.

'You'll be fit by the time the new season starts. Who do you support?'

'Chelsea – and the Boston Breakers.'

'I've heard of the first, though I'm an Arsenal man myself, but who are the others?'

'An American team – they're in the women's soccer league.'

'The good news is that the leg won't stop you playing for them one day if you're good enough. Take it slowly and you'll be back on top form.'

Ginnie and Michael were both waiting when she came out. They had respected her wish to go in alone but immediately rushed to her side when she emerged to help her along like two living crutches.

'I'm OK. Everything works.' She waggled her arm and leg to prove it.

'Wonderful. Let's go for a pizza to celebrate,' suggested Michael.

'Since when did you eat pizza, Dad?' Darcie asked in amazement, looking at her sports-jacketed father with his neat moustache. He would be more at home in a country pub or a Michelin-starred restaurant.

'I thought you'd prefer it to pickled cabbage and beer.'

'I do.'

'Don't we all,' muttered Ginnie.

'Let's go then.' Michael jingled the car keys. 'I thought, Darcie, we could all have a look at the route your cruise ship is taking. Remember me once telling you the legend of the curse of Tutankhamen? You'll get to see his tomb in the Valley of the Kings. And, I've brought you a few more books on Egypt to tell you about the other sights you'll see.'

When Darcie got back to her room, she dumped the travel books on the bed, her mind full of the exciting places she was going to visit. Dad had turned up trumps with his purchases, as well as displaying a rarely glimpsed lighter side by throwing in *Death on the Nile* by Agatha Christie.

A knock on the door. Darcie opened it to find a young soldier outside.

'Yes?'

'Miss Lock?'

She nodded.

'This came for you in the army postbag today.' He passed her a heavy suitcase. 'It's been checked. Nothing to worry about.'

Thanking him, she shut the door and put the case on the bed. It was a Louis Vuitton in red leather of the kind she'd seen on the trolleys of supermodels as they swanned their way through airports in front of the world's paparazzi. A manila label was tied to the handle.

For my granddaughter.

What was this? She didn't know that she even had a grandfather! Quickly, she opened up the case. Inside was another note, this one written on pale blue paper.

> *Dear Darcie,*
> *My old friend, Gladys Smith, asked me to send*
> *on some things you left behind in Kenya. I also*

enclose a little gift of my own. I don't suppose
your parents will be pleased, but what are
grandfathers for if not to lead the younger
generation astray?
With love,
Christopher Lock
P.S. I look forward to meeting you at long last
when you are next in London.

That was it.

The first communication she'd ever had from a grandfather she'd never met and he'd written so little! Not a word about himself – apart from the fact that he was friends with her old MI6 mentor from Nairobi, Gladys Smith. That was not so surprising as the one thing Darcie did know was that Gladys was a family friend and had acted as godmother at her christening.

She delved deeper into the case and found all the things that had survived from her first mission – phone, camouflage jacket, penknife, headband with its microphone, her specially adapted little black dress.

She was surprised that Gladys had made such a sentimental gesture as to send her these mementoes. Right at the bottom she came across a heavy shoe box she didn't recognize. It had 'Rollerblade TRS Treseder' written on the side. Her grandfather had even guessed her shoe-size correctly. Opening the box, she pulled out a pair of black and white skates – 'for aggressive skating', said the blurb.

'Hey, Mom, Dad, guess what?'

Darcie burst in on her parents who were both tapping away on their laptops.

'What's got you so excited, honey?' asked her mother, not looking up.

'I got a note from my grandfather – I suppose that's your father, isn't it, Dad? – though you never told me, of course – anyway, he's sent me some well cool rollerblades.' Darcie held them up by their laces. 'Oh yeah, and a Louis Vuitton suitcase.'

Michael and Ginnie Lock were both looking at her in horror.

'He's been in contact?' said Ginnie.

'He sent you those?' Michael asked.

'Yeah. He said you wouldn't approve.' Darcie grinned.

'How like your father to send her rollerblades when she's just recovered from breaking her leg,' Ginnie remarked acerbically to her husband. 'So she can break the other one perhaps?'

'What did he say in the note?' Michael asked.

Darcie shrugged. 'Not much. Said he hoped to see me next time I'm in London.'

Michael took the boots and examined them.

'What are you looking for? Unexploded bombs or something?'

He said nothing.

'What does he do, this mysterious grandfather of mine? He said he knows Gladys – he sounded really fun.'

'Fun? My father, fun?'

'He gave me those, didn't he?'

'My father never gives anyone anything without a reason.'

'Yeah, well, maybe the reason is that he's taking an interest in me.'

'What else is in the case?' Michael pressed her.

'Just a few things I left behind in Nairobi – oh, sorry, but I'm not supposed to use that word, am I?' Darcie said sarcastically.

'Of course you can mention Kenya when we are alone and safe like now, Darcie,' her dad said patiently.

'What's he up to, Michael?' Ginnie asked. She moved to her husband's side and took the blades from him. 'This holiday was his idea, wasn't it?'

'He claimed it was the prime minister's brainwave,' Michael replied.

'Why does he have to be up to anything?' fumed Darcie, snatching her blades back.

'You don't know him, Darcie,' Michael said, shaking his head.

'No, I don't – thanks to you two,' Darcie slung back, and stormed out, slamming the door behind her.

Still fuming, Darcie put on the rollerblades and, just to spite her parents, decided to practise on the basketball court outside the guest lodgings. Ignoring the ache in her leg, she tottered along, holding the wire mesh, then let go. Her legs immediately went in different directions and she collapsed.

'Hey, Zebra, up to no good as usual?'

'Stingo!' Darcie cried out with delight as her former SAS bodyguard in Nairobi limped across the court towards her. His sandy hair had recently been cut so short that she could see the pink flush of his scalp beneath. 'What are you doing here?'

'Same as you, I guess. Came for the sawbones to check me out. I thought you had a broken leg?'

'I do – did.'

Stingo hauled her to her feet and looked pointedly at the blades.

'OK, bad idea. I just wanted to annoy Mom and Dad.' Darcie leaned over and unlaced them.

'That's something you'll never grow out of,' Stingo said, his blue eyes twinkling. He gestured towards a bench at the side of the court, and they sat down to bask in the late afternoon sunshine.

'Oh? What did you do to annoy yours?'

'Joined the SAS, of course. My parents are vegetarian, sixties-style hippies who think spending their Sundays on their organic allotment is enough excitement for them.'

Darcie snorted. 'How come they had you? Are you adopted?'

'I often wonder but my mum swears I'm theirs.'

'So what do you talk about round the kitchen table?'

'Not much to be honest. Politics – definitely not. Food – a minefield. Career – completely unmentionable. I think last time I went home we talked about the weather and the favourable conditions for Brussels sprouts. So, are the parents giving you grief then?'

Darcie shrugged. 'Not really. We just don't see things the same way.' She paused for a moment. 'No, that's not it – the real problem is, they've been lying to me about everything and now a bit of truth has broken through, none of us are quite sure what to do with it.'

Stingo rubbed his leg, easing the stiffness. 'My advice is "roll with the punches".'

'What's that supposed to mean?'

'What do kids say now? Go with the flow? Don't get all chip-on-shoulder about it. You can't change your parents.'

Darcie glanced sideways at the battered face of one of her best friends, guessing he was speaking from experience. 'What did the doctor say about your leg?'

Stingo had been shot on a hunt in Kenya where he had been the big game for a smuggling gang – the same people who had next tried to throw Darcie to the lions.

'It's fine. I'll probably limp a bit but I'm told that'll make the ladies think I'm more interesting. I was lucky it was just a hunting rifle, rather than a semi-automatic – not too much mess inside.'

Darcie winced. 'So are you going back on duty?'

'Yep. We've been given a new assignment.'

'But you can't tell me where.' She stated it as a fact, knowing it wasn't possible.

'No more than you can tell me where you're going.'

'I'm just going on holiday.'

'You deserve it. All you need to do is to remember to keep your head down, your kit clean and your boots polished, Zebra.'

On the 1st of August, Darcie walked through the customs at Naples airport feeling very conspicuous with her new suitcase. She needn't have worried: she was following an Italian family, voluble mother shepherding two long-limbed teenage girls with the kind of hair you normally only saw in shampoo adverts. The customs officials only had eyes for them and let Darcie through with barely a glance.

Stepping out into the glass and steel arrival hall, Darcie paused before the sea of faces waiting by the exit. It was the first time she'd flown on her own and, though she was trying to look confident, she really felt overwhelmed. Her instructions were to look out for the representative from Fresh Start Travel who should be waiting for her on the other side of the barrier.

At first she didn't see him. This was because the

huge sign he was displaying bore the name Miss Logan – her new identity and surname, chosen to hide her from Madam Tsui's assassins. It was not a name she yet recognised as her own. She'd walked straight past him before she realised her error. She'd have to stop making such basic mistakes, she told herself. From now on, she *had* to get used to answering to Logan rather than Lock – one more thing she could blame her parents for!

'Hi, I'm here,' she said breathlessly, arriving in front of the dark-haired, olive-skinned man holding the sign.

'Darcie Logan? I'm Carl Deneuve, one of your guides. Welcome to Italy.' They shook hands. 'That all your luggage?'

'Yes.'

'Thank my lucky stars. My first client of the day came with a mountain of things – we had to travel in several cars.'

He walked Darcie briskly out to the short-stay car park and flashed his keys at a white Mercedes.

'You're fourteen, is that right?' His accent was

not quite American, Darcie noticed, French Canadian maybe.

'Yes.'

'You're the youngest then. Most parents wait till their children graduate before sending them on the tour, but I'm sure you'll all get along fine. If anyone gives you a hard time, just come to me.'

'Gives me a hard time? Is that likely? I thought this was a holiday.'

He loaded her case in the boot and they got into the car. He slammed the air conditioning on high, turning the atmosphere icy compared to the hot pavement outside.

'To tell you the truth, yes, it is.' He reversed out into the stream of traffic, hooting and gesticulating at the taxi drivers trying to cut him up. Once on the road he glanced sideways at her. 'How much do you know about us?'

'I know it's an educational cruise – a kind of finishing school afloat, Dad said.'

'Did he? Well, that's right, I suppose. But there's a

bit more to it than that. Most parents send their kids to be finished because they don't particularly like the rough edges their earlier education has given them. I'm sure that's not the case with you' (he looked doubtful), 'but you'll find some can be ... er ... challenging to start with.' Darcie looked worried so he added, 'Don't be concerned, we work hard at team building and by the end of next week you won't recognise the troublemakers.'

Darcie stared straight ahead at the heat-shimmer dancing over the road. Had her parents thought she needed 'finishing'? She knew her mom in her heart of hearts would've liked a different kind of daughter, but not her dad surely? But why else would they send her? It left a sour taste in her mouth to think that, after everything she'd been through, they had betrayed her by their lies again. They'd plotted this together and said nothing to her. She'd had enough. From now on, she'd never trust them. Never, ever again. They'd been so great in Paris and Germany; she felt sick to the stomach knowing they'd been planning this all along.

Eyes on the road, Carl hadn't noticed his passenger's white, pinched face. 'You're the last to arrive,' he continued. 'We're having a little get-together this evening at the hotel. We set sail tomorrow, so tonight's the night if you want to see something of Naples, though, in your case, you'll have to be escorted by an adult. Naples is not a safe city – not like what you're used to at home, I imagine. Where are you from?'

'All over,' Darcie said sullenly.

'Your dad a diplomat – or is it army?'

'Diplomat.'

'Tough being moved around like so much baggage, hey?' probed Carl.

'I guess.' Darcie shrugged.

Carl let the conversation drop as they drew up outside a white hotel with black wrought-iron balconies. It commanded a breathtaking view of the Bay of Naples, glittering gold in the late afternoon sunshine. The volcano Vesuvius loomed on the horizon, a threatening dark presence. Yachts and pleasure craft skimmed across the bay, white dots scoring the mirror surface with their wakes. But Darcie had no desire to admire the view: she just wanted to shut herself in her room and be alone.

Carl dealt with the check-in and handed her a key.

'First team-building exercise starts tonight at six. We'll expect you in the meeting room.'

'OK.'

Carl frowned as Darcie trailed after the bellboy. He was surprised: she'd seemed quite unspoiled to start with, but now he wasn't so sure. Oh well, he thought, turning to catch a few minutes to himself before the next session, that would all soon change. The Fresh Start course had not failed anyone yet.

Darcie had never been inside such a stylish hotel room: fresh-cut flowers on the antique table by the window, plasma television hidden behind a screen, a rose-pink sofa, and a double bed with a white satin counterpane. But the elegance was wasted on her as she sat on the floor, not even bothering to take off her jacket. She was tempted to ring her parents and have it out with them, there and then. Something held her back: the thought that they were relieved to be shot of their problem daughter, hoping she'd come back reformed to fit neatly into their lives as the perfect child for a diplomatic couple.

If that's what they thought, they had another thing coming.

Looking back, she worked out what must have happened: her parents had told everyone how worried they were after her ordeal in Africa; even the prime minister had felt it necessary to give his advice and suggested this course as the cure. It was so embarrassing, not to say insulting. Only her grandfather had seen through the plan and sent her the rollerblades and note to encourage her to have some fun. And fun was what she intended to have.

With this defiant thought, Darcie up-ended her suitcase on the bed and chose her scruffiest clothes: the Chelsea shirt and a pair of ripped jeans. Much-worn trainers completed the outfit. Now she was ready to team-build her own way.

Her shyness returned as Darcie found her way to the meeting room. Carl had cleared the tables to one side and placed cushions in a circle.

'Hey, Darcie, come and join us,' Carl said cheerfully, patting the cushion beside him. He had a soft ball in front of him which he was rolling restlessly to and fro. Young people began to drift in. Most, Darcie noticed, looked as though they'd rather be anywhere else. A baggy-trousered black boy had an iPod in his ears which Carl deftly confiscated before he knew what was happening. He slumped next to Darcie and swore.

'You'll get it back later,' said Carl calmly.

Darcie wondered if she should say something to the boy but he beat her to it.

'Who's the kid?' the boy asked Carl as he chewed on his gum.

'This is Darcie Logan. Darcie, meet Jon Lee Vermont.'

Darcie resented being called a 'kid'. She gave Jon Lee a slight nod, but nothing more.

'How old are you, kid?' Jon Lee asked.

'Fourteen.'

He laughed. 'Who's babysitting her tonight then?'

'That's enough, Jon Lee,' said Carl sharply.

'The person who's detailed to toilet train you,' Darcie slipped in.

'Now, Darcie, let's not start off on the wrong foot,' cautioned Carl.

Jon Lee gave her a withering look and turned to the boy on his other side, leaving her stranded on the beach of no-conversation. Darcie knew she hated Fresh Start already.

The last 'client' to arrive did so in spectacular fashion. First came the screams outside.

'No way! I am not going in there.'

'Shelly, your father said that either you take this course or you go on retreat to a convent on Corsica.' The second voice belonged to a woman who was clearly unimpressed by the girl's firework display.

'My father sucks.'

'Shelly, is it going to be the convent or are you going to give this course a chance?' the woman replied briskly.

The door now flew open and in stomped a flush-faced Shelly Morris, accompanied by two harassed security agents and a woman wearing a Fresh Start T-shirt. Darcie recognized the president's daughter instantly from the blading incident in Paris.

'Hi, fellow inmates,' Shelly growled, slumping on to a cushion opposite Darcie.

'Thanks for joining us, Shelly,' said Carl evenly as if none of them had heard the altercation. 'And this is my partner, Gina.' He waved to the woman in the T-shirt. She gave the circle a bright smile, uncannily like Carl's. 'Now, let's make a start. Though some of us may be better known than the rest,' he grinned at Shelly, 'we're all going to begin as equals. Forget anything you think you know about the people in this circle. We are here to make a fresh start. As of today, the slate is clean.'

Shelly yawned. Darcie sympathised: she felt pretty bored by this pep talk too. It was the worst adult-pretending-to-be-your-best-mate stuff she'd ever heard.

'I'm going to pass the ball around the circle,' Carl

continued. 'When you catch it, I want you to say your name, your age, where you're from and then tell us a couple of things that you'd like to share about yourself.

'OK, I'll kick off. I'm Carl – that's Carl with a C. I'm from Montreal originally, now living in London. I like tennis and ancient history.'

He threw the ball quickly to a blonde boy on the other side of the circle next to Shelly.

'Hi, I'm Hans from Vienna. I'm eighteen. I ski pretty good but am lousy at everything else. I have a foul temper.'

It had been shrewd of Carl to choose the Austrian first, Darcie decided. He'd played it straight with no mocking at what was asked of him. Hans chucked the ball to the girl sitting on the other side of Carl. And she passed it on to a girl named Karin. And so it continued. Darcie sank further into despair: everyone seemed so confident and all were several years older than her. What could she tell them about herself? There was nothing she was allowed to say.

The boy next to her saved her from an immediate answer by snatching away the ball aimed at her.

'Howdy partners. My name is Jon Lee Vermont – that's Jon with a J, Lee with an L and Vermont with – what the hell, you get the picture. I am sweet sixteen and never been kissed, so if any of the lay-dies want to change that, I'm available afterwards.' He waggled his eyebrows, making the girls laugh. Carl coughed warningly. 'I am the man – *the* man – if you wanna know anything that is hap-pen-ning in my neigh-bourhood – that's the Bronx in the great big juicy apple itself. What the hell am I doin' here? Big Daddy-O Vermont kicked me out and sent me here to improve myself. Question: how can you improve upon per-fec-tion?'

This speech brought whistles and cheers from the circle. Even Carl smiled.

'Thank you, Jon Lee. Pass it along.'

Jon Lee threw the ball hard at Shelly. She caught it and chucked it at her nearest bodyguard.

'Hey, Mike, wake up: there's a head case from the

Bronx throwing things at me,' she said sarcastically. Then turning back to the ring, she flashed Jon Lee a wide smile. Her voice see-sawed between girlish and harsh. 'Shelly Morris reporting, sir!' She snapped a salute to Carl. 'Prisoner number 401 according to the door of my padded cell.' Jon Lee and Darcie laughed. 'I'm seventeen years old and I live in a sweet little old house in Washington that some dork painted white. My father's a moron but, hey, somebody must love him because he rules the world. And I've been sent here to stop him having to answer dumb questions as to why Americans should trust him to run the country when he can't control his own kid. You know something: I think that's a great question and maybe one day he'd find time to give me the answer.' She stopped, realising she'd revealed more than she intended. 'Can we finish this stupid game now?' she whined. 'Everyone's done their thing, Carl with a C.'

Carl shook his head. 'Not yet. Darcie hasn't had her turn yet. Pass the ball, please.'

Shelly turned round to see her guard holding the

ball out to her. 'Oh my, I forgot.' She put her hand to her mouth, acting like Dorothy from *The Wizard of Oz*. 'This, Munchkins, is Mike, he's from Washington too, and he hates my guts. He's been sent to Fresh Start because his boss loathes him and this is the assignment from hell. He has absolutely no sense of humour.'

Mike's face was impassive as he held out the ball. Shelly grinned and took it from him. She threw it lazily towards Darcie. It rolled to a stop in the centre so that Darcie had to get up to fetch it.

'I'm Darcie Logan. I'm fourteen.' Several people sniggered. Darcie flushed, feeling humiliated. 'I'm from everywhere, I s'pose, and I've got to disappear to nowhere because otherwise I'm dead.'

An awkward silence followed this statement. Darcie knew it made her sound pretty messed up, but it was an approximation of the truth. She'd already promised herself she wasn't going to invent a complicated back story – she didn't want to play her parents' game.

'Er, thank you.' She could see she'd got Carl really worried now. 'Do you want to add anything –

about your interests, that kind of stuff?'

Darcie thought for a moment. She looked across the circle at Shelly, wondering if she remembered her from Paris. 'I want to learn to rollerblade.'

Carl beamed. 'That's good – set yourself a target, something to improve upon. Right, let's go eat. Seventeens and over, if you're going out after dinner, you're to sign in and out with me. Any younger clients are to see me first for permission if they want to join any of the older students. Curfew for everyone at eleven.'

Darcie had already resigned herself to the fact that no one would want to 'babysit' her, as Jon Lee had put it. She noticed that he had sat himself next to Shelly at dinner; being the second youngest at sixteen, he too needed an escort before he could go out. The two Americans had identified each other as like-minded rebels and now put their heads together. Darcie took the empty chair next to Hans and spent the next hour listening to tales of his exploits off-piste. At least he wasn't rude to her; he barely seemed to notice her. Perhaps his parents had sent him on this cruise in hopes Fresh Start would stop him boring everyone rigid? If so, early signs were not promising.

After dinner, Carl and Gina retired with their coffee to their 'office': two chairs in the lobby where they could monitor the comings and goings.

'What do you think then?' Gina asked, stirring sugar into her expresso.

'We've seen it all before, Gina. Even Miss Tough-Girl USA – just because she's famous, doesn't mean she can't change.'

'And Jon Lee Vermont?'

'Mouth as big as the Bay of Naples, but he'll mellow.'

'So it's going to be easy.' Gina laughed and pushed back her shoulder-length reddish-brown hair. They both knew it was never that.

'Tell you the truth, it's the kid I'm most worried about. Did you notice her scars? It looks like she's just walked through a glass door or something. What does her file say?'

Gina shook her head. 'That's the odd thing – nearly

nothing. Recommended by someone very senior in the British government. Recent traumatic accident but we're not to ask anything about it.'

'What do you reckon – car crash?'

Gina raised a sceptical eyebrow. 'Maybe, but why the secrecy?'

'Self-harm then?'

'Possibly. We better keep a close eye on her. Where is she now?'

'She' had been about to go to bed but had been waylaid by Shelly in the dining room. Jon Lee was hovering behind his new partner in crime, smirking.

'Hey, Kiddo, where you going?'

'Back to my room.'

'What? Miss the last chance to party before we get banged up on that barge?'

Darcie shrugged. 'I don't have a choice. I'm not allowed to go out without an adult.'

'Then come with us two.'

'You're hardly adults.'

53

'You forget that I go round with two albatrosses strapped to my neck. Mike and Bernie will babysit us all.'

Darcie had seen the kind of babysitting they did in Paris and in her current mood that promised to be very entertaining.

'If you're sure you don't mind me tagging along?'

'Mind? Course not. Get changed: I can't go round with you dressed like that. We're going to hit the town, girl.'

When Darcie came down in her black dress, Shelly was sitting on the sofa with Jon Lee being grilled by Carl and Gina.

'Now, if you take Darcie out, you've got to act responsibly,' Carl was lecturing.

'When have I ever not done so?' Shelly said, wide-eyed.

'Let us say, your reputation has preceded you.'

'But, Carl with a C, you said that we all begin with a clean slate at Fresh Start. Don't tell me you didn't mean it – that this whole thing is fake?'

She's clever, thought Darcie. Carl could do nothing if he wanted to retain any respect for his course.

'OK, Shelly, I take your point. Be back by eleven.'

Jon Lee leapt up. 'Yo, Kiddo, we've sprung you from gaol and are ready to go.'

Shelly took one arm, Jon Lee the other and they frog-marched Darcie from the building.

'Talk about lamb to the slaughter,' said Carl, shaking his head.

'Don't worry, nothing too bad can happen,' said Gina, settling down to check the itinerary for the next day. 'Those security guys don't look as if they'd let anyone mess with them. They'll at least bring them all back in one piece.'

Outside on the street, the security agents were jittery. This was just the kind of night they hated: no planned route, Shelly allowed to be spontaneous, and all in a city they didn't know.

'I s'pose you guys would like a beer?' Shelly asked them innocently.

They weren't fooled. 'We don't drink on duty, Miss.'

'Lemonade then. Let's go to a pizza place – I'm starving.'

Darcie, who had only just eaten, was surprised that Shelly could be hungry so soon – until she caught the look exchanged with Jon Lee. They walked a few hundred metres down the street and turned into a busy restaurant.

A waiter bustled over. He was about to tell them they were full when he recognised the customer. 'Terrace or inside, signorina?' he asked obsequiously.

Darcie hoped they'd sit outside. The view across the bay was beautiful and a cool breeze was blowing inland.

'Inside please. My friends prefer it.' Shelly nodded to the security men. The two guards looked relieved – there were fewer variables inside a building, limited entrances, a chance to anticipate trouble.

They were shown to a table near the back.

'Lemonades all round?' asked Shelly.

Darcie was amazed. She'd expected Shelly to at least

try ordering a glass of wine to push the boundaries a bit.

'*Pronto*,' said the waiter, rushing off.

After five minutes of slurping the lemonade, Jon Lee got up.

'This Jon has to go to the john,' he announced and disappeared through the swing door into the Gents. His habit of making everything he said sound such a big deal was beginning to annoy Darcie.

'You know, I think I need the washroom too,' said Shelly. 'Wanna come, Kiddo?'

Darcie was about to refuse when she felt a kick under the table.

'Sure, I'll come.'

She followed Shelly into the Ladies.

'Right, time to make our escape,' said Shelly. She climbed on the cistern and opened the window.

'What?'

'You don't think I'm gonna hang around all night with Tom and Jerry in tow? Gimme a hand.'

Darcie pushed her up until Shelly reached the window ledge.

'I checked this place out earlier. Can you climb in that cute dress – it looks a bit tight?'

'I can climb.'

'Pass me my purse.'

Darcie held up the bag and watched as Shelly wriggled through the narrow window. She knew she had a choice: she could go back like a good little girl and tell the bodyguards that their charge had gone AWOL or she could follow. If she went back, Shelly and Jon Lee would punish her for betraying them, turning the rest of the cruise into a nightmare. Besides, she understood why Shelly might like to have a few nights to herself – to be a normal girl and not some-one's daughter. If even her security team didn't know where she was, no terrorist would, surely?

Making a decision, Darcie pulled herself up on to the ledge. She was in better shape than Shelly – slimmer and fitter – so she managed the window with no difficulty. She dropped down to the ground to a surprise hug from Shelly and Jon Lee.

'Well done, Prisoner D. We thought you might give

us away to the guards,' said Shelly, giving her a salute.

'I won't say it didn't cross my mind,' admitted Darcie with a grin, 'but then I'd miss out on all the fun, wouldn't I?'

'You sure would. Now to make good our escape – we go along this alley, out by the side of the restaurant and head for the city centre – one at a time. I'll go first, then Darcie, then Jon Lee.' Shelly whipped a baseball cap out of her pocket and pulled it low over her face.

Darcie understood now why Shelly had chosen a table inside. The protection guys were still staring at the washroom doors, wondering when the girls would stop chatting and come back to finish their drinks. She gave Shelly thirty seconds to get away, then followed at a quick walk until she was out of sight of the well-lit restaurant terrace. Breaking into a jog, she ran until she saw the baseball cap wearer waiting by a bus stop. Jon Lee joined them after a few minutes.

'Any sign?' Shelly asked.

'No.' Jon Lee grinned. 'Mission accomplished.' He

raised his palm for Shelly to strike, then offered it to Darcie. 'High five, Kiddo.'

Darcie hit her hand against his, feeling a wild laugh bubble up inside her. Carl had said the evening was about team-building – they'd certainly made a start on that.

'I thought we'd try the Vesuvius Club,' Shelly announced, leading them confidently through the labyrinth of streets that formed the centre of old Naples. 'A backpackers' website said it was the place to go.'

They paused in a small courtyard where an old fountain splashed into a shell-shaped bowl. Down the next street, Darcie could see the flashing neon sign of the Vesuvius Club – a volcano erupting – and two bouncers standing on the door.

'OK, Kiddo, it's your eighteenth birthday,' Shelly told Darcie.

'You're joking – they'll never fall for that,' Darcie protested.

'They don't have to believe you and they won't care

as long as you have the right answers to excuse them of the responsibility. Just like my father.' She pulled at Darcie's ponytail, letting the hair tumble down. 'There – hide behind that if you have to. Ready, Jon Lee?'

Jon Lee nodded. 'Thunderbirds are go, First Daughter of the Empire.'

Shelly glanced nervously at Darcie, sensing she was the weak link. 'Just follow our lead.'

The threesome walked towards the bouncers, Shelly in front. They challenged her in Italian. She smiled and shrugged, indicating she didn't understand. The nearest man tapped the notice behind him: *Sopra 18*. Shelly nodded and pointed to herself and the others, starting to walk through. Darcie felt her arm caught.

'Too young,' the bouncer stated in halting English.

'What?' Shelly said incredulously. 'It's her birthday.' He looked blank. 'Eighteen today. You know, "Happy Birthday to you, Happy Birthday to you . . ."'

Jon Lee joined in until the caterwauling made the bouncers smile.

'Happy Birthday, de-ar Darcie,

Happy Birthday to you!'

'*Compleaño*.' The bouncer let go of Darcie. 'OK, you go in.'

'See, what did I tell you?' said Shelly triumphantly as she paid for the three of them. 'They couldn't care less.'

They squeezed their way through the crowds of young people gathered by the bar in a cavernous room pounding with music. Flashing lights pulsated in time to the beat as a DJ directed operations from a massive consol. Jon Lee spread his arms and took a deep breath.

'This is my kinda place. See you later – don't tell Pater – gotta get a mate or – I'm outta here.' He plunged on to the dance floor and was soon paired up with a tall girl with long brown hair.

'Are you going to dance?' Shelly shouted in Darcie's ear.

'Maybe. I think I'll just sit down first.' Darcie retreated to an empty table in a corner, wanting to acclimatize.

'OK. I'll check on you in ten.' Shelly followed Jon

Lee and was swallowed up in the crowd.

Darcie was very pleased she was wearing black: it made her almost invisible as she sank into her corner. Part of her wanted to dive straight into the thick of things to prove she could be cool and confident, the other wanted to go home. Wondering what to do now, she looked at her watch – 22.45. They'd have to be going soon. She felt relieved that she didn't have to make a decision.

'Hey, Kiddo, I've brought someone to meet you.' Shelly turned to two Italian boys with perfect smiles. 'This is Toni and this is Luigi – or maybe it's the other way round. Say hi, guys.'

'*Ciao*,' the boys said together. They looked at least twenty.

'Now, I'm keeping Toni, but why don't you talk to Luigi? His English is OK. Luigi, why don't you get Darcie a drink?'

'What you like, Darcie?' Luigi asked.

'Er, orange juice please,' Darcie said shyly. 'But we have to go in a minute.'

'Go?' said Shelly, taking a seat at the table. 'We've only just got here.'

'But the curfew?'

'What do you think they'll do to us if we're late? Chuck us off the course? Great! You're supposed to be on holiday. Chill – have some fun.'

'But I think I'd better get back. You stay – I'll be fine.' Darcie felt slightly panicky. Now she was here, she realised she really didn't know how to 'chat' to Luigi. She was way out of her depth and had forgotten how to swim.

'Sit still. You can't walk out on Luigi now he's getting you a drink.' Shelly waved towards the bar where the Italian boy was standing next to Jon Lee. 'Do you have any idea how much a juice costs in here?' Darcie shook her head, feeling miserable. 'The least you can do is let him practise his English on a real live specimen.'

'He just wants to practise his English?' Darcie asked with relief.

'Yeah, of course. You've got a dirty mind, Kiddo, I'm surprised at you.'

Darcie blushed, then looked away because Shelly had started whispering in Toni's ear. From the giggles, she doubted they were discussing irregular verbs.

'Orange juice for the signorina,' said Luigi, producing a drink with a flourish.

'Have you been learning English long?' Darcie could've thumped herself – what a lame question! She took a sip of her drink and winced. It tasted unpleasant but she was thirsty and wanted to finish it so she could leave. She gulped it down.

'All my life – so I can meet a girl like you.'

'Please, spare me the compliments,' said Darcie, laughing nervously. 'You sound like you've been reading bad romantic novels.'

'You no like my compliments?' Luigi looked offended.

'They're very good – for the right girl. But not me, Luigi.'

Luigi clasped his hands to his chest. 'I love it when you say my name! Say it again.'

'Luigi.' Darcie began to giggle. It seemed so funny to be sitting with the daughter of the President of the

United States in a nightclub with an Italian boy she didn't know. 'Louis-Louis-Luigi.'

Shelly looked across at her and smiled. 'You all right, Kiddo?'

'Perfect. Perfection. Perfecto. Perfectissimo.' Darcie slumped against Luigi and continued to giggle. Her bones felt as if they had turned to liquid.

Shelly picked up the glass and sniffed it. 'What did you put in that drink?' she asked Luigi shrewdly.

He shrugged. 'Your friend buyed it for her.' He nodded over at Jon Lee.

Shelly swore. 'Great. It was vodka, wasn't it? I just hope it's him who carries her back to the hotel. We'd better go before she pukes.'

Hauling Darcie to her feet, Shelly towed her through the dancers, resisting Darcie's attempts to start jigging to the music. She tapped Jon Lee on the shoulder.

'Your problem,' she said bluntly, transferring Darcie from her arm to Jon Lee's. 'We're going.'

'So soon?' complained Jon Lee.

'You're the one who bought her the drink.'

'Can't we just leave her in a corner to sleep it off?'

'She's not at the sleepy stage.'

Darcie was swaying in time to the booming music. Jon Lee grinned.

'Hey, no longer so depressed, Kiddo? Not want to die today now?'

'Stop making fun of her: she's only some poor sad kid. She'll want to die tomorrow with the hangover she'll have.'

'I didn't know you were so responsible, Sister Shelly.'

'I have my moments. Now, come on.'

Together they half-carried Darcie to the exit.

The president's daughter had her head down or she would have spotted the reception committee waiting for her outside. One step on to the pavement and cameras flashed from all directions. Shelly dropped Darcie to put her hands over her face. Darcie toppled on top of Jon Lee, still giggling. The press pack swarmed over them, stepping on fingers and toes to get a good shot. They only moved back when Darcie was spectacularly sick over the man from the *Sun*.

*

The next morning, Darcie lay in the darkened hotel room wishing the world would come to an end. She didn't want to get up to face the consequences of what had happened. Her head ached; her mouth tasted like a burial ground; she still felt sick. Shelly had come to visit her earlier. Her approach was to pass the whole evening off as a big joke. Dumping a pile of newspapers on the bedside, she poured Darcie a tumbler of water and told her to drink as much as she could.

'Not a bad way to start your life as a clubber, Kiddo – front page on all the scandal sheets the world over.'

Shelly left Darcie to leaf through the papers and find out the worst. Most led with a picture of Shelly hiding her face from the camera, but many followed up with a shot of Darcie and Jon Lee rolling on the floor. Darcie's face was clearly discernible. The articles all told a similar, sorry story.

First daughter in club brawl – Shelly Morris and two friends gatecrash over-18s club, spilling out on to the streets of Naples in scenes of violence and drunkenness.

The President's biggest problem is not re-election but his own daughter, say the American public.

Mediterranean cruise for problem kids falls at first fence – Shelly Morris is still up to her old tricks, this time leading a fourteen-year-old off the rails.

Blame the parents? You bet, say 9 out of 10 Americans.

Someone hammered on the door.

'Get up, Darcie. You're to be in the meeting room in five minutes.' It was Carl – no longer sounding so patient. Darcie guessed he'd just received the worst publicity for his company ever and spent all morning dealing with journalists.

Darcie considered staying where she was but knew that was not a solution. She might as well get this over and done with. She pulled on some clothes. As she did so, her mobile phone fell out of her pocket. She had four messages in her inbox. She flicked through them:

09.01 Ring us! Mom and Dad

09.30 Please ring us!! Mom
and Dad

09.45 Ring now or else! Mom
and Dad

Or else what, Darcie wondered? Or else we'll be even crosser than we are already? Was that possible?

The last message was from Stingo.

10.14 Congrats: uv just blown ur cover big time. What the **** do u think ur playing at? Drinking? Boys? Clubbing? Fighting? I didn't think u would be so stupid. If u want 2 survive, u can't afford a teenage rebellion now. Grow up.

Darcie threw the phone on the bed. She knew it was her fault – she'd chosen to go to the club – but the photos and write-up made her look far worse. A wild thought struck her: she could run away. She could walk right out of the hotel and not come back. Thinking about it, it seemed the best way to deal with the security breach. Her cover had failed – she needed a new one and this time she'd choose it for herself. Goodbye Fresh Start, goodbye death threats from Madame Tsui, Goodbye Darcie Logan. She could simply disappear.

Picking up her small backpack, she stuffed a few belongings inside, deciding to leave her passport and anything that connected her to Darcie Logan behind. She had a few hundred Euros. That would be a start. Taking a last look around her, she slipped out of the room.

On the bed, her phone whirred:

11.15 Please please ring. We are frantic. Mom and Dad.

Downstairs in the meeting room, Jon Lee and Shelly stood sullenly in front of Carl and Gina.

'You were out of order last night,' Carl said. 'You've let yourselves down and disappointed us. Being the oldest, Shelly, I hold you most to blame.'

Shelly shrugged. 'I didn't twist anyone's arm, Carl. They came because they wanted to.'

'Yeah, I had a ball,' grinned Jon Lee.

'Did you think about Darcie at any stage? She completely went over the edge. Don't you think you might have encouraged her?'

'Yeah, well, it wasn't her fault.' Shelly rubbed her neck awkwardly. 'She wanted to get home before curfew but I made her stay. Then someone spiked her drink and it all got out of hand.'

'So you took a vulnerable fourteen-year-old to an over eighteens' club, watched while she innocently got drunk and then let her be photographed rolling on the floor with our all-American boy here?'

'Hey, she should be proud to be seen with me. Some lay-dies would kill for the honour.'

'Cut the bull, Jon Lee. This is not remotely amusing. And where is Darcie? I called her a quarter of an hour ago.'

'I'll check on her,' said Gina.

A minute later, Gina dashed back in. 'The room's empty. I think she's run away.'

Carl thumped his forehead. 'Great. Don't just stand there, you two: you made this mess, now get out there and find her. She can't have got far. Gina, send the others out to look for her too. I'll alert the police.'

Christopher Lock read through the press cuttings as he sipped his coffee, a puzzled expression on his face. He'd misjudged his granddaughter. He had thought her too sensible to behave like this. There must be more of her American mother in her than he had realised. Darcie had left him with a security nightmare. Every Tsui operative from Milan to Cairo would know exactly where she was. Should he pull her out?

He looked at the pictures again.

Well, she had certainly bonded with Shelly Morris as he intended. He needn't have bought the rollerblades after all. Despite – or maybe because of – her disgraceful goings-on, Darcie was now in prime position for the task he had allotted her. The Americans had rightly guessed that the first daughter would go AWOL as often as she could; it looked as though his grand-daughter would accompany her on these unplanned expeditions and when she did, he'd know exactly where she was, thanks to the tracking device in her phone. The Americans would be very grateful – and he would make sure he squeezed every last drop of gratitude out of them before he had finished. It would be nice to have the upper hand for once.

He poured himself a second cup of coffee from the cafetière and tapped a shortbread biscuit on its plate to make sure no buttery crumbs fell on his desk.

Looking at it another way, had she known about her mission, he might even have encouraged Darcie to behave like this as part of her cover. Perhaps it was the old Lock instinct to find the right path after all?

The phone rang. He pushed aside his cup to answer it.

'Yes?'

'Don't you dare tell your secretary not to put me through again, Father. This is an emergency.' Michael was shouting into his phone. 'I've been awake all night following the news. I suppose you've seen it too?'

'Indeed I have. I am most surprised.'

'And I was "most surprised" to find I'd sent my daughter on a course for problem rich kids! Do you have any idea what she must think of us? She'd just saved my life – and the lives of many others – and I reward her by packing her off to boot camp.'

'It's hardly boot camp, Michael.'

'Call it what you like, but I know what I would think if I were her. She's not answering our calls – that speaks volumes.'

'She's probably just recovering from her hangover. I must send her my recipe for a pick-me-up.'

'This is not a joke, Father. When are you bringing her out?'

'Bringing her out? What are you talking about?'

'Do I really have to spell it out for you? She's in danger.'

'Michael, she is safest where she is. The *Pharaoh* is already on the high seas and guarded by US air and sea cover. I am confident that no harm can come to her.'

Christopher Lock glanced at his watch – he was bending the truth a little but he was good at that.

'Father!'

'What do you expect me to do, Michael? I can hardly send in a helicopter to airlift her out. Let's review the situation when she reaches the next port.'

'Review the situation! You bring her home, you hear me?'

'Why don't we let her decide? Sorry, I have to go. I've got a call on the other line.'

Once the initial excitement of escaping had passed, Darcie felt pretty stupid out on the streets of a foreign city with absolutely no idea where to go. Her initiative fizzled away and she drifted down to the harbour, wondering if she should just go back. That seemed even more pathetic.

She made her way through the crowds and found a bench at the dockside. The easiest thing seemed to be just to sit in the sun and wait for something to happen.

It was Shelly who found her an hour later. The president's daughter signalled the security team to hold back while she took a seat next to Darcie. One bodyguard discreetly radioed to Carl.

'Hey. Walking out on us?'

Darcie shrugged.

'I'm sorry, Kiddo, I hadn't realised you were so depressed.'

'I'm not depressed.'

'Then why are you crying?'

Darcie furiously wiped the tears away. 'I can't tell you.'

'But it doesn't seem to be doing you any good bottling it all up, does it?'

'Why the spiked drink, Shelly? Were you and Jon Lee making fun of me?'

'No!' Shelly protested. 'OK, maybe. We thought it would be funny to take you out to walk the wild side with us. But, hey, the drink wasn't my idea.'

'No, you just wanted to watch me make a fool of myself.'

'You have to admit, that was kinda funny.'

Darcie got up. Shelly pulled her back down by her T-shirt. 'Look, I'm sorry. Let me do some good for once – at least, help me feel less bad by giving me the chance to listen to you.'

Darcie cradled her head in her hands. She wanted to tell someone and she seemed very short of friends at the moment.

'Can you keep a secret?'

'I live in the White House, remember. The walls drip with secrets.'

That was true. The daughter of the President of the United States was probably one of the few young people in the world to be unruffled by issues of national security. Taking a risk, Darcie sketched out what had happened in Nairobi, concluding with the confrontation with Madame Tsui that had left her at the top of the drug smuggler's list of targets.

Shelly looked doubtful. 'Is this all true? I don't want

79

to fall for some nutcase story. You're not here because of mental problems or something?'

'No, I'm here because no one knows what to do with me.'

Shelly's face cracked into a broad grin. 'Sister, welcome to the club. You're a target for one bunch of killers? Well, every terrorist from here to Baghdad would love to have a crack at me. Misfit at home? I wrote the book on that. You hang with me, Kiddo, and we'll be OK. I don't let them know but those two bodyguards do have their uses. They can look after you too.'

'Thanks.' Darcie's despondency began to lift. She had thought she was the only girl in the world facing death threats, but now she realised she was not alone. In fact, given the choice, she'd rather be herself than Shelly. At least she knew who her enemy was.

'So, Darcie-whatever-your-real-name-is, are you coming aboard the SS Alcatraz? See if we can make Carl say that he's more than "disappointed"? I'm aiming for "very displeased" but Jon Lee thinks "livid" is possible.'

Darcie laughed. 'OK. I thought we'd made him go off the scale already.'

'No way. We've only just started. There's still a long way to go.'

The Fresh Start minibus carried the party of twelve young people and their guides down from the hotel to the luxury yacht, the *Pharaoh*, waiting for her passengers at the dockside. The vessel looked more like a miniature cruise liner: a sharp white prow, darkened glass windows, even a small pool on the sun deck. It looked very exclusive – something from Shelly's world, not Darcie's.

Carl optimistically hoped that boarding in the sleepy hours after lunch would keep the curious away, but nothing would deflect the attention of the press pack from the story of the moment. A line of Italian police kept reporters at bay but they were still close enough to shout their questions.

'Shelly – what did your father say to you this morning?'

'Did you drink alcohol last night, Shelly?'

'Take drugs?'

'You were fighting over the boy, weren't you?'

Shelly gave the onlookers a two-fingered salute. Jon Lee swooped up from behind and kissed her on the cheek.

'See, no hard feelings, man,' he said, laughing. He posed for photos until Carl hauled him away.

Darcie hurried on board with her head down, taking advantage of the bustle to hide herself.

'Right,' said Carl, once they were all gathered on the deck, 'thanks to our celebrity guests, we're setting sail immediately. No more shore leave until we reach Cyprus.' A groan went up from the group. 'Gina has the list of cabins – check it, take your stuff below and then report to the saloon in fifteen minutes. That's when Fresh Start really begins.'

'That sounds ominous,' Shelly whispered to Darcie.

Carl clapped his hands. 'Don't stand there looking at

me like sheep – move! Darcie, can I see you for a moment?'

Darcie had been expecting this. When she'd returned to the hotel with Shelly, she had only been asked to prove to two Italian police officers she was safe and well and had then been sent to her room to pack. Carl and Gina had obviously decided to give her some space. That space had just disappeared.

Carl ran his hands through his hair. 'Look, let's sit down.' He led her to two deckchairs side by side on the sundeck by the pool. It wasn't a good choice: they were now almost flat on their backs, staring up at the hotels on the cliff above the port. 'I heard what went on last night – it seems it wasn't your fault.' He paused, but Darcie said nothing. 'But running out on us was dumb. What did you think you'd achieve? Most kids are sent here because they keep running away from their problems rather than facing up to them. This is where we draw the line. This is your chance to deal with the problems.'

Darcie still didn't say anything. She wasn't sure

what it was she was supposed to deal with. Her problems did not seem of her own creation so neither was the solution in her hands.

'I'm not going to wrap you in cotton wool just because you're younger than everyone else.'

Silence.

'Darcie, are you even listening to me?'

'I am listening. You're not going to wrap me in cotton wool.'

'That's right. But if you want to pull another stunt like you did today, can you please at least think about talking to one of us first? You went straight to the nuclear option of running away without even considering what else could be done, didn't you?'

'I s'pose I did.'

'For better or worse you seem to be bonding with Shelly and Jon Lee. That's OK, I'm not here to patrol your friendships, but I will say "be careful". As you've already formed a team, we decided to put you in the same group, but I've allocated you a cabin near Gina and me on the other side of the boat. I don't want any more late night high-jinks. In the evening, you are under curfew: you're to be in your cabin at 10.30 until I say otherwise. That's the penalty for breaking curfew last night.'

'OK. That seems fair.'

'Good.' Carl smiled at her. 'Now let's put yesterday behind us, shall we? Start again? You might even enjoy yourself if you give it a chance. In the saloon in five, OK?'

'OK.'

When Darcie got to her room, she found someone had got there first. A tall glass of what looked like orange juice stood on the bedside table.

'If you're going to be on my team, I prefer you trashed,' read the note.

Darcie tore up Jon Lee's message and poured the contents of the glass down the sink. Some hope that this might be enjoyable.

The twelve students sat in easy chairs around the dance floor in the saloon, waiting to find out what Carl had in store for them. They had all been issued T-shirts which placed them in four different coloured teams. Shelly had already ripped the sleeves off her yellow vest; Jon Lee had scrawled over his in black pen, customising it with *Beware the yellow peril*. Darcie felt very self-conscious to be the only team member sitting dutifully, too obviously the good little girl.

'I told you yesterday that everyone here has a chance to start again,' announced Carl. He was smiling broadly. Darcie wondered whether the moment for his revenge on the new intake of spoiled rich kids was nigh. 'I meant it literally. We here at Fresh Start think that the greatest motor of change is a new way of looking at life – to view yourself and the way you behave from another perspective.'

Darcie's eyes drifted to the window. They were passing Capri. She wished they'd had time to visit this beautiful island but that had been cancelled for fear of the press besieging them again. Still too near Naples, according to Carl.

'Here's how we do it,' Carl continued, 'we take a leaf

out of the book of the Ancient Egyptians. You're on board the *Pharaoh*. Each day some of you will be pharaohs, living at the top of the social ladder, your every whim obeyed – a bit like what you're used to at home, I guess.'

You guess wrong, thought Darcie.

'After them come the courtiers, next the servants, and finally the slaves. If it's your turn to be pharaoh, you sit around and do nothing, issuing orders; if courtiers, you make sure the pharaohs are comfortable and then can have a pretty good time too; if servants, you cook the meals and serve drinks; if slaves, you clean – dishes, toilets, even feet if someone asks.'

Several in the circle laughed.

'That's gross!' said Shelly.

'Maybe, but think about it. You all get a turn. One day a pharaoh with smelly feet, next a slave. The person you made clean up after you might just make your life as miserable as you did his – or he might make it worse.

'One more thing – there are penalties for breaking

the rules or refusing a reasonable order from someone of a superior caste for the day.'

'Yeah, like what?' growled Jon Lee.

'That's to be decided by the other teams. Every evening we will hold a court to review the day's progress, presided over by the pharaohs, naturally. They can choose – within reason – what the punishment is to be. And everyone in that team shares it – even if only one person was at fault.'

Darcie had a very bad feeling about this. She could see no chance of her team-mates getting through an hour, let alone a whole day, without breaking rules. Shelly accept an order? He had to be joking.

'That's not fair!' said a Swedish girl with white-blonde hair, sitting next to Hans. She had the stick-thin looks of a supermodel and a sour expression – though why she was unhappy when she looked the way she did, Darcie couldn't guess.

'No, Karin, it's not,' replied Carl. 'But that's life. You're all too bright to need it spelt out. Don't you think it is better to have some of your rough edges smoothed on board the *Pharaoh* than to wait for the much harder school of life to do it to you? That's what your parents think. And all of you are heading for a crash with reality if you don't change direction now.'

'Sure, I'll change direction,' muttered Shelly. 'Turn the boat round and let me off at Monte Carlo. I'll apply for political asylum to escape my father.'

The Americans on board laughed sympathetically.

Carl ignored her. 'I think most of you will agree that, in view of the fact that certain people have deprived us of the chance to visit Capri, yellow team will be taking first watch as slaves; red, you're servants; green, you're courtiers; blue, you are today's pharaohs. This watch ends tomorrow evening, so lucky blues get extra time on the top of the ladder.'

'Yes!' Hans and Karin high-fived with their third team-mate, a Nigerian boy called Femi.

Darcie was surprised that Jon Lee and Shelly hadn't protested. She glanced sideways and saw them whispering.

'A list of basic duties is pinned to the galley door.

Other duties are at the discretion of the higher castes.'
Carl gave a grim smile. 'Enjoy.'

Darcie checked the list and groaned. The slaves had the greatest number of chores – bed making, floor mopping, cleaning bathrooms, fetching and carrying for the servants. It looked as though yellow team could say goodbye to sitting down for the foreseeable future.

'Bad luck,' said Hans, slapping her on the shoulder. 'But now I think of it, fetch me my sun-cream, slave; it is on my bedside table, cabin twelve. I will be on the deck.'

'OK, Pharaoh,' replied Darcie. She didn't have a problem with this part of the game – after all, she'd remember every time someone sent her scuttling off and could save up her revenge. The most annoying aspect was that she felt like a mouse in Carl's behavioural experiment. She suspected that even those who protested were already allowed for and their conduct anticipated. If she could only think of a way to beat the maze – the week ahead could be very entertaining, but so far her mind was a blank.

When she returned to the deck, she saw Shelly and Jon Lee stretched out on recliners next to Hans.

'Here you are,' Darcie said, putting the bottle down by the Austrian.

'Thank you.' Hans yawned and sat up. He glanced sideways at Shelly then looked at Darcie with a smile. 'Here, slave!' He tapped Shelly on the shoulder. 'Rub this on my back for me.'

'Get lost,' growled Shelly. 'I'm not playing these dumb games.'

Hans frowned. 'You have to.'

'No, I don't.'

Hans got to his feet and picked up his towel. 'So you're going to eat the food prepared by other students; enjoy rooms cleaned by someone else; and lay in the sun all week?'

'Yeah, that's about it. They should employ someone to do these things – there's enough people wanting a job, for Pete's sake. They shouldn't expect us to slave for each other. If you're stupid enough to play along, that's your problem.' Shelly turned over, letting her hand drape over the side of the sunbed.

'What about you, Jon Lee?' Hans was trying hard to control his temper – the veins on his neck were bulging.

'Jon Lee is going to sleep,' the New Yorker mumbled from under the baseball hat that he'd pulled over his face.

'What about the punishment?' Hans pressed. 'If you anger everyone, we are bound to give you one.'

'Get lost, Hans, you're beginning to bug me,' said Shelly lazily.

'I'd like to see someone try to punish me,' added Jon Lee.

'But what about your team-mate? What about Darcie?' Hans twisted the towel viciously in his fists.

Shelly lifted her sunglasses for a moment and stared straight at Darcie, offering her an unspoken challenge to join the rebels. 'That's up to her.' She replaced the shades and settled back down.

Hans glanced sideways at Darcie. This refusal to play

fair clearly infuriated him. Darcie sensed he was building up to an explosion of outrage. But what could she do?

'You two are the most arrogant, selfish people I have ever met! You're both . . .' He relapsed into his native tongue, letting out a stream of German.

Jon Lee didn't need to speak the language to know he was being bad-mouthed. He whipped his cap off and jumped up. 'You are really bugging me, Hulk-man. Like she said, get lost!'

Hans threw the towel at Jon Lee. 'Make me!'

'My pleasure.'

'Stop this!' shouted Darcie, barging between them. 'Just calm down!'

'Butt out, baby-face.' Jon Lee shoved her roughly sideways and threw a punch at Hans. Darcie stumbled over a sunbed, lost her balance and fell into the pool. The shock of the cold water forced a scream from her before she went under. She came up spluttering.

'She's drowning!' shrieked Shelly, tumbling off her recliner. Hans and Jon Lee were oblivious to the drama, locked in their private battle. 'Darcie!'

'I'm all right,' coughed Darcie, splashing her way to the side. She stood up. The water barely reached her shoulders. She felt ridiculous.

Shelly gave a relieved laugh and held out her hand. 'You had me scared for a moment there.'

By now, the fight had attracted the attention of the rest of the crew. Carl came running, grabbed Hans by the back of his shirt and hauled.

'Help me!' he gasped.

Femi stepped in and pulled Jon Lee none-too-gently off his team-mate. The American boy's nose was bleeding but the big-framed Austrian was unhurt.

'I'll get you!' hissed Jon Lee, wiping the blood away.

'Any time, shrimp,' jeered Hans.

Carl looked furious. He turned from Jon Lee, to Hans, to the wringing-wet Darcie. 'What has been going on here?'

'They won't join in,' said Hans, pointing at Shelly and Jon Lee. 'They are leaving Darcie to do all the work.'

Carl ran his fingers through his hair in exasperation.

'What has that got to do with fighting? You disagree? OK. Wait until the court this evening. But you don't come to blows about it. That's what you've got to learn, Hans, before you end up really hurting someone.'

Hans looked crestfallen. 'Sorry,' he muttered.

Carl turned to Darcie. 'How did you end up in the pool?'

'I . . . er . . . tripped.'

'No, she didn't,' countered Jon Lee. 'She was trying to stop us so I pushed her out of my way,' he said proudly, baiting Carl to be angry.

'I'm pleased that at least one of you had the decency to try and prevent violence. As for you two, I'm *very* disappointed . . .'

'Only "very",' Shelly whispered to Darcie. 'Jon Lee will be really annoyed he didn't score higher. Waste of a bloody nose.'

Darcie couldn't help smiling.

'We'll deal with this later at the court,' said Carl, tight-lipped. 'Darcie, go get changed.' He pointed at

John Lee and Hans. 'And you two – keep away from each other for the rest of the day. Hans, I think we'd better have a chat about anger-management in my office. Now.'

6

Alone in her cabin to change into dry clothes, Darcie considered her options. For better or worse, she was on board this vessel for at least a week. She could either sit out with Shelly or try to get something from the Fresh Start formula. OK, she was angry with her parents for sending her into this madhouse, for wanting to change her into someone they found more acceptable, but she still was going to visit the pyramids, it wasn't all bad news.

The books her father had given her lay on her bedside table. She flicked through the top one but her mind was really on her parents. Should she ring them? She hadn't answered their text messages, at first because she was ashamed of herself, then because she wanted to avoid a scene. No, she'd leave it. Let them cool off and allow time to pull herself together. She knew that she'd been very down for the last few weeks. That wasn't her normal self at all. She had to come to grips with her new life as Darcie Logan, like it or lump it.

What about Stingo? Should she answer his text? She decided to let him stew a bit longer. He hadn't paused to find out what had really happened. He deserved no reply.

She pulled a new yellow T-shirt out of its cellophane wrapper and held it against her chest.

Maul it about? Rip off the sleeves?

Too corny. If she did that, she'd look as if she was copying Jon Lee and Shelly. She needed to find her own way of dealing with this.

Besides, she'd proved that she could look after herself in Kenya, hadn't she? She was no one's baby. They weren't going to get the better of her. Jon Lee was just a spoiled kid who thought rebellion meant being rude and annoying people. So did Shelly in her own way. They both mocked her for playing the Fresh Start game, but they were playing it too even if they didn't realise. A real rebel would remake the rules to fit their agenda.

It was then Darcie had a brainwave: the perfect revenge on all of them – on Carl with his formulaic responses to everything, on Shelly and Jon Lee for the way they treated her, part pet, part butt of their jokes. And the best thing of all, she thought as she checked her appearance in the mirror, in this case, revenge really was sweet.

Darcie knew she couldn't put her plan into action until she'd finished serving her time as slave. She was kept busy the rest of that day. As the only one from yellow team on duty, she had to do all the fetching and carrying for the servants who were cooking supper. She knew they were giving her an easier time than they might as their resentment was directed towards Jon Lee and Shelly, both of whom were still lying by the pool, pretending to take no notice of the others.

'You again?' asked the store-room manager as Darcie went below for the tenth time to fetch some lemons. She had already discovered after her third visit that he was a young Egyptian called Antar on his first voyage. He had a friendly smile and excellent English, learned, he claimed, by listening to the BBC World Service at night. Tall for his cramped quarters below decks, he had to hunch as he moved around.

'Yep, me again,' she replied.

'What's it this time?' he called as he disappeared inside the store.

'Lemons. Red team are making pasta with green vegetables. Actually, Antar, can you get me some parsley while you're there? They haven't asked for it but I took a look at the recipe when they weren't watching.'

'Of course.'

He came back with what she had asked for, plus a large slab of parmesan cheese. 'That will save you another trip,' he said.

'Thanks. You're my hero.'

'I wouldn't go so far as to say that.' His eyes, large and dark brown in his suntanned face, laughed at her. 'Just forward-planning – like you. Here, take a break for a moment. The wise slave does his work slowly and never shows his real thoughts to the masters.' Antar tapped the box of tinned tuna next to his stool. 'Do you want a Coke?'

'Thanks.'

He opened two bottles and passed her one. 'So, how is it going upstairs?'

'Trouble's brewing,' she said simply, taking a gulp.

'More trouble? You mean *more* than a brawl outside a nightclub and a fight by the pool?'

Darcie blushed. 'You know about that do you?'

'Everyone on the crew knows about that. How is Miss America behaving now?'

'Doing nothing – that's the problem.'

'I see.' Antar smiled sympathetically. Darcie noticed that he had a small tattoo on the base of his throat – a stylised crocodile, like the ones she'd seen in her books about Egyptian hieroglyphics.

'What's that?' she asked, pointing.

Antar touched the mark self-consciously then did up the top button of his shirt to hide it. 'Oh, nothing.' He now stood up, putting down his half-finished bottle of

Coke. 'You know, I had better get on with my work. Come and see me any time, Darcie. Let me know how things are going in yellow team, won't you?'

Returning to the galley, Darcie wondered about the crocodile – it seemed a most intriguing choice for a tattoo.

She handed the lemons over to the cooks. They were preparing the meal under Gina's supervision.

'Hey, slave-girl,' said Gina, 'can you fetch us some parsley – I forgot to ask.'

Darcie produced her bunch with a flourish. 'Next you're going to ask for some parmesan, aren't you?'

Gina glanced down at the recipe. 'You're right.'

Darcie placed the cheese on the counter.

'I'm impressed, slave-girl,' grinned Gina. 'Go and take five outside.'

Leaving the red team to their steaming pots, Darcie emerged on to the welcome cool of the deck. The pharaohs were playing cards; the courtiers were chatting; Jon Lee and Shelly appeared to be asleep. Hans looked up as she approached an empty chair.

'Hey, come here.'

What now, she thought?

'What is your command, oh great and wise ruler of the universe?' she intoned, bowing mockingly.

Hans laughed. 'Nothing. We just wanted to ask you something. Sit down.'

Darcie perched beside him, glancing at Femi and Karin curiously. Blue team were up to something.

'Do you like swimming?' Karin asked softly.

Darcie thought they must be teasing her about her dip earlier in the day. 'As you saw, I don't waste any opportunity to get wet. Why?'

'You'll find out. Just come to the court wearing your swimming costume – and don't tell the rest of yellow team – that's a command,' grinned Hans.

19.00, At sea off Amalfi, Italy: Overnight showers, 18°C
The yacht anchored that evening in a bay near some spectacular cliffs. Houses and churches clung to the rocks like a colony of nesting birds. Shafts of the setting sun fell obliquely across the water, making the

crowd gathered on the deck shade their eyes as the pharaohs assumed the three chairs placed centre stage. Blue team had entered into the spirit of the occasion by placing towels over their heads, Egyptian-style.

'Silence in court,' shouted a boy from green team, thumping the deck with a hockey stick.

Hans stood up. He was thoroughly enjoying himself, having discovered for the first time that delayed revenge was better than immediate anger. Planning this particular vengeance had obviously made his day.

'It has been brought to our attention,' he announced, 'both through complaints from our servants and courtiers, and from the evidence of our own eyes, that certain members of the slave community have not been carrying out the orders of higher castes.'

Shelly and Jon Lee were not standing with the others. They were talking loudly to each other by the rail, again pretending not to be interested in what their fellow passengers were doing.

'One was also seen pushing a fellow slave into the pool. We have therefore decided that a fitting punishment is for them to be made to . . .' he paused dramatically . . . 'walk the plank!'

Red, blue and green team cheered. Even Carl and Gina could not hide their smiles. Shelly's protection team looked positively ecstatic.

'Not very Ancient Egypt, Pharaoh,' commented Carl.

'We didn't think you'd let us feed them to our pet crocodiles,' explained Femi.

'OK,' grinned Carl. 'You can carry out the sentence – it seems reasonable to me.'

Hans clapped his hands and two servants produced the boarding ramp. They slid it into place.

'Who's to go first?' asked the boy from green team, approaching Shelly and Jon Lee. Darcie stood back behind Hans, anticipating that it was suddenly about to get very stormy.

'Don't you dare touch me!' yelled Shelly, pushing the boy away.

'Get her!' called Hans.

Karin and two girls from green team ran forward, tackled Shelly and pulled her over to the plank.

'One, two, three!' chanted the crowd – and the president's daughter was pushed over the side, falling into the bay with a big splash. She came up swearing at those laughing as they leaned over the rail to watch.

Jon Lee meanwhile was wrestling with the boy from green team and two others. Unlike Shelly, who had put up only slight resistance, he acted as if he were fighting for his life.

'Back off!' he screamed, taking a wild swipe at them.

Hans strode across, picked Jon Lee up in a fireman's lift, marched back to the plank and threw him over the side. Jon Lee went down with arms and legs flailing, hitting the water with an untidy smack. The crowd cheered and hooted.

Darcie was eager to get this over and done with. She stripped off her T-shirt and stood on the plank, waiting for Jon Lee to resurface. He didn't come. The laughter faded as those nearest the rail started to mutter.

'Can he swim?' asked Karin, her face pale.

Darcie didn't wait to hear the answer. She dived from the end of the board and slipped beneath the waves. The salt stung her eyes but she could just make out somebody thrashing about some metres away, bubbles escaping from his mouth in a silent scream. She swam to Jon Lee, grabbed his arm, then kicked strongly for the surface. She broke into the air, took a gulp and bobbed down again so she could push Jon Lee up. He gasped and struggled as he reached the surface, pushing Darcie back under as he tried to climb up her like a ladder. They both sank.

'Don't!' she spluttered as she emerged, dragging him up with her. 'Trust me – stop kicking.'

Jon Lee's eyes were wide with terror. He no longer looked the arrogant teenager, but a frightened boy.

With two splashes, Hans and Carl jumped in the sea beside them.

'I'll take him,' said Carl, attempting to slide his arm under Jon Lee's neck.

But Jon Lee refused to let go of Darcie. His grip was painful, making red welts on her arm. Still panicking, he pushed her under as he struggled against Carl. Hans grabbed Jon Lee's arm and prised him off Darcie.

'Stop that! You'll drown her,' Hans shouted, ducking Jon Lee to get his attention.

When she came up again, Hans and Carl were towing Jon Lee to a rope ladder that had been let down the side. Hands reached down from above to help pull Jon Lee in. Shelly had already reached deck and was screaming at anyone who'd listen.

'He'll sue you, you morons! You almost killed him!'

Shelly's spiked hair straggled over her face, her make-up ran down her cheeks, and she'd lost a sneaker.

Darcie rewarded herself by diving back under the water and swimming a few relaxing strokes away from the boat. It was tempting to carry on swimming to the beach but, reluctantly, she returned and was the last one up over the side.

Jon Lee collapsed on to the deck, coughing out sea water, but seemed otherwise unhurt. Dripping from his unexpected dip, Hans rounded on Shelly.

'How were we to know he couldn't swim? Did he ask when he pushed Darcie into the pool? Did he care if she could swim or not?'

Karin passed Darcie a towel. 'You all right?' she asked.

'Fine, thanks.'

Several other people she didn't know well came over and congratulated her on her quick action.

'That was cool.'

'Where did you learn to dive like that?'

'You're wasted on yellow team – come and join red.'

'Good work, Darcie,' said Carl, pushing through the crowd to give her a one-armed hug. 'Now go get dry – I seem to be telling you that a lot, don't I?'

Darcie smiled. 'Yeah, this voyage is getting a bit repetitive.'

'You might find it boring, but I'm certainly not: you keep on surprising me. Try not to do anything else heroic before supper, OK? I don't think my nerves can take it.'

The next day, Shelly and Jon Lee did not emerge on deck but spent their time sulking in the saloon watching DVDs and foul-mouthing everyone who came near them. When Darcie came to say hello, Jon Lee did not even mention the fact that she had saved him: he looked through her, complaining she was blocking his view. Shelly, however, was not so ungrateful.

'Mean swimming, Kiddo,' she said. 'Want to learn to rollerblade?'

'What, now?'

'Yeah, why not?'

'Maybe tomorrow. I'm a bit busy today.'

'Still playing along?'

'I guess.' Darcie held up the mop she was using to wash the decks.

Shelly gave a disgusted shrug and turned back to the screen. 'I'm surprised. I thought you had more guts than that.'

Darcie had had enough. 'It's better than sitting on my backside all day letting the others do the work.'

'Ouch!' mocked Shelly. 'You do have claws. Go on and play then – don't let me keep you.'

Later, Hans confided that the yellow team were only getting meals because no one wanted to deprive

Darcie of the food she had helped prepare.

'I was all for bread and water rations for them,' he told her in his serious manner, 'but it didn't seem fair that you'd have to share it. Can't you put in for a transfer to our team so we can really teach them a lesson?' His appetite for revenge had not been dampened by half-drowning Jon Lee.

'You know the rules, Hans. I'm stuck in yellow till Carl says otherwise.'

'If I were you, I would mutiny.'

'Don't worry – I'm planning to.'

The punishment at that evening's court was very mild compared to the previous night. Yellow team were relegated to taking their meal outside and barred from the post-supper entertainments in the saloon. Darcie sat apart from Shelly and Jon Lee, trying to enjoy the cool breeze and sunset as she ate her rations. In the darkening east, the sea rippled like grey silk under the oyster-shell sky. Behind her the sun sank in a gold blaze, melting into the horizon. When it rose again, she'd be a pharaoh.

7

Apart from yellow team's overnight promotion to the top of the social ladder, everyone else had moved down a rung.

'It's good for you,' Carl told the students at breakfast. 'We could plan it the other way round, of course, but we think it is better to know that tomorrow things will be worse rather than better. That knowledge helps moderate your behaviour.'

Shelly and Jon Lee walked out, leaving Darcie in sole charge of the top table.

'I guess that means we will all be dancing attendance on just one pharaoh today,' Carl said wryly, bowing to Darcie.

At least Jon Lee and Shelly weren't going to take part just when it suited them, thought Darcie, watching them go. It would make her plan unworkable if they had decided to be pharaohs.

'Right,' announced Carl, clapping his hands.

'There's a lot to do – get going.'

Red team shuffled wearily to their feet. As the slaves, they knew they had a depressing day ahead.

'So, Darcie, how are you going to spend your holiday?' Carl said, taking a seat beside her.

'Oh, doing this and that,' Darcie replied vaguely.

'You've certainly earned some time off.'

Bernadette, an Irish girl whose red hair clashed horribly with her T-shirt, approached them.

'What's your cabin number, Pharaoh?' she asked Darcie sulkily. 'I've been told to make your bed and clean up.'

'No need,' Darcie replied brightly. 'I've done it already.'

Bernadette gave her a surprised look. 'You're not supposed to do that.'

'Just habit,' Darcie shrugged.

'So, Carl, can I have the key to do your cabin?' Bernadette held out her hand.

'Sure.' Carl patted his pockets and then dropped the key into her palm.

'Bernadette, do you need any help?' asked Darcie.

'Are you joking? All these cabins to clean and the others have been sent off by green team to shell peas.'

'OK, I'll come with you.'

Carl caught her by the arm. 'Er, Darcie, I don't think you've quite got the idea. You're the pharaoh – you just get this one shot at it.'

'You mean I'm not allowed to help Bernadette?' Darcie asked.

'Of course you're allowed; it's just not how the game's played.'

'That's OK then.' Darcie got up with a smile at Carl's astounded expression. 'Better get started if there's so much to do.'

Darcie blended in with red team very happily all morning, singing favourite songs with Bernadette while they cleaned the cabins, then mucking about with the rest of the trio as they washed down the decks. None of the other teams could reprimand the slaves for jousting with the mops while they had the pharaoh with them. Red team was having a brilliant time.

Carl sat down beside Gina in the saloon, gazing out at the antics on deck.

'What's going on?' asked Gina, looking up from her paperwork.

'It's yellow team.'

'You mean Jon Lee and Shelly?'

'No. As expected, they're still pretending not to take part – they'll tire of that eventually. It's the kid.'

A mop-head slopped against the window, accompanied by shrieks of laughter from Bernadette.

Gina joined him at the window and saw Darcie pursuing a red T-shirted boy with a wringing wet sponge. 'Looks like she's having fun. Nothing wrong with that.'

Carl scratched his chin. 'No, but she's doing the slaves' chores with them – not taking advantage of her time as pharaoh at all.'

'Perhaps she's too shy to order everyone else around?' suggested Gina.

'She doesn't look shy to me,' said Carl as Darcie caught up with the boy and squeezed the sponge over his head as he fended her off with his mop.

'Then what's she doing?'

'I think,' said Carl slowly, 'I think she's being very clever.'

'What?'

'I hate to say it, but I think she's sabotaging Fresh Start.'

Gina grimaced. 'You'd better have a word with her then.'

'I intend to.'

Carl strode out on to the deck to find that blue team had joined in the sponge fight. Shelly and Jon Lee were watching from a safe distance, but even they were laughing as Hans received a face-full of water from Darcie.

'I'll get you!' growled Hans good-humouredly, grabbing a mop from Bernadette and chasing Darcie round the pool.

'You'll have to be quicker than that,' shrieked Darcie, as she dodged the mop-head, jumped over a recliner – and collided with Carl. He caught her by the shoulders. Red and blue team stopped in their tracks, exchanging guilty looks.

'I'd like a word, Pharaoh,' said Carl tersely. 'Carry on with your duties, red team. Courtiers, I expect to see you keeping your servants under control.'

Carl marched Darcie into the saloon and gestured for her to sit in an armchair. He remained standing over her. 'Just what do you think you're playing at?'

'I was just having fun,' said Darcie meekly. She'd anticipated that Carl would react like this. All she had to do was stand her ground – he could not accuse her of doing anything wrong.

'Don't give me that – I know what you're up to.'

'Oh? What's that?' She curled her knees up to her chest and looked up at him innocently.

'You're trying to ruin our system.'

'Am I breaking any rules?'

'No,' Carl admitted reluctantly.

'Have I upset anyone?'

'No.'

'So what am I doing wrong, Carl?'

'You're not playing the game properly. How will you make progress unless you experience the four stages in society? You won't learn to show consideration for others.'

'You think I don't respect other people?'

'You tell me – you must have been sent here for a reason. Someone must have thought you had something to learn and I can tell you, young lady, that there's not been a single student on Fresh Start who hasn't been an arrogant berk in real life. You hide it well, but maybe you're just about the worst of the lot.'

That hurt.

'I'm sorry if you don't like my behaviour, Carl, but as you said, I'm not breaking your rules.'

'Obeying the letter is not the same as following the spirit, Darcie. You know that. I am very, very disappointed in you.'

Darcie let the silence stretch between them, before asking:

'Can I go now?'

Carl nodded.

Darcie walked out on to the deck. Hans came over to her and put a comforting arm around her shoulders.

'Did he give you grief?' he asked with concern.

'No, I think I gave him grief.' Darcie turned to Shelly who was standing not far away. 'I got a result – a "very, very disappointed". Aren't you impressed?'

'You devious little thing,' said Shelly in admiration. She threw aside her magazine. 'I wish I'd thought of it first.'

'Still time to join in if you want,' grinned Darcie. 'Hans, how about a rematch with the mops?'

'You're on!' The Austrian relieved Bernadette of her deck-cleaning equipment.

'Count me in!' announced Shelly.

'You know,' said Darcie, 'this would be even better on rollerblades . . .'

That evening, the pharaoh ascended her throne, decked out in a robe that Shelly had pinned together from bedsheets. Darcie looked round the smiling faces of her Fresh Start colleagues.

'I would like to use this court to announce the winners of the jousting competition held on the sun-deck this afternoon. Winner of the mop freestyle was Hans Voss of blue team.'

Hans stepped forward to receive the prize of a plastic bucket, bowing as he acknowledged the cheers of the crowd. He put it on his head like a helmet.

'Undisputed winner of the wheel-mounted mop was Shelly Morris.' Darcie presented the president's daughter with a wet sponge.

The onlookers cheered again. Shelly looked pleased to find herself unexpectedly the object of approval rather than annoyance. Even her security team were applauding as she took a bow, that was until they had to duck as she threw the sponge at them.

Darcie searched for Jon Lee among the spectators, but he had chosen to boycott the event. She wondered what he would do now she had stolen his partner in crime. Whatever it was, she could only hope he did not bear her a grudge . . .

*

By the time the yacht approached Cyprus, Fresh Start had descended into a very enjoyable chaos. Darcie's revolt against the division of labour spread. A competition began as to who could do the most chores in the most riotous fashion with prizes at each evening's court being awarded to the most outrageous. Specialisms were encouraged as everyone tried to show off their skills. Shelly turned out to be a fantastic cook – something she had picked up in the White House, she explained, as she had spent a lot of time hanging out in the kitchen when fancy dinners were being prepared. After a truly memorable risotto, she was unanimously elected as head chef for the duration of the voyage and relieved of all cleaning duties.

'She can't do that!' Carl had protested on finding Shelly presiding over the galley for the third day in a row.

'Why not?' asked Darcie. 'Each day the pharaoh appoints her as chef. On the day she is pharaoh, she decides she wants to spend it cooking. What's the problem?'

Carl just shook his head, watching his carefully laid scheme veering off course like a boat with a broken rudder. He could not think how to bring it back on the route he had plotted. Unless, he thought, he got rid of the unlikely ringleader.

Darcie was appointed liaison with the store-room manager as it was recognised that she was most popular with the crew and seemed to be able to wheedle supplies from Antar that he had sworn point-blank to others he had not got.

'You seem to have caused a little revolution,' Antar told her one afternoon as they had their customary drink together. 'The Fresh Start people are very unhappy.'

Darcie shrugged. 'But everyone else is happier, don't you think?'

'There is no doubt about that. Just be careful: it is not wise to make enemies.' Antar leaned back and closed his eyes; he looked more tired and somehow sadder than at the start of the voyage.

'Are you OK?' Darcie asked.

'I am fine. Perhaps I am not as good a sailor as I thought.'

'Are you missing home?'

Antar shot her a quick look from under his half-closed eyes. 'Maybe.'

'What's it like? Where is it?'

'You wouldn't have heard of it,' Antar said dismissively.

'Try me. I'm interested.'

'Few westerners are – they think all Arabs are terrorists.'

'That's just a stupid caricature,' said Darcie, thinking of her polo-playing friend Kassim, from Nairobi. 'Tell me something about yourself.'

'There is little to tell. I went to college in America and I am now travelling far from home. I am noboby special. What about you? Where is your home?'

Darcie sighed. 'I don't have one at the moment.'

'That is not right. Everyone needs a home. Your home is where your people are – your parents, your relatives.'

'Exactly my problem.' She smiled at his puzzled face. 'Don't worry about me – I'll end up somewhere, I expect.'

The *Pharaoh* sailed into the port of Limassol at dawn. Darcie woke to find houses, hotels and people just outside her porthole. Beyond the rocky shore, a row of scraggy palm trees waved in the stiff breeze: thick trunks sporting green, spiky topknots like punk haircuts. White low-rise blocks of apartments lined the esplanade, beach towels set out to dry on balconies like bunting. It would be good to set foot on land again. Life on board was mostly enjoyable, but she felt in the background the oppressive disapproval of three people: Carl, Gina and Jon Lee. There was no escaping them at sea.

There was a tap on her door.

'Darcie?' It was Carl, using that pained voice he now always employed when addressing her.

She opened the door and he handed her a fax.

'This just came. It seems that your grandfather has decided to check up on you.'

'My grandfather?'

'Don't sound so astonished. He said he was here on holiday and wanted to take the opportunity to see you. Didn't you know?'

'No.'

'He's going to join us on our trip to the amphi-theatre.' Carl paused. 'I . . . er . . . I want to ask him to consider taking you out of Fresh Start.'

'What!' This was the last thing Darcie wanted – to meet her grandfather for the first time and have his ears assailed with complaints about her behaviour. 'That's not fair! I've not done anything wrong!'

'Do you really believe that?'

'But I haven't broken the rules – not since that first night in Naples.'

'But you have spoiled it for everyone else with your clever game-playing. No one's learning anything – except how to muck around.'

Darcie turned away so he couldn't see that he had

upset her. Was he right? It seemed to her that they had all learned how to get on with each other. Surely that was worth something?'

'So you're expelling me?'

'Not exactly. I would like you and your grandfather to consider whether it would not be better for you to leave us here. The decision is yours. If you stay, I can't see how I can get the course back on track. Fresh Start has never failed anyone in the past, but I fear it has failed you. My advice is that you now go.'

'So the mouse that beat the maze is being chucked out,' Darcie said, half to herself.

'Mouse?' Carl guessed what she meant and glowered at her. 'I don't regard you as an experiment, you know.'

Darcie shrugged, not believing him. 'Whatever. I'll think about quitting, but I'd prefer it if you didn't involve my grandfather.'

Carl scented a weakness: perhaps Darcie knew that the old man would naturally gravitate to his side? 'I have to, I'm afraid,' he replied.

'Why?' Darcie asked.

'You need to talk this through with someone who knows you well and has your best interests at heart.'

'That rules out my grandfather. I've never met him.'

Fresh from his interview with Darcie, Carl sought out Gina in the office.

'That girl is more of a mystery than ever,' he said, sitting down at the desk and calling up Darcie's details on the computer. 'She just told me that she's never met this grandfather of hers.'

'You know these diplomatic kids – new city every few years. Perhaps her parents haven't gone home for a while?' suggested Gina.

'For fourteen years? I can't believe that.'

'Maybe the family quarrelled?'

'Possibly.' Carl tapped at the keyboard, scrolling through the very few details they had on their most troublesome client. 'And do you know what else she said?'

'Go on.'

'She said that I was treating her like the mouse that defeated the maze – accused me of chucking her out of the experiment.'

Gina snorted.

'I don't treat them like that, do I? I believe in Fresh Start – we've had good results in the past.'

Gina massaged Carl's tense shoulders as he hunched over the screen. 'Well, maybe she has a point. Perhaps we have become too rigid – expecting the course to follow the same pattern each time.'

'But I owe it to the other parents to achieve the right result for their kids. I have no way of predicting what will happen if we let that girl stay.'

'I agree it would be safer to let her go.' Gina smiled. 'I can't help admiring the kid, though. She's got a group of eleven of her peers all following her without even appearing to want to be the leader – not bad going. And she seems to have cheered up – that's good.'

Carl grimaced. 'She had cheered up, but I think I've just upset her again by telling her that we don't want her to continue.'

'Don't beat yourself up about it. She'll bounce back – she's proved that much already.'

'Yeah, you're right.' Carl closed the screen displaying Darcie's file. 'I'll have words with this grandfather of hers. I think it would be better to be safe than sorry as far as Darcie Logan goes.'

8

Darcie slung her rollerblades round her neck as she disembarked from the minibus that had taken the group to the Roman amphitheatre at Kourion. The sun was already hot on her back as she followed the others to the shade of a palm tree.

'Why did you bring them ashore?' Shelly asked her, tapping the rollerblades. 'Not much chance to skate round here. Anyway, it's too hot.' They looked up at the raked seating that formed a crescent around the stage, light glaring off the white stone. A group of acrobats in sequinned green suits were clustered in the sun-bleached centre under a banner: Cirque de L'Est – Circus of the East. A woman juggled at the side of the stage, waiting for her chance to rehearse.

'I just wanted to thank my grandfather – show him that I got his present. That looks interesting.' Darcie nodded towards the circus troupe.

'Performance isn't until this evening when it cools

down,' said Gina, appearing at Darcie's elbow. 'Perhaps we'll come back to see it if there are tickets left.'

'That'd be great,' said Shelly, watching the juggler throw six balls in the air and catch them as they ran down her back.

Darcie said nothing, wondering if she would still be part of Fresh Start by the time the performance began. Part of her would be sorry to leave her new friends.

'I came to tell you, Darcie, that your grandfather rang to say he is waiting for you up on row eleven.' Gina pointed up into the auditorium where an elderly man wearing a white hat could be seen sitting in the sun.

Darcie felt a swoop of nerves like missing the bottom step in the dark. This was the first time she was going to meet someone other than her parents who shared the same blood as her – one of her people, as Antar would have put it.

'OK,' she said hoarsely.

'Your grandfather? What's he doing here?' asked Shelly with interest.

'I don't know – I've not met him before.' Shelly raised a brow. 'But he gave me the rollerblades,' Darcie said hurriedly, offering the one piece of information she did know about him.

'He sounds fun.'

'The minibus leaves in two hours,' continued Gina, also watching the man on the eleventh row. Carl was making his way towards him, his arm held out to shake hands.

Darcie groaned. Her grandfather would be set against her before she even had time to explain what had been going on.

'It'll be OK,' said Gina, taking pity on the ashen-faced girl before her. 'Carl just wants to have a quick word.'

Darcie swallowed – her throat felt like sandpaper – and set off up the bank of stone steps.

'So you see, Mr Logan, I really think your grand-daughter has gained all she can from Fresh Start. I would like you to consider removing her from the course today and taking her back with you.'

Carl finished his piece and found himself staring into the pale blue eyes of Darcie's grandfather. The old man's gaze was like a late frost. Carl felt the tender green shoots of his argument blacken and curl up.

'Do I understand you correctly, young man? You are telling me that my granddaughter has done nothing more than subvert your little brainwashing strategies?'

'Hardly brainwashing, Mr Logan.'

'But she saw right through all your management-speak mumbo-jumbo and has allowed everyone to have a whale of a time.'

'I don't know about that –'

'I do. I say "Good for her". I would have thought the less of her if she'd tamely submitted to your scheme. A true chip off the old block – that's what she is.'

Carl could see that he was going to get nowhere on this tack.

'But you must have seen what she got up to in Naples. Surely the family is worried about her? With the benefit of hindsight, it's clear Darcie is too young for us.'

'Too young? What utter drivel! It's you that is getting too old to work with young people if you think a bit of under-age drinking a sign of incurable delinquency.'

'I wasn't suggesting that she –'

'I should hope not. Then I can tell you that the family is not the least bit concerned. She is doing splendidly. If she's beaten your system, I suggest you go back to the drawing board and think where you went wrong. She's good for you. You should be thanking us for sending her to you. Ah! Here she is now.'

Christopher Lock stood up as his granddaughter approached them hesitantly.

'I was just telling Earl here –' he began.

'Carl,' corrected the Fresh Start man irritably.

'Yes, that's what I said. I was just telling him how well you are doing on his little course. Earl says you've cracked the code – well done you, eh? I am impressed.'

Darcie did not know what to say. 'Er . . . thanks, Grandad.' It felt so strange calling him that – like a foreign word in her mouth.

'Not at all, my dear. Now, Earl, my granddaughter and I have a lot to discuss.'

'In that case I'll make myself scarce,' Carl said huffily. He turned and stalked back down the aisle.

'His name *is* Carl, you know,' Darcie said as she sat down next to the stranger, 'not Earl.'

'I know,' said Christopher Lock with a small smile, 'but it was very amusing to watch him get all hot under the collar, wasn't it?'

'So you don't want me to leave the cruise?'

'Heavens, no. Though your mother and father have instructed me to say that you can give it up if you want.'

'Has Carl been complaining to them too?' Darcie asked in despair.

Christopher looked out over the tumbling acrobats and milling crowds of tourists, pleased that she had leapt to this conclusion without him even having to prompt the thought. He wouldn't have to explain that they were worried for her safety. 'Not that I know, but we do not talk much, as you have probably guessed.'

He turned to her and held out his hand. 'I'm pleased to meet you at last, Darcie. It's been too long in coming: you've grown up and I've only seen you once or twice and then only as a baby. We've got a lot of lost time to make up.'

Darcie shook his hand, only realising now she was up close that he looked so very much like her father – he had the same eyebrows, same jawline. Even his voice was uncannily similar.

'I'm afraid I don't know anything about you,' Darcie said apologetically.'Mum and Dad never mentioned you.'

'Your mother does not approve of me – thinks I'm a bad influence. But there's not much to know about me anyway, my dear. I'm a boring old fuddy-duddy who spends far too much time in his club and not enough time with his granddaughter.'

'Is there a . . . a Mrs Lock – my grandmother, I mean?'

'There was. She went her separate way some years ago.'

Darcie wasn't sure if that meant she was dead or

divorced, but felt too shy to press him for a clearer answer.

'It's just me now, I'm afraid. But that's enough about my life. Tell me all about yourself. I hear you have some interesting new friends. Carl was quite put out by your facility to make allies.'

Darcie laughed and began to describe her colleagues on the *Pharaoh*. She wasn't surprised that he showed most interest in Shelly – after all, who would not be intrigued to find out more about the president's famously wayward daughter?

'So they spiked your drink, eh?' Christopher mused when she'd finished. 'In your line of work, you have to be very careful about that sort of thing.'

'My line of work?' Darcie looked puzzled.

Christopher cursed himself for forgetting she knew nothing about the mission he had devised for her. 'I meant your all-engrossing task of enjoying your youth,' he amended. He took a second look at her, congratulating himself that the Lock family had turned out another top-notch specimen: fit, healthy, pretty.

'And you should enjoy it while you may. Thus speaks the old man whose prime is long since passed. They're already scheming at the office to put me out to grass.'

Darcie had assumed that he must be retired so was surprised to learn that he was still working. 'What do you do?'

'Oh, it's very dull. Foreign relations, business, you know the sort of thing.'

'Not really,' admitted Darcie with a smile.

'That's how it should be. No need to worry about all that at your age.' It was time to change the subject. 'How about an ice cream and then you can show me how you're getting on with my present.' He waved at the rollerblades.

As they made their way down to ground level, Christopher leaned on Darcie's arm, and began to wheeze gently. Acting had always been his favourite part of the job of a spy, so he had decided before he left England that the part of grandfather necessitated the adoption of a slight limp and walking stick. His tailor in Savile Row had run him up a dapper blazer and trousers suitable for the Mediterranean, and suggested the finishing touch of a panama hat. Christopher reflected on how enjoyable it was to be back on active service after all those years at his desk.

Darcie was also enjoying his company, but for very different reasons. She had quickly warmed to her grandfather. His defence of her conduct with Carl was the first point in his favour, and then his interest in her settled the matter. The only shade to an otherwise sunny relationship was that she had a concern that he was over-exerting himself: his breath had become laboured and he was more hunched than ever.

'Why not sit in the shade, Grandad, and I'll get the ice creams,' she suggested.

'Thank you, my dear.' He pressed some money into her hand. 'Something plain for me – dicky tummy according to the doctor.'

While Darcie was away, Christopher invented a few more medical symptoms to sprinkle into the conversation – a dodgy ticker was a must, possibly a vague war wound to explain the limp. He was so used to living a loveless life surrounded by colleagues who didn't care two hoots for him that he was determined to exploit his one opportunity to be with someone who would be bothered about him for himself. She was a sweet girl. He really must make the time to see more of her and help her develop the first-rate skills she had already demonstrated.

Darcie came back with two vanilla ice creams and they chatted about the amphitheatre as they ate them. Relishing his role of a wise old bird, Christopher told her all that he could remember from his schooldays about classical theatre.

'A lot of this is fake, of course,' he added, waving his stick at the banks of stone seats, 'a replica built on the ruins of the old – archaeological guesswork. Now, what about that skating? Let us find somewhere for you to show me what you're made of.'

They found a quieter alleyway round the back of the amphitheatre and Darcie buckled on her new blades.

'I'm not that good yet,' she warned him. 'I've only practised on deck.'

'This should be easy then,' he said encouragingly. 'At least the ground keeps still.'

Darcie glided up the alley and stopped clumsily at the end. Christopher was disappointed: he had been hoping for something more impressive but she really wasn't very good at all. He was about to say something, but stopped himself in time, remembering it wasn't in character.

'A good start. Well done,' he called.

'No, that was rubbish. I'll get better in a minute,' replied Darcie, beginning the return journey.

Christopher noted her honesty with approval. At least she didn't over-estimate her own skills: a vital ingredient in the make-up of a good agent.

Darcie skated smoothly down the pathway. As she approached the end, she saw the juggler appear round the corner, still practising hard, this time tossing knives in the air. Darcie wondered how the juggler could do this while walking without losing a finger. Not wanting to make the woman break her concentration, Darcie ground to a halt and turned, staggering slightly.

Wheesht! A knife whistled past her ear and clattered into the wall next to her.

'Dive!' shouted her grandfather, running towards her, all trace of a limp gone.

Darcie threw herself sideways as two more knives hit the path where she had been standing only moments before. Rolling over, she saw her grandfather race past, stick whirling, as he charged towards the juggler. The woman hurled a knife at him. He swerved and the weapon hit the flapping lining of his jacket, cutting a rent in the grey silk. Darcie caught sight of movement at the other end of the alleyway. Was it help? This hope vanished when she saw three of the acrobats sprinting towards her with less than friendly expressions. Scrambling to her feet, she skated after her grandfather, determined at all costs to protect him. She knew full well who had sent these people after her and she was not going to let them hurt an innocent old man with a heart condition and numerous other frailties.

Head down, she propelled herself towards the

juggler. The woman had one knife remaining which she was about to throw at Christopher. Seeing the danger, Darcie outstripped her grandfather, ducked down and cannoned into the juggler, throwing her back against the wall with stunning force. Darcie pulled herself to her feet and seized the knife from the woman's hand.

'Watch her!' she shouted at her grandfather, shoving the knife into his palm. 'Get behind me.' She grabbed his cane and placed herself protectively in front before he had time to protest. Already the first acrobat had reached them. He leapt in the air and tumbled towards Darcie, aiming to kick the stick from her grip. Holding the cane like a fencing blade, Darcie tensed, chose her moment and struck. The tumbler received a whack across his head, lost control and crashed into Darcie. Rollerblades went flying and both he and Darcie ended up in a heap on the floor, the cane spinning out of her hand. Dazed, she was too slow to regain her feet before the other two acrobats reached her. One jumped, pushing her to the ground again, as the other helped his colleague to his feet with a spring. The first man's face was marked by an ugly red mark across his cheek and he shouted angrily in Chinese, pointing at Darcie. The acrobat standing over Darcie now produced a small revolver from his back pocket and levelled it at her forehead.

'Madame Tsui say "goodbye",' he said coldly in broken English. He clicked the safety catch.

Whack! The flat of a sword knocked the man's arm sideways. The gun went off and the bullet buried itself in the ground six metres away. A second stroke and the man dropped the gun from his paralysed hand. Christopher Lock swiftly bent, picked up the weapon and trained it on the acrobats, a thin sword still grasped in his other hand.

'That last shot will bring everyone running. I suggest you leave quickly and tell Madame Tsui not to mess with my granddaughter again or I'll personally come after her. Understand?'

It was not clear how much the men comprehended but they knew enough to drag the juggler to her feet and flee. As they disappeared out of one end of the alley, the monument guards arrived on the scene, guns waving in the air, shouting in rapid Greek. They got completely the wrong impression, thinking Christopher the assailant as he was the one with the revolver. By the time Darcie and her grandfather had picked themselves up and made themselves understood, the circus performers had disappeared. The guards took the gun but returned the sword stick now sheathed once more in its case, warning the Englishman that he should not carry it in public again.

'Good job I did though,' said Christopher, hobbling for real this time as he made for a café. 'First time that old heirloom's come into use. I think I'll leave my sword stick to you in my will, Darcie.'

Darcie was too shaken to smile. 'Are you all right?' she asked anxiously, feeling guilty that she had just put her grandfather through that ordeal.

'Never felt better in years. What about you?'

'I'm OK.' She wasn't really, but she wanted to be brave for her grandfather's sake. She couldn't get out of her head the image of the gun barrel pointing straight between her eyes. 'You're probably wondering what all that was about.'

Christopher took a table under an umbrella and ordered himself an expresso and a mineral water for her.

'There's no need to explain, my dear,' he said calmly when the waiter had moved off. 'Your father said some business associates of his had a score to settle with the family. I suppose that was them?'

She nodded. 'It's all my fault for getting my face in the papers in Naples. Do you think I should leave the cruise? Perhaps I should go underground again?'

It was a tricky question. Had Christopher not had other plans for her, he would have advised her to withdraw now her cover was so clearly compromised. On the other hand, they would never get another chance like this again: an agent best friends with a key target, perfectly positioned to be of immense use to MI6. He stirred his coffee to buy himself some time.

'I think there's no safer place for you to be than on the high seas,' he said at length. 'I'll have a word with your father, see if his employers can't organise some discreet protection for you when you next come ashore.'

'So you know who my father works for?'

'Of course. Not that we discuss his work when we see each other. I'm very hazy about the details, but if his organisation has got you into this, I'll tell him that it's their responsibility to see you safely through.'

'Thanks, Grandad, I appreciate that.' Darcie checked her watch. 'I'm supposed to be joining the minibus.'

'That's the spirit – straight back into the saddle after a fall,' he said cheerfully. Darcie wondered how he could shake off what had just happened so lightly. 'You best stay quietly on board for the rest of your stay in Cyprus. I assume it's well guarded as this Shelly is a fellow passenger?'

Darcie nodded.

'Here's my number so you can keep in touch.' He pressed a card into her hand. 'I look forward to seeing you again soon, but no more excursions for the moment, I fear.'

'I agree. I've quite lost my appetite to see the circus this evening,' said Darcie with a shaky smile.

'I can't think why,' laughed Christopher, patting her on the back as she rose to go. Darcie walked off in the direction of the minibus. She turned once to look at the man sitting in the sun, now with a mobile phone in his hand. She waved. He nodded then began to speak urgently into the handset.

9

Back on board the *Pharaoh*, Darcie began to wonder about her grandfather. It was strange that he had not been more upset by the events in the alley behind the amphitheatre. He had mentioned something about an old war wound: perhaps he was used to being under fire? But she certainly wasn't. Her hands were still shaking hours after her brush with death. Her grand-father might be right that the safest place for the moment was the *Pharaoh* – but only until they next docked. She wished she had someone to talk to or, even better, someone to give her a hug and tell her it would all be all right. The only person she could think of was Shelly.

Darcie went in search of the president's daughter and found her with Jon Lee in her cabin. They were both getting ready to go out for the evening.

'Hey, how was Grandpa?' Shelly asked as she layered her mascara to make her lashes thick and long.

Jon Lee made no sign he'd even noticed her come in.

'Fine, thanks.' Darcie hardly wanted to explain what had really happened with Jon Lee in earshot. 'Can I have a word, Shelly – in private?'

'Sure. Jon Lee won't tell anyone – I've already told him about your little identity problem.'

'You what?' Darcie backed away. This wasn't what she'd wanted at all.

Jon Lee flopped back on Shelly's bed. 'Yeah, you worked for those government creeps, didn't you, Kiddo?' he said.

'It wasn't what you think,' Darcie said defensively.

'What do I think?' asked Jon Lee, twirling his baseball cap on the end of a finger. 'That you're on the side of the authorities. You're one of the enemy. You're sent here to spy on us, aren't you?'

'Give her a break, Jon Lee. I told you, she did it for her dad.' Shelly checked her appearance and turned to face her audience of two. 'What d'ya think?' She was wearing a T-shirt that depicted her father with satanic horns.

'That's bad!' Jon Lee said approvingly.

'Are you coming?' Shelly asked Darcie. 'You can talk to us then.'

'I can't believe you told Jon Lee,' said Darcie, still caught up in the fact that her secret had so casually been betrayed. 'I trusted you.'

'Are you saying you can't trust him, Kiddo? Because that's a really harsh thing to say about a fellow team member,' said Shelly.

'What? That I can't trust the guy who spiked my drink? Who pushed me in the pool? Sorry, I must have missed the "earning your team member's trust" part of this team building exercise. When did that happen?'

'She's right, Shell, I'm totally unreliable: you shouldn't have told me. I'd probably sell her out to the nearest Tsui hitman if the price was right,' said Jon Lee coolly.

'He's only joking,' Shelly said, throwing a cushion at him. 'So, are you coming out with us, Kiddo?'

'I'd rather sit in a bath of scorpions.'

'Ouch – vivid phrase – very pharaonic – well done,

The Babe,' Jon Lee crowed with laughter. 'Mind if I borrow it for my next song?'

The door slammed. Darcie had gone.

As the *Pharaoh* headed for Alexandria, Carl was increasingly perplexed by his youngest client. Against all the indications, the kid's grandfather must have told her to behave because she spent the next part of the voyage fulfilling her duties to the letter. The chaos she'd begun continued as everyone else abandoned the hierarchy Carl had tried to introduce, but she just faded into the background, letting others take the lead in the evening's court. She never won the plastic bucket or the wet sponge; she never seemed to be around when everyone else was having fun. It was as if she had lost interest in beating the system.

'I don't like it,' Carl commented to Gina one evening as the off-duty Fresh Start participants sang under the stars to the accompaniment of Femi's guitar.

'What don't you like?' Gina asked dreamily, enjoying the cool night breeze and the fragments of song drifting in through the open doors of the saloon.

'Darcie. She's not here again and no one's noticed.'

Gina tutted. 'Look, you didn't like it when she was leading this anarchy; now you hate it when she's keeping to herself and behaving impeccably. You can't have it both ways, Carl.'

'I wanted her off the course, remember, not beaten into submission.'

'Don't be ridiculous: you didn't beat her into submission, Carl.'

'Didn't I? Something happened after I spoke to her grandfather. He's an odd man – I thought he was completely on her side, but maybe that was just for show. He must've said something to her: she's not been the same since we came back from that trip. She hardly leaves her cabin.'

'You did give her a curfew, remember?'

'Yeah, from 10.30 – not all day, every day, when she's not specifically asked to do something else. And what's worse is that none of them seem to be looking out for her.'

'Well, I did see Hans and Karin go knocking on her door last night. She said she had a headache.'

'But her team-mates – where are they?'

This question was answered by a change of pace to the music. Jon Lee had come down from his high horse and was entertaining the others with his 'greatest hits'. Gina flinched – most of it would have had to be bleeped out if it were broadcast. Shelly had taken over on guitar.

'I had noticed that they're not talking to Darcie. But you did say that friendship wouldn't last.'

'I wouldn't say it was ever a friendship. Shelly took an interest in Darcie for a while but she doesn't care enough about other people to stay the course.' Carl moved to the window to watch the rap artist at work. 'And Jon Lee never cared – his only agenda is tormenting someone younger than him.'

'So what are you going to do?'

'I dunno, Gina. Talk to her I suppose. My nightmare is that she'll start harming herself again.'

'We don't know that she's into that stuff.'

'Don't we?'

*

Darcie was sitting on her bed rubbing her bare arms thoughtfully. The silver scars were very obvious in the overhead light, a perpetual reminder of Madame Tsui if she needed one. Tracing one line from her wrist to her elbow with a fingertip, Darcie asked herself when was the last time she felt really safe? Thinking back, she realised it had been when she'd had Stingo at her side. It wasn't that there was no danger then too, it was that he had given her confidence, something that was totally lacking now. She was scared of mixing with the others, afraid they all knew about her, worried that somehow her past would catch up with her from the least expected direction, as it had in Cyprus. It seemed simpler just to keep her head down and stay out of the way.

Problem was: the loneliness was unbearable. But she's tried confiding in someone once, and look where that had led!

Needing a friend – any friend – even a soldier who always thought he knew best, she pulled out her phone. There was a signal. It was time she answered Stingo's text.

> Hi. I feel ☹ Tell me something
> 2 cheer me up. Zebra.

She smiled as she signed her old code name. It had been given to her by the SAS team protecting her on a weekend safari in Kenya. After they'd failed in that task they'd adopted her as their unlucky mascot.

She was pleased to find that her message was answered almost immediately.

> Glad ur still talking 2 me.
> Greetings from the team. Not
> much else 2 do on desert
> training than look at the stars
> and text so I'll see what I can
> come up with. Best. Stingo.

Darcie smiled, imagining Stingo asking round his

squad for something to amuse her. He'd have to edit it to make it decent to send, she had no doubt, but that only made it funnier. It felt good to be back in contact with a real friend at last. She waited, the phone lying in her lap.

The ringtone sounded just as someone knocked at her door. Reluctantly, Darcie put the phone aside, message unread, and opened the door a crack. It was Carl.

'Hi, Darcie.'

'Oh, hi, Carl.'

'Are you all right?'

'Fine.'

'Can I come in?'

She tried to think of an excuse, failed to come up with one, so stepped back to let him enter.

Carl took a seat at the small desk under the port-hole; Darcie sat back on the bed, burning to read the message. How long would he stay?

'You've been very quiet recently,' Carl began.

'I s'pose so.'

'Something you want to talk about?'

What could she say? I almost got murdered the last time we were ashore? I jump any time someone even vaguely Chinese-looking comes near me, fearing Madame Tsui has sent them to finish me off? He'd think she was seriously paranoid if she came out with that.

'I . . . er . . . suppose I'm homesick.'

Carl smiled understandingly. She was just a child after all – nothing complicated, just a kid missing her parents.

'First time you've been away from your folks?' he asked.

'In a way.'

'Tell me about them: do you get on OK?'

'Sometimes. I've been through a lot with Dad.' Darcie remembered the fierce, protective love her father had shown for her when they had been captured by a militia group in Kenya. They had never been so close before or since.

'But your mum?' Carl queried, trying to tease his way through the tangled history of his client.

'We're . . . it's complicated.'

'From what I've seen on Fresh Start, all mother-daughter relationships are – at least until you emerge from the tunnel of the teenage years and can become friends with each other as adults.'

Darcie doubted she'd ever really know her mother – Ginnie would continually slip away from her, assume another character to fit some new role she was playing for her country. 'Perhaps.'

'But if you're homesick, you won't make yourself feel better by hiding in your cabin.'

'I thought you preferred me to keep out of the way. You don't want me here, do you?'

Carl was about to lie but Darcie's gaze was so frank he could not bring himself to insult her intelligence. 'No, I don't, but neither do I want you to feel miserable on your own.'

'Thank you, but you don't need to worry about me. I've been thinking – I'll probably leave the course in Cairo, head home like you suggested. It's not safe.'

'Not safe? What do you mean?'

Darcie tried to laugh off the comment. 'Oh, it's just that it's not safe for me to continue messing up Fresh Start. Like you said: you can't predict the results with me around. I'm not enjoying myself; you don't want me; I'd better go.'

Carl scratched his head. He couldn't figure her out at all. Talking to her now, she seemed so mature, not at all the severely messed-up kid he had persuaded himself she must be.

'That's a very grown-up way of looking at things. We're going on a desert circuit soon after our arrival in Cairo. If you're leaving us, you'll have to make up your mind if you do so before or after that as you'll be out of contact with civilization for a few days.'

'What do you think is best?' She touched her phone subconsciously: Stingo was in the desert somewhere; she'd always wanted to see a sea of sand. It was very unlikely Madame Tsui would be able to reach her there.

Carl was feeling warmer towards his youngest client than he had for many days. 'It's up to you, but if you think you'll enjoy the trip, then I have no objection to you coming along. And when we get back – you might even decide to stay. The desert changes people, they say.'

'And you – will you want me to stay?'

'Who knows? Perhaps your grandad was right: you're good for me – you make me think outside the box.'

'I thought you didn't like me.'

'It's not that I don't like you, Darcie, it's just that you . . . well, you make things much more difficult. To tell you the truth, Gina and I are rather in awe of your subversive abilities.'

Darcie laughed. 'Thanks, Carl, I'll take that as a compliment.'

'So, are you coming top side? I can't recommend the music, but the atmosphere is nice enough.'

'Thanks, but I'll stay here. I've got a message to read. I might come up later.'

'Oh yeah, that reminds me. You're no longer under curfew. In fact, I positively encourage you to stay up and socialize – I think you need it.'

'Maybe.'

Carl left her and Darcie immediately made a grab for her phone.

> *Midge sAz that hearing how*
> *miserable some1 is alwys*
> *cheers him up. So, here goes.*
> *We R baked, thirsty, sand in*
> *every orifice and have 3 dAz 2*
> *go on our survival course –*
> *surely that makes U feel betA?*
> *Stingo.*

Darcie smiled.

Tell me about the desert, she tapped in, then sat back to wait for the answers to scroll across her screen.

10.00, Washington DC, USA: Sunny, humidity high, 31°C
'There isn't much choice, is there?' said Ginnie Lock mournfully as they leafed through the selection of jobs she and Michael had been offered. 'We'd get a much

more interesting post if one of us sat this round out.'

Michael stared out of the coffee shop window at the traffic-clogged street. He hated Washington at the best of times, particularly in the summer. Tempers frayed and the air smelt of exhaust. He was missing the wide African skies and people who had time to greet you. No wonder Darcie was angry with them both for pulling her out of Kenya so suddenly.

'They said they could find me something that'd be good for my career if I came back to HQ for a while – that'd mean living in Washington. Can your people offer you anything in the British mission here?' Ginnie continued.

Michael pulled himself back to the present. His tea – undrinkable in any case – had gone cold.

'Sorry, darling, I was miles away.'

Ginnie reached across and took his hand. 'She'll be OK. Once she lands in Cyprus, they'll pull her out and bring her home.' Her grip suddenly tightened. Michael turned. Ginnie was staring at the headline on the inside page of a magazine that a woman at the next table was reading. *Dad from Hell?* – it showed a picture of Shelly grinning drunkenly, wearing a T-shirt with her father's face on it. Ginnie leaned over and tapped the woman on the arm. 'Excuse me. Would you mind if I took a look at that?'

The woman shrugged. 'Sure. You know, if that were my girl, I'd tan her hide.' She flourished the magazine at Ginnie.

Taking it from her, Ginnie swiftly read the article. 'The manipulating, old . . .' she said softly, then stopped, remembering her company. 'Thank you.' She handed back the magazine and bent closer to Michael. 'That's the last straw! She's already passed through Cyprus! You phone that man and ask him where she is!'

Swallowing his rage, Michael punched in his father's direct line. It would be late afternoon in the UK – he should still be at his desk.

'Lock,' a voice said curtly.

'It's Michael.'

'Ah, Michael, I was expecting your call.'

'Where is she?'

'Where is whom?'

'Goddamit, you know who I'm talking about.'

'I took the liberty of dropping in on my grand-daughter a few days ago to find out what she wanted to do. She told me she wanted to stay the course so I let her.'

'You did what?'

'Visited my granddaughter. It's not illegal to try and get acquainted with your close relatives, you know. You should try it some time.'

Ginnie watched Michael's face turn purple. She grabbed the phone from him.

'Christopher, it's Ginnie.'

'Ah, Ginnie, how delightful to hear your voice.'

'Cut that out. You don't have to pretend with me. Get her out now, you hear me? I want her back here with us.'

'I don't think you quite understand. Darcie has said she wants to stay, so I am happy to let her continue with her mission.'

'Her mission? What are you talking about?'

'She's keeping an eye on someone for me. It's all above board – approved by your masters as well as mine – surely you can't object to that.'

'Of course I object!'

'Then I suggest you take it up with the Secretary of State – she's all in favour.'

'I don't care if the president himself has authorised this –'

'Oh, he has – you can be sure of that.'

'I want her out.'

'Then I suggest you ask Darcie to leave, not run crying to me. Do you ever talk to your daughter directly, Ginnie?'

'How can you do this – exploit a child like this? What's wrong with you, Christopher?'

'Darcie is a very mature, competent young lady. I have every confidence in her.'

'How can you say that? You don't even know her.'

'Oh, but I do. I've seen her in action – she's very brave and thinks quickly.'

'You've done what . . .?' The penny dropped.

'What happened in Cyprus?'

'Nothing to get worried about: we just had a little brush with some people and emerged victorious.'

'It was Tsui, wasn't it?' Ginnie's face was ashen. Michael was crouched forward, trying to hear what they were saying.

'Should you really be talking so openly, Ginnie?' Christopher asked.

Even though Ginnie knew he was only saying it to wrong-foot her, she couldn't help glancing over her shoulder. 'Tell us what happened,' she hissed.

'I'll send Michael the report. You'll both be very proud of her.'

Ginnie didn't know what to do with her anger: she felt like hurling the phone across the café. Reining her feelings in, she asked coldly:

'When does she next arrive in port?'

'The ship should be reaching Cairo any day now.'

'Right.'

'And, Ginnie?'

'Yes?'

'I really would think twice before interfering – for your sake. The president will be very displeased.'

Ginnie cut off her father-in-law's smug voice by ending the call. 'We've got to get to Cairo,' she said bleakly. 'This has all gone too far. I don't know what he's persuaded Darcie to do, but it's got to stop.'

Michael nodded. 'I'm sorry about my father. We should never have trusted him to pull her out. The only way is to do it ourselves.'

Ginnie gave him a weak smile and squeezed his hand affectionately. 'You can't help that old rogue – thank heavens, you're nothing like him.'

Michael kissed her. 'You know, that's the nicest thing you've ever said to me.'

10

The yacht passed through the Egyptian port of Alexandria and headed up the Nile river. When not keeping a low profile chatting to Antar in the store-room, Darcie spent many happy hours watching the banks, catching glimpses of life by the water's edge. At times they passed though modern villages of concrete blocks and scraggy palm trees, then they would float back in time to mud brick houses, farmers ploughing with oxen, children playing in the water. The land fringing the Nile was a jewel-green, but in the distance the arid hills reminded Darcie that she was back in Africa. Like northern Kenya, the landscape could seem barren but would hold unexpected oases. She could picture the camel trains and the ancient tombs. Stingo had told her that camels could survive in the desert for up to ten days without drinking, whereas a human will die in two. She had begun to imagine herself sitting on camelback out in the middle of nowhere – in a place where there was no chance of unexpected attack. The thought was very soothing.

Hans approached her.

'Hi. What are you doing?'

'Just wishing,' she smiled in return.

'Be careful what you wish for in case it comes true, my grandmother always says.' He sat down. 'Carl said you might like to come with us blues on the desert trip. What do you think?'

Darcie felt her spirits lift. 'Can I really?'

'Yeah. He said he made a mistake putting you in yellow and you deserved a break.'

'Thanks.'

He patted her on the back. 'Think nothing on it. We all wanted to have you – it is the blues who are the lucky ones and yellows who are the losers.'

That evening, Carl held a special briefing to prepare the Fresh Start participants for the desert. Entering the saloon, Darcie felt very conspicuous wearing her new blue T-shirt. Shelly gave her a resentful look; Jon Lee rolled his eyes, but the coldness of their welcome was more than made up by the enthusiasm of Hans, Karin and Femi.

'We're here,' said Carl, pointing at a map projected on a screen behind him. 'We are setting out for the desert immediately, leaving the sights and sounds of the capital until our return when, doubtless, our appetite for civilisation will have been sharpened.' He didn't add that the American intelligence service had advised this unexpected variation to the schedule on the grounds of security. It was best to keep anyone monitoring the progress of the president's daughter in the dark. 'Our trip will take us south-west of Cairo, through the Bahariya Oasis, and out to what they call the White Desert. We'll be travelling in four-wheel drives – one to each team –'

'What, no camels?' interrupted Hans with a note of disappointment in his voice.

Carl laughed. 'How long do you think we've got, Hans? I'm sure we'll see plenty of camels but we've only got a couple of days for this trip. Also, we have security concerns – and I'm not just talking about Miss Morris.'

Darcie's heart lurched: did he know about her?

'Any westerner is a target these days,' Carl continued. 'To get permission to travel out to the deserts we have to follow strict conditions laid down by the authorities and we'll be travelling with an armed guard. Still, we are all hoping for a problem free visit that'll be good for all concerned.'

Darcie relaxed. This wasn't about her. She now wondered what discreet protection her grandfather had planned to talk her father into providing. She should ring her grandfather to let him know about this – and her thoughts about leaving after the trip.

'Travelling in the desert is no joke – really. Jon Lee, even you need to listen to this. We're here at the hottest time of the year. Temperatures can reach well over one hundred degrees fahrenheit – you'll quickly fry outside your air-conditioned vehicles. We've planned our days so that we do our sightseeing in the evening and at night while the moon's up. Remember, accidents can happen even to the best prepared tour. If you get stranded in the desert with a broken-down vehicle, you need to know what to do to survive. The rules are: stay together, follow the advice of our local guides, treat the people and places with respect.'

A pleasurable frisson of anticipation ran round the room. Few had ever been in so hostile an environment – it promised to be an exciting adventure.

'That's all for now,' Carl continued. 'Pack up your kit as instructed – there's a list on the galley door. Don't stint on warmer clothes just because it's a desert – the nights can be cold.'

Darcie rose to go but Shelly caught her arm.

'What's all this?' she said, tugging on the T-shirt. 'Abandoned ship?'

'Sort of,' Darcie replied awkwardly. 'Yellow just wasn't my colour.'

'You take everything too seriously, Darcie. Jon Lee was only joking when he said he'd sell you out.'

'Oh, was he?'

'Lighten up.'

'Perhaps we just don't share the same sense of humour, Shelly. To me, being hunted down by assassins is not very funny.'

Shelly raised her eyebrows. 'You're so paranoid. That Chinese woman's probably forgotten all about you by now.'

Darcie realised that the president's daughter had no concept of anyone else's importance except her own. She was in no mood to put Shelly right. 'Let's drop the subject, shall we? You and Jon Lee will get on fine without me – better probably. I'll be OK in with the blues.'

Shelly shrugged. 'Suit yourself. Don't say I didn't try.' Turning her back, Shelly marched off to Jon Lee at the bar.

Well, you didn't really try, did you? Darcie thought, watching Shelly go.

At dawn the next day, five white vehicles waited on the quayside, flanked by an escort of two army trucks. Darcie climbed into the back of a Land Rover with

Karin and Hans as Femi sat up-front with the driver. She watched as Shelly's security team shepherded their charge into an identical white 4×4. Jon Lee sauntered behind, saw Darcie and gave an ironic wave. Three Egyptian soldiers stalked between the cars, looking at every occupant with suspicion. Darcie felt a pang of pity for them: it could be no easy detail to guard a bunch of high-profile westerners with the government breathing down your neck.

Darcie used the time to text her grandfather.

> *Off to the desert 4 3 days.*
> *Have armed guard so OK.*
> *Thinking of leaving course*
> *when get back. Any advice?*
> *Darcie.*

She didn't expect to get an answer immediately – it was the middle of the night in London. She did, however, notice that there were several new messages from her parents. She could guess what they were about. Why spoil the beginning of the only true bit of holiday she was going to get on this trip? She'd read them on her return. Instead she sent her parents a quick text.

Desert bound. Thinking fly home on return. P.S. Where is home these dAz?

She was rather pleased with the postscript, knowing full well that her parents could not offer her one at the moment. It was good to remind them of their short-comings as they were so quick to bring hers to her attention.

Antar came down the gangway carrying a large hamper. A young Egyptian boy Darcie hadn't seen before followed with another. Hans rubbed his hands enthusiastically.

'Lunch!' he said as the hampers were loaded in the spare vehicle. Antar climbed in, as did the boy. 'Perhaps we won't have to do our own cooking in the desert?'

'I wouldn't bet on it,' said Darcie. 'I can't see Carl

letting us miss out on the full campfire experience.'

The first stop they made in the relative cool of the morning was to admire the pyramids of Giza. These were much more impressive than Darcie had expected – bigger and more brutal than the romantic pictures she had seen in brochures. She stood at the base of the Great Pyramid of Khufu and measured herself against the first row of stone blocks, trying to imagine what it had been like to be one of the slaves hauling the rocks here from the quarries in the desert all those centuries ago. The thought of all that suffering made her shudder. It did not seem a good omen for the start of their venture into the desert.

As the sun rose, the tour returned to their vehicles and left the pyramids behind. They bumped their way for what must have been hundreds of kilometres though a rough no-man's land, seeing little to relieve the monotony of the landscape except the odd way-marker or an outcrop of rock. The rough track to the Bahariya Oasis shimmered in the heat haze. Darcie dozed fitfully, her bare arms chilled by the refrigerated atmosphere of the car. It was hard to believe that if she put a foot outside it would be like stepping into an oven. Later, feeling bored, she checked her phone – there was no signal. Not that she had expected there to be one, but she would have liked to know what her grandfather thought about her idea of leaving Fresh Start. She half hoped he might even invite her to stay with him for a while, seeing how her parents had no fixed abode.

Hans interrupted her thoughts by tapping her on the arm.

'Darcie, now is the time to confess. Did you do that to hide the needle marks?' he asked. Karin was watching her with interest, chewing on the end of one of her long blonde braids.

'What?' Darcie didn't understand what he meant.

'We made it a rule in blue team to be honest with each other why we're here,' Hans continued. 'And we have heard nothing about you. I am here because I got angry and thumped someone. He is still in hospital.' He grimaced at the memory.

'And I'm here because I got caught shoplifting,' Karin said brightly, pushing her hair back over her shoulder. 'It became a bit of an addiction. I didn't need anything – I just liked the thrill. My mother wanted me to find a different way of getting a kick – and a desert safari sounded exactly that.'

Femi turned round in his seat to look at her. Slim-faced with round glasses, he had the look of a scholar. 'And I killed someone,' he said, no trace of his usual smile. 'Driving while not exactly sober, I hit a tramp who was lying on the road. So whatever you've done, it can't be worse than that, can it?'

'We guessed – what with you being so young – that it must be drugs,' said Hans.

'Carl and Gina think it's self-harm,' Karin said knowledgeably. She saw Darcie's shocked expression. 'I heard them discussing you – they think you're a real mystery.'

Darcie couldn't bring herself to lie to them, but she appreciated their interest in her.

'I can't explain everything,' she began, 'but it's

nothing to do with drugs. I got caught up in an explosion. I was thrown clear but I used my arms to protect my face, I guess, and they caught the worst of it. I don't remember much else.'

Hans whistled. 'Were you playing about with chemicals or something?'

'No!' said Darcie indignantly. 'I just got in the way of someone else.'

Karin frowned. 'So why are you here?'

'I'm not sure. I s'pose I'm not the daughter my parents want.'

'That's mean – really mean: to throw you in with all us head cases!'

Femi and Hans smiled grimly. 'Thanks, Karin,' said Femi sardonically.

'You know what I meant. Did they realise what they were sending you to?' asked Karin.

This question pulled Darcie up short. Had her parents known? It had been her grandfather's suggestion after all and he had been very keen for her to see it through to the end. In Cyprus, he seemed to be under the impression that Fresh Start was all some glorified game with a tour of the pyramids thrown in for good measure. Had he unintentionally misled her parents to think the same?

'Now you mention it, I'm not sure. Our life was a little complicated right before I came here.' She fingered her phone – promising herself that she would read her parents' messages as soon as she had a moment. She was beginning to suspect that she might have got it wrong. She remembered her parents saying that her grandfather had heard about the cruise from the British prime minister, but how could he have done? What did Christopher Lock do in foreign relations that brought him into the orbit of leading politicians? None of this made sense.

'If they didn't know, it was one expensive mistake,' said Femi, turning round to face forwards again. 'You pay a small fortune for the Fresh Start treatment – but perhaps Carl and Gina would say it wasn't enough for all the aggro we give them.'

Once attention moved from her, Darcie swiftly

ran through her parents' messages:

> *Sunday 17.30 Darcie,*
> *Whatever your grandfather*
> *has persuaded you to do,*
> *don't do it. He is a dangerous*
> *man. We are coming to Cairo*
> *to fetch you. Will arrive*
> *Monday evening.*

Her parents were coming today and she was already miles away. But what did they mean about her grandfather?

> *20.50 Please reply to last*
> *message. Abort your mission.*
> *You are not his agent – you*
> *are our daughter.*

What mission? Her parents weren't making sense. Did they mean the mission to improve herself – but what had that to do with being an agent? And hadn't they agreed in the first place to send her on this mad tour? Darcie slipped the phone back in her pocket, her mind still trying to solve the puzzle.

They had a brief rest stop in the oasis of Bahariya, a huddle of earth-coloured houses among the palms, the only spot of green for miles. At dusk, the convoy set off for the desert.

'Just think – there are 680 000 square kilometres of this,' said Hans in awe as the last houses were left behind and the Empty Quarter began. He was sitting up front with their driver, Ahmed. 'Nothing between here and Libya – and even that is just a made-up border – a straight line drawn in the desert by colonialists.'

'680 000 kilometres . . . that sounds big,' said Darcie, 'I can't imagine it.'

'Well, think of Central Europe – Germany down to Greece – and pretend it is all desert and then you are getting close.'

'Wow.'

'Get stranded out here and I guess that is it – goodbye. Too far to walk to civilisation – few people passing – you are food for the crows.'

'Not that there are any crows,' added Femi.

'OK – you're food for scarab beetles,' said Hans. 'Or snakes.'

'Or more likely you'll bake on a sand dune until you end up as a sun-dried mummy,' suggested Femi with relish.

'Yuck. Will you two shut up,' said Karin, shuddering. 'You're planting horrible ideas in my head.'

Hans gave one of his loud laughs.

'Don't worry, lady,' said the driver. 'Nothing happen to you. Too many of us for you to get lost.' He nodded at the army truck kicking up the dust in front and then at the one travelling at the rear of the column.

19.00, The White Desert: Clear skies, full moon, 24°C
The plan was to explore the desert by moonlight and bivouac under the stars. Darcie's excitement grew as a landscape of black rocks gave way to the chalk of the

184

White Desert. She felt they had not only left civilisation behind, but also Earth itself. The terrain looked like the surface of an alien planet and it was no stretch to imagine spaceships or Martians appearing over the horizon. In the setting sun, the chalk outcrops glowed with a strange fluorescent light, seeming to float above the pale yellow sand. Some looked like dollops of whipped cream dropped from heaven; others recalled animal shapes or towers. One leaned like a drunken toadstool on an impossibly narrow stalk.

The army truck in front signalled a halt: this was where they were to camp. The Land Rovers drew up in a circle and the passengers got stiffly out, clothes clinging uncomfortably to sweaty skin. Darcie flapped her blue T-shirt to unstick it from her back and took her first few breaths of desert air. A stiff breeze was blowing, hot and dry. She felt she had stepped out into a hairdryer. The heat was so sapping that she could imagine her energy streaming out of her like thin hairs unwinding in the wind. She knew if she stood still any longer she wouldn't be able to move. Seeing Antar struggling to get his hamper out of the back of the vehicle, she grabbed hold of Hans and towed him across to help.

'Need a hand?' she asked Antar.

The Egyptian started on hearing her voice. He darted a look at her then lowered his eyes. 'No, thank you, Darcie. I will manage.'

'Come on, my friend, I will take an end of that,' insisted Hans, moving to the other side of the hamper.

Antar was about to refuse, thought better of it, and nodded. Together they hefted the basket to the floor.

'It is heavy,' said Hans. 'What is in it? Something tasty, I hope?'

'You will find out later,' said Antar evasively. 'I think your leader wants you.' He pointed at Carl who was waving the students into a circle around him.

'Not very friendly today, is he?' Hans commented as the two of them made their way over to Carl.

'Yeah. He's not normally like that,' she replied, glancing back over her shoulder. Antar was watching her, but turned away when he saw her looking. Was it something she'd said? Had she in some way offended his honour by suggesting he couldn't manage to carry the hamper on his own?

Darcie was diverted from her concerns about Antar by an intriguing new arrival that Carl introduced to the group.

'Our friend here is a Bedouin, one of the nomadic people who have lived here for centuries, so there is no better person to show us the ways of the desert.'

The Bedouin made no comment but bowed solemnly, his long white robes brushing the sand. His face had the look of old leather – tough and wrinkled.

'He is going to take us on a hike in the moonlight,' continued Carl, 'returning here for a late supper.'

Karin nudged Darcie. 'Great! That means someone else must be cooking.'

They walked in pairs, Darcie with Karin, Hans and Femi just behind. Ahead she could see Shelly and Jon Lee flanked by the two security agents. The men looked almost relaxed to be out in the open, guarded by two truck-loads of soldiers in the rear. At least there was no way for Shelly to run out on them.

The guide led the party through a haunting land-scape. Now that the full heat of the day had passed into twilight, the ground was shedding the heat it had accumulated. The sand was still hot underfoot but no longer scorching to the touch. By a common instinct, no one spoke as they walked, allowing the absolute silence to be fully appreciated. It was so peaceful that the loudest noises Darcie could hear were her own breathing, the rustle of her trousers as she walked, and her heart beating. People seemed so insignificant placed against this landscape; her worries and concerns dropped away like grains of sand brushed from her clothes. As the sky turned from the orange flush of sunset to navy blue night, the first stars came out. A full moon rose, floating dramatically into view over a rock shaped like a lion's head.

'Wow,' breathed Hans softly. 'This is the first truly perfect moment in my life!'

Darcie knew how he felt. The world seemed to have stopped for a moment just for them. It was magical.

11

After two hours of walking behind the Bedouin guide, the Fresh Start hikers returned to the campsite, hungry and pleasantly tired. Darcie was looking forward to stretching out in her sleeping bag to count the stars. Climbing the last dune, they gazed down upon the welcome sight of the circle of vehicles and the flickering light of a campfire.

Hans's stomach rumbled audibly. 'What do you think is for supper?' he asked.

'Something spicy, I hope,' speculated Darcie.

'Something cold,' said Femi, licking his lips. 'Did anyone see a cool box? I could do with a long iced drink.'

As they approached the camp, Antar was sitting on the hamper, waiting alone by the fire. He didn't look up even though he must have heard them approaching. That didn't seem right.

'Where are the soldiers?' Darcie asked Karin in a low voice.

Her companion shrugged and stretched her long arms wearily over her head. 'No idea. Out on patrol? Let's hope they didn't eat everything before they went.'

Darcie wasn't the only one to be wary about the emptiness of the camp: one of Shelly's bodyguards broke away from the party and jogged to the front of the column to reach Antar first. From his gestures, the guard appeared to be asking the same question Darcie had just put to Karin. Antar pointed in the direction of the truck. On the ground, propped up against a wheel, a soldier was sleeping, gun across his lap. The bodyguard swivelled round to shout at the man. As soon as the security agent turned his back, Antar stood up, opened the hamper and took something out, concealing it in the folds of his robe. Darcie didn't like the suspicions that then entered her head.

Getting no response to his calls, the security agent ran over to the soldier and prodded him. Nothing. He knelt down and shook his shoulder. Still nothing.

Darcie's heart picked up its beat. She stopped

walking so abruptly that Hans and Femi bumped into her.

'What's the matter? Stone in your boot?' asked Hans.

'Something's wrong,' she said.

Red team walked past them, laughing unconcernedly, thoughts fixed on supper. The second bodyguard, however, had caught Shelly's arm and was holding her back, hand to his holster. The first was talking heatedly to Antar, demanding an explanation. Carl and Gina hurried over to join the discussion.

Following Darcie's gaze, Hans had by now also noticed the odd signs. 'What do you think is happening?'

'I think –' began Darcie, but she didn't have time to finish her sentence as a burst of gunfire sounded from behind them. Several young people screamed and ran forwards; others, Darcie included, threw themselves flat. Squirming round on the sand, she looked behind and saw a horseman appear on the horizon, gun pointing in the air. He squeezed the trigger again, releasing a shower of bullets. The bodyguard at

Shelly's side returned fire, but his defence was cut short: three men appeared from behind the army trucks and shot him in the back. He spiralled round and fell on the ground, clutching his side. Shelly stood rooted to the spot, staring – she made a clear mark for any sniper. Quick to see the danger, Jon Lee pulled her down. Darcie expected to hear the other bodyguard put up some resistance but he was wrestled to the floor by Antar, a gun pointing at his head.

By Antar.

Antar was the traitor in their midst. With the bodyguards down, the tourists didn't stand a chance against armed men.

'What do we do?' hissed Femi, his eyes wide with panic.

'We do whatever they ask,' replied Darcie. 'Do nothing to anger them.'

Hooves thudded down the bank beside them, showering them in sand.

'You! Get up!' A rider on a white stallion was gesticulating at them, ordering them to join the others already sitting with their hands on their head by the fire. The uninjured security man had been tied up; the Bedouin guide, Jon Lee and Carl were carrying the one who had been shot down the sand dune under the watchful eye of one of the gunmen. Shelly had her own armed guard and was sitting some distance from the others. There was no sign of the soldiers. Looking at the empty bowls heaped around the campfire, Darcie guessed what must have happened. Antar had probably poisoned or drugged the guards' food – they would have had no reason to be suspicious of him.

The group stumbled down the slope and sat cross-legged on the sand next to the others.

Just stay calm. See how things develop. They don't appear to want to kill us, Darcie told herself. Let's keep it that way.

The horseman reined in his mount to a stop in front of the party of twenty terrified people. He wore a long dark robe and his face was almost completely shadowed in the folds of a scarf thrown over his head and shoulders. All Darcie could make out were a pair of tanned wrinkled hands on the bridle and eyes glittering under black brows. She looked anxiously over to the campfire and saw that Antar was now wordlessly but efficiently administering first aid to the gunshot victim. Another armed man walked through the ranks of young people, watching for any sign of resistance.

'Greetings from the Brotherhood of the Martyrs for Truth,' the horseman now began in English. His voice was cultured and polite – a strange contrast to his wraith-like appearance. 'We have no intent to keep you long or to harm you. We have come to fetch three guests and then you may go on your way.' He gave a shrill whistle. Two of the men disappeared behind the trucks and returned with the young boy who had been helping Antar earlier. They brought with them five horses. 'We want now the group called yellow team and we go.' He looked to Antar, who confirmed this with a nod. 'Shelly Morris we have.' The man's eyes fell on Jon Lee, conspicuous in his T-shirt. 'You, join her.' He waved his gun towards Shelly. Looking sick with terror, Jon Lee scrambled to his feet and went to join his team-mate. They locked hands.

'Where is the third?' barked the spokesman, scanning the ranks of young people for the tell-tale T-shirt.

'They are enough, Khaled,' said Antar in a hoarse voice, speaking up for the first time. He repeated it in Arabic – making gestures suggesting they should leave.

'No!' said the leader. 'We must take the three allies. The USA,' he pointed to Shelly, 'the UN – you said the boy is from its headquarters, no?'

Antar nodded reluctantly. 'Yes, he is from New York.'

'And then the faithful follower, Britain, our old masters. You told me there was a third. Where is the British guest?'

Darcie sank down as far as she could behind Hans. Her team-mates shuffled slightly to shield her.

'Khaled, we do not need another,' repeated Antar. 'We are wasting time.'

The leader swung down from his horse and marched

over to Antar. He hissed something in Arabic, all too obviously a threat, and then wheeled round to gaze hawk-like at the captives.

'It does not matter who we take. Let us make our pick. Stand up, all of you!'

Everyone shuffled to their feet.

'Sit down if you are from Africa, Asia or the Americas.' The man seemed to be enjoying himself. He even slapped Femi on the back as he took his seat on the ground again. Darcie, Karin, Hans, Gina, Bernadette, a Russian boy and a Spanish girl were left standing. 'So here are the Europeans,' he said with a grim smile. 'Who do we have here?' He approached Hans and jabbed him in the chest with the barrel of his rifle. 'Where are you from?'

Hans stood to attention as if on parade, gazing over the man's shoulder. 'Austria,' he said loudly and with pride.

Khaled shook his head. 'Too small. Sit down.'

He went up to the other boy. 'You?'

'Russia.' The boy looked as if he was close to tears.

The man tapped him on the shoulder. 'Not you. Too complicated. It will have to be one of the women.'

He rejected Karin, Bernadette and the Spaniard, leaving Gina and Darcie still on their feet. 'And you two?'

Darcie thought how strange it was that she had to declare a tie to a country she had hardly ever visited.

'I'm half British,' she said quietly.

'British,' said Gina firmly. 'It's me you want.'

The man stared at the older woman for a moment then turned back to Darcie. 'What is your other nationality?'

Darcie hesitated, wondering what was best to say. He didn't seem to want any more Americans. She knew she was the one he had been looking for from the start, but it would be taking her sense of fairness too far to volunteer to be taken captive. Having no idea how it would affect her chances, she opted for the truth.

'American.'

The man prodded Gina on the shoulder. 'You!' – Darcie felt a huge wave of guilt and relief. 'You, sit. We take the girl.' Relief was replaced by shock as Darcie was pulled away from the others.

'Why not me?' protested Gina, reaching out to grab Darcie. 'She's only a kid!'

The man knocked her arm aside. 'That is why I take her. American and British public will care more about her than you. Sit down or I will shoot you – and I do not want to shoot a woman.'

Gina subsided on to the sand, shaking with fear and anger. Hans sat with his fists clenched, looking close to an explosion.

Please God, may he do nothing rash, Darcie thought desperately.

But it was too late. Like a snake uncoiling, Hans leapt to his feet and swung a punch at Khaled, sending him sprawling into the dust. There was a sharp burst of gunfire. Darcie threw herself down. When she dared to open her eyes, she found Hans lying beside her. Dead.

It had happened so quickly: one moment Hans was alive and thinking about supper; next he was spread-eagled on the sand, murdered. Looking up, Darcie saw Antar lower his gun. He seemed almost surprised at what he had done, staring at the body of the Austrian boy as if expecting him to spring up and say it was all a joke. But from where she was, Darcie could see that there would be no getting up after the wounds Hans had sustained. She reached out to touch her friend's face, her fingers trembling.

'Up!' Khaled was back on his feet, standing over her with his dark robes flapping in the breeze.

Darcie couldn't make herself move. Her body had shut down completely.

He pointed his rifle at her. 'I said "get up!"'

Antar called out something in Arabic. Darcie wondered if he was telling the man to shoot her or be gentle – either was possible now she knew he was not what he had seemed. Slowly, she dragged herself to her feet, her head swimming. She feared she was about to faint.

With Hans's death, the mood changed. Gone was the pretence at pleasantries. Khaled pushed her towards Shelly and Jon Lee, shouting at his comrades to hurry. He lifted Darcie on to his horse and climbed up behind. Shelly was put on a mount in front of Antar; Jon Lee sat with a third man. Seeing everyone was saddled, Khaled turned to address the silent crowd of spectators.

'We go now. Do not try to follow. If we catch sight of anyone – or even hear an aircraft overhead – we will kill one of our guests, understood?' He looked down at the body of Hans but said nothing, knowing that he had made his point. 'Tell your governments that we demand the release of Abu El-Gebel and the withdrawal of all foreign troops from the Middle East. Tell them they will hear more from us soon.'

Spurring his horse, Khaled turned its head to the west and galloped off across the desert, gripping Darcie in an iron embrace, his comrades following. As they cantered out of sight, Darcie heard the people they had left behind begin to wail and shriek as they came out of their numbed silence. She wanted to shriek herself to release some of the horror inside her, but instead closed her eyes, imagining Karin, Carl, Gina and Femi clustered around Hans in the vain hope there was something they could do. The protection guys would be on their sat phones calling for help. As the news broke that the president's daughter had been abducted and a boy killed, the eyes of the whole world would turn to this little-regarded patch of the desert. But what would they see? Even the most powerful satellites would find it almost impossible to spot a small band of horsemen in the Empty Quarter. Darcie had no doubt that the most powerful nation on earth would want to mobilize every helicopter, ship and aircraft within reach to scour the desert for Shelly, but if they sent any help either she or Jon Lee would be killed.

Khaled barely seemed to notice he was still holding a girl in front of him. After ten minutes of galloping, he waved his arm over his head, signalling a shift in direction. Continuing on this route, the landscape began to change. The pinnacles of chalk formed peaks like the surface of whipped egg-whites, turning the desert into a choppy sea of stone. Khaled steered his horse expertly through these obstacles, heading for the moonlit hills on the other side of the valley. He reined his horse to a halt under the shadow of a cliff face and swung off the saddle.

'Get down,' he said gruffly.

Darcie slid clumsily to the floor. She was shaking so much she could barely stand. As they dismounted, Shelly and Jon Lee looked in a similar condition. Khaled strode over to Shelly.

'You – your father will do anything to have you back safely, no?'

Normally, Shelly would have shrugged and said something rude. Today she whispered: 'I hope so.'

'We will see, won't we, how much the American father loves his little daughter? You are not good girl, we know, but while with us, you will behave like best daughter. If you don't, one of your friends will be killed.'

In the distance, Darcie heard the sound of a helicopter. She flinched. It couldn't be the Americans so soon, could it?

Khaled pointed upwards. 'Those are our friends – a little diversion. Your father will think we are going to Libya when he catch sight of that.'

The noise grew louder. The sand began to swirl in a mini-dust storm. Antar and another man ran on to a patch of flat earth and set out a circle of landing lights. Darcie screwed her eyes up against the grit. When she opened them again, a battered black helicopter with slowly rotating blades crouched on the ground. A door opened and a package was thrown to the ground. Khaled exchanged a few words with the pilot, gave a wave, and returned with the bundle. He untied his parcel and threw each of the prisoners a long robe and head scarf.

'Put these on and hand over any electric devices and watches.'

The helicopter's engines were whining as it prepared to take off. By the time Darcie had slipped the new gear over her head, the aircraft was flying off into the west. Antar's boy was examining Jon Lee's iPod with great interest; he had stuffed the phones he had collected from Shelly and Darcie into a duffel bag.

'If anyone's watching, they will think we went that way,' Khaled said with satisfaction as the helicopter faded from sight. He appeared to enjoy keeping them abreast of just how hopeless their situation was. 'Now we disappear into the desert and keep them guessing until our demands are met.'

Darcie stared down at her boots, all but hidden beneath robes that swamped her. He couldn't seriously believe that the president would pull troops out of the Middle East? She remembered her father telling her once that governments did not pay the ransom demanded by terrorists as success would breed more hostage-takings. Then again, no one had ever got this close to the president before so it was impossible to guess what would happen. Her eyes met Shelly's. She could tell that the American was thinking along the same lines. But whatever happened over the next few days, it was hard to imagine all three of them emerging from this unscathed.

'We ride till dawn,' announced Khaled. 'Let us go.'

At dawn, they found shelter in a cave hidden in a line of rocky hills. If Darcie had had the stomach to appreciate it, the view was magnificent: an undulating ocean of sand stretching as far as the eye could see. The three hostages had been placed together in the back of the cave, one waterskin to share between them.

'You must make that last all day,' warned Antar as he dumped it down at their feet. He still had not met Darcie's eyes.

Jon Lee immediately grabbed the water and took many gulps, quickly followed by Shelly. When it came to Darcie's turn, she found the container already half empty.

'I think we should go easy on this,' she said.

Jon Lee glared at her. 'Why? They won't let us die of thirst – we're too valuable to them as hostages.'

Darcie wondered that he could be so dense. 'Look, this is the desert. They are clearly planning to hide out here for some time and will ration the water. Shelly may be of value to them, but frankly, Jon Lee, you and I are not. If they have to cut back to make the water go round, they might just get rid of one of us.'

Jon Lee licked his cracked lips and hunched his shoulders in a sulk, but she thought she had got through to him.

'OK, Kiddo, how shall we ration it?' asked Shelly, her voice shaking a little but she seemed to be rallying now they were back together again.

The first thing Stingo had taught Darcie about desert survival had concerned water. He had often been on desert manoeuvres and had enjoyed regaling her with the grisly details of life in the sand.

'We should have as little as possible to start with as we all drank plenty yesterday. We need to keep covered up –'

'But I'm already boiling!' protested Shelly.

'I know, so am I, but the less skin we expose, the less sweat we'll lose. I remember being told that long robes are supposed to trap air between the cloth and our body – it's the coolest we are going to get out here.'

Shelly nodded. 'That makes sense. I'm going to take off my T-shirt – no point in wearing clingy layers.'

Darcie followed her example. After a few minutes, Jon Lee did likewise. They heaped the two yellow and one blue T-shirt on the cave floor.

'What do you think is going to happen?' Shelly asked Darcie anxiously.

'I don't know. I mean, how could I?'

'Well, you're the one . . . you know, used to this sort of thing. You're the professional, aren't you?'

Darcie swallowed hard, feeling close to tears. It was bad enough being kidnapped and threatened with death without being made into some kind of expert on life-threatening situations by a girl several years older than her. Darcie didn't want anyone to rely on her – she'd much prefer to be the one following someone who really knew what they were doing. Perhaps then she might be able to cope.

'Look, I don't really know anything.'

'You knew about the water.'

'Yeah, well, I have a friend who told me a few things.'

Shelly massaged her stiff legs. 'Then that makes you the authority. You don't fool me, Darcie. I know you were sent to spy on me. It made me so mad when I first found out back on Cyprus, but now I'm glad.'

'What?' Darcie looked over her shoulder nervously – this idea wasn't something she wanted her captors to overhear. Things were bad enough as they were. 'Don't be stupid – I'm not a spy. I told you all about that – I got involved once – for my dad – end of story.'

'So why did you meet that MI6 guy on Cyprus? My security team recognised him.'

'He's my grandfather – not a spy.'

'Oh yeah? Pull the other one. That old man's a top guy in the British Secret Service.'

'No.' Darcie put her head in her hands. Could it be

true? 'I thought he was my grandfather – I mean he even looks like my dad. He told me he was.'

Shelly rolled her eyes. 'You don't need to keep pretending, you know. It's a bit beyond that, isn't it? Don't you have some James Bond gismo up your sleeve to get us out of this?'

'Of course I haven't and I'm not pretending!' Darcie blurted out – too loudly as she drew Khaled's attention to their discussion.

He strode over to the threesome. 'Too much noise. You!' He pointed at Darcie. 'Over there.' He placed her next to Antar, who was stretched out on a blanket to sleep. 'You two.' He pointed at Jon Lee and Shelly. 'No more talk.'

Darcie lay down on the ground using her T-shirt as an inadequate pillow. She turned her back on everyone and faced the wall. Perhaps if she slept she would wake up and find this was all a bad dream?

But try as she might, she couldn't sleep as, piece by piece, the puzzle fell into place. It explained her parents' last messages warning her about her grandfather and telling her to abort her mission. They must have found out what everyone else knew but her: she had been put on the cruise neither as a reward nor a punishment. She was being used as a source of information on Shelly. But her 'grandfather' – who was he? Was he really related to her or had he just pretended to get her to talk about the president's daughter? She remembered that her parents had never questioned the blood tie, but that didn't mean anything – they had spent a lifetime lying to her.

Whatever the truth, she was left with two unpleasant possibilities: she was in this situation because someone at MI6 had pretended he was her relative and sent her blind into danger, or Christopher Lock was who he and her parents said he was and he had still thought nothing of putting his granddaughter at risk.

05.15, London, England: Overcast, 15°C

At that very same moment, Christopher Lock was staring mutely at the photos of the Austrian boy that the American reconnaissance team had brought back from the scene of the abduction. He had not anticipated that the American and Egyptian security could be so lax; he had not for one moment really believed his granddaughter to be in danger. The threat from Tsui had been manageable – just one of the inevitable hazards gathered during the career of a spy – but to allow Darcie to become entangled in an attack by a splinter group of Egyptian nationalists – that was unforgivable! He didn't blame himself, of course: it was those fools in the CIA. Where was their wonderful intelligence when it was most needed? Why had no one spotted the connection between Antar Abdul Al-Rabeeah and the fanatics known as the Brotherhood – madmen who had some dream of restoring the monarchy? Khaled Al-Jafry was one of the most wanted men in Egypt, a ruthless but charismatic man, unhinged by torture while in gaol. So what on earth was his second cousin, Antar, doing in charge of all the food and drink for an expedition into the desert? That should never have been allowed. The Egyptian's security clearance should have been checked and double-checked. Instead Antar was allowed to serve up a meal that knocked the soldiers out for hours – one was still in a coma.

And now his Darcie – his lovely Darcie – was stuck in the desert with a bunch of cut-throat fanatics. Christopher's hands began to shake and a lump formed in his throat. He could lose her – he could lose his only granddaughter. Until he met her, he had not realised just what that meant to him.

He picked up the phone and dialled the switchboard at Number Ten.

'It's Lock here. Can you tell the prime minister I have to speak to him at once.'

He waited a moment as the call was put through.

'Prime Minister? Lock here. Sorry to wake you. Yes, yes, thank you for your concern. It is about the . . . er . . . situation. No, there have been no new developments. Yes, I know that the Americans have warned us off in no uncertain terms . . . I understand your position – and that of the president – entirely.

We all know we must tread carefully.' He took a breath. 'But that's just it, sir, can we trust the Yanks to do that? After all, it's our girl that'll be the first to get … if something happens. The political consequences will be terrible if the truth comes out about Darcie.' He paused, letting this subtle threat sink into the sleepy prime minister's brain. 'What do I propose? I recommend that we bring in a discreet team of our own – some people who can work without drawing attention to themselves – just in case.'

The prime minister said something long-winded about the impossibility of going behind the Americans' backs. Christopher Lock rubbed his hand across his forehead, cursing the spinelessness of his political masters.

'If I may be so bold, Prime Minister, you forget that we hold the ace – the tracking device in my granddaughter's phone. The signal's blocked, suggesting she must be underground at the moment, but it was working well until a few hours ago. We know exactly where they are – certainly not on that helicopter as the Americans would have us believe. They're still in the desert, not in Libya, thank heavens.'

The prime minister mumbled something about diplomatic headaches until he finally got round to asking for Lock's advice. Christopher leapt in, the plan already fully formed in his head.

'What do I have in mind? I have the perfect team already in theatre. No, not in Egypt – of course, I haven't jumped the gun, sir. We have some of our best men on a training exercise in the Emirates, preparing for deployment in Iraq. They know our girl from Kenya. We can trust them to do everything possible to extract our agent safely – if and when it comes to that. And we can use the fact that we have a tracking device to bring the US onside. It's not the first time they have had to work alongside us.'

A child wailed in the background at Number Ten as the prime minister deliberated.

'She's only fourteen, sir,' Christopher added hoarsely. 'We owe her this much.'

There was a pause as the prime minister decided Darcie's fate.

'Yes, I understand. Thank you, sir. I'll get on to it right away.' Christopher Lock ended the call and immediately rang SAS headquarters.

11.45, Somewhere in the desert, United Arab Emirates:
Hot, 40°C

Stingo was dozing in the heat of the day when Midge woke him. He had been anticipating a long shower, a cold beer and clean clothes when they completed their survival course that night. He opened his eyes to find his commanding officer standing over him in the shelter they had made next to their vehicle. His expression was enough to tell Stingo that something serious had happened.

'Sir?' said Stingo, jumping to his feet.

'Wake the others. Briefing in two minutes.'

In less than that time, the nine members of Stingo's team were crouched in a circle. After a week in the desert they all looked rough and dirty, a bunch of bandits rather than crack troops. Midge, their silver-haired captain, looked round the circle. He did not see the grime but eyes hungry for news. He dived straight in.

'We're being diverted to Egypt. A small group of terrorists known as the Brotherhood have abducted the daughter of the president of the United States and two others.'

A few of the men gave disbelieving whistles.

'They're hiding out in the desert, threatening to kill one of the hostages if any rescue attempt is mounted.'

'Why us?' asked Merlin. His black skin had been turned grey by the dust and his lips were cracked, but his mind had not suffered. 'The Yanks would want to keep this their show, wouldn't they?'

'One of the hostages is British.'

'It's Darcie, isn't it?' Stingo had been sitting silently at Midge's right hand. He had worked it out as soon as Shelly Morris was mentioned. 'What the hell does the Firm think it's doing pitching the kid into that situation?'

'For once, I quite agree with you, Stingo. MI6 have messed up again. Yes, it's Zebra. She has no idea that the Firm was using her, nor that her phone's fitted with a tracking device. Think what you like about the rights and wrongs of that, at least we can use it to our advantage now.'

Merlin glanced sideways at Stingo and saw that his friend was boiling with fury.

'What are the kidnappers demanding?' asked Merlin.

'Release of one of their men –'

'That should be manageable.'

'– Oh yeah, and the small matter of withdrawal of all foreign troops from the Middle East and the restoration of the Egyptian monarchy.'

There was silence.

'So understandably London thinks our kid won't make it unless we come up with a plan,' Midge continued levelly, though anyone who knew him as well as these eight men could tell that he was crackling with suppressed anger. The ones really to blame never got to put their necks on the block – it was always the innocent that suffered. 'When the chips are down, they don't trust the Americans to take care of anyone but the first daughter; they want us to fight Darcie's corner for her.'

'When are we off?' Knife asked, already on his feet.

'Immediately. Pack up the camouflage. We've a plane to catch.'

15.00, Cairo, Egypt: Hot and dry, 35°C

Ginnie and Michael Lock were sitting shell-shocked in an unregarded corner of the American Embassy's emergency control room in Cairo. They had arrived expecting to take their daughter back with them, only to find that she had become involved in an international incident. Around them, the diplomats and military were in overdrive, shouting into telephones, cursing computer screens and running about the communications centre with the latest satellite imagery. Technicians were still erecting the big display screen that was supposed to give them daylight coverage of anything that moved out in the desert as long as any satellites were overhead, but so far the surveillance had yielded nothing but an empty helicopter heading into Libyan airspace. Colonel Gaddafi's men had searched it on landing and sworn they'd found nothing.

'The Brits put the last position somewhere here,' they heard a CIA official tell the US Defence Attaché. Michael watched as he pointed out a spot just south of the area known as the White Desert.

'Where are they going? What's our best guess?' asked the military man.

'Going nowhere, we guess. But we don't think we can reach them without first being seen – the locals say there's high ground round there with many caves; it'd take us some time to pinpoint them and by then we might have casualties.'

He meant Darcie and the American boy might be killed, thought Michael. He reached across and took his wife's hand.

'This has always been my worst nightmare – her out

there and us unable to help,' whispered Ginnie. Her grip on his hand was painfully tight.

'Mr and Mrs Lock?'

They looked up and saw that a secretary was offering them some coffee. She doesn't look much older than Darcie, thought Michael.

'Thanks.' He took a cup in a shaking hand.

'When you've finished that, you might like to talk to our visitors,' the secretary said. 'They're being briefed in the ambassador's office.'

'We'll come right away,' said Ginnie, standing up. Anything was better than sitting uselessly on the sidelines like this.

They followed the secretary down a corridor and through a door into an elegant office. The ambassador sat behind a shining desk, a smart man in uniform standing at his shoulder, and seated in front of them a rag-tag bunch of unshaven, weather-stained men in dusty camouflage.

'Michael!' Stingo leapt to his feet and shook Darcie's father's hand fervently.

Michael's face broke into the first smile since he had heard the news of the abduction. 'Stingo! It's good to see you. Thank God they sent you. This is my wife, Ginnie.'

Stingo shook her hand. 'I'm very sorry, Mrs Lock. But Darcie's a great kid. She'll keep her head, you can be confident of that.'

'Thanks . . . er . . . Stingo. Darcie told me about you.'

'Mrs Lock, Mr Lock, do please take a seat,' said the ambassador, coming out from behind his desk. 'We were just winding up our briefing. Later today, our British friends here will be joining the American Special Forces stationed in Farafra. That's the closest oasis to the last known position of our targets. Can I offer you my personal assurances that we are taking no risks – no one will do anything to endanger the lives of our young people? Captain Mahoney –' Midge nodded at Michael and Ginnie, 'and his team are here as back-up – just in case. Our belief is still that this situation will be peacefully resolved.'

Stingo raised his eyebrows sceptically, but resisted

the temptation to disagree openly.

'I hope you will accept my hospitality until this is over. That way you'll be able to follow everything closely.'

'Thank you,' said Ginnie.

'And I hope you understand the necessity of steering clear of the press. If they . . . er . . . got wind of your daughter's particular role in the affair it would put her at even greater risk.'

'Particular role!' spluttered Michael. 'You make it sound as if she has contributed to the disaster in some way.'

'I didn't mean that, I assure you. We all know that Agent Lock, I mean, Darcie, is ignorant of her assignment. But, nonetheless, it puts her in greater danger.'

'What do you mean? She's ignorant that she's being used to monitor Shelly Morris?' fumed Michael, his hands flexing convulsively.

'Of course. Didn't you know?' The ambassador glanced uneasily at his aide.'

'No, *we* did not.'

'But, even so, we're not going to say anything to the media,' said Ginnie, placing a restraining arm on her husband. 'Can you promise us that your staff will be equally discreet? The world's press has descended on Cairo: do they know the consequences of a careless word in the wrong ear?'

'They do, Mrs Lock. No one beyond a small group of people in the British and American governments knows anything about this. You can rest assured that your daughter's secret is safe.'

15.30, Empty Quarter: Hot, 41°C

Darcie woke up in the hottest part of the afternoon to find Jon Lee staring at her from the other side of the cave. Their abductors were huddled together at the entrance, sorting out some kind of machine. She propped her back against the rock wall, conscious of a raging thirst.

'Can I have the water?' she croaked.

Jon Lee threw the canteen to her, letting it fall short so that she had to scramble up to get it. It was empty.

'Where's it all gone?' she asked.

'Must've evaporated,' said Jon Lee.

'He drank it,' Shelly cut in, coming into view from the back of the cave.

'Yeah, only after you took more than your fair share,' grumbled Jon Lee.

'So you left none for me?' Darcie quivered with anger. They were no longer playing games on the *Pharaoh*; water was life or death out here.

'You mustn't cry, Babe: it'll waste water,' said Jon Lee flippantly, turning his back on her.

Why was he punishing her like this? Darcie wondered. Weren't they all in this together?

'Don't be mean, Jon Lee,' said Shelly wearily. 'She's not to blame.'

'So why didn't her people stop this happening?' he asked bitterly. 'If she's supposed to be the *intelligent* one among us, why did she cosy up with Antar and let him fool us all into thinking he was all right?'

Shelly shrugged but gave no answer. Perhaps she had been thinking this too.

'You both seem to think I knew what was going on, but I didn't,' said Darcie. 'Actually, I'm pretty gutted to find I've been used by someone I thought I could trust.'

'*Actually, I'm pretty gutted,*' parroted Jon Lee cruelly.

Shelly looked doubtful. 'So you really didn't know that man was MI6?'

'Of course not.'

'Don't believe her – she's a professional liar, remember,' said Jon Lee.

Darcie was feeling too wretched and thirsty to argue. She closed her eyes. Her life seemed irretrievably messed up: mistrusted by those she was with and betrayed by those nearest to her. Why should she even bother to try and survive this?

Why? asked a voice in her head. Because you're not a quitter. You aren't to blame and you know it. Jon Lee is just scared and angry and you are the only person around for him to blame. You owe it to your real friends – to Hans – to yourself – not to give up.

Feeling as if she was wading through concrete, she turned her exhausted mind to their predicament, forcing herself to think through the various outcomes. Negotiations can't have even properly begun yet – there hadn't been time. The kidnappers had made impossible demands, but maybe they'd settle for less and let the three hostages go? If that was the case, she just had to sit tight and wait it out.

On the other hand, if things turned nasty, their chances depended on the mood of their captors. If it were possible, they should try not to anger anyone.

She looked up. Antar had left his comrades and now crouched down beside her. He took a canteen of water from his belt and put it surreptitiously in her hands.

'They drank yours,' he said, casting a scornful look at Jon Lee and Shelly who were watching Darcie with suspicion. 'Share mine.'

'Thanks,' Darcie whispered. She didn't know what to think about Antar – he had murdered Hans, yet she had not forgotten he had also tried to prevent a third hostage being taken.

'I am sorry about that Austrian boy. I did not want

anyone to get hurt,' he said softly as if he could hear her thoughts.

'Didn't you?'

He turned away from her. She thought he had aged several years over the last twenty-four hours. 'No. This is not about killing. I am doing this for Egypt. We want a country that stands on its own feet, not one that bows to the foreigners.'

'But why this? Why us?'

He didn't answer her directly. 'Abu El-Gebel is a good man – he should never have been put in prison. And they should not have tortured Khaled. There is no justice. No one was listening.'

'And you think they'll listen now?'

Antar stood up. 'The whole world is waiting on our every word.' He beckoned Shelly over. 'Come: we want you to speak to your father.'

A video camera had been set up in the entrance to the cave. Khaled came towards them. Without his scarf over his face, Darcie saw that he was a gaunt-looking man of around thirty, missing a few teeth at the front. A round burn mark scarred his left cheek. He gave Shelly a handwritten speech to read out then led her into place. The president's daughter looked so different to the image that had appeared on the front pages last week – with no make-up, she seemed young and vulnerable.

Shelly read through the words they had prepared for her and shuddered.

'I can't say that. Please don't ask me to.'

Khaled strode to the back of the cave and seized Jon Lee by the elbow.

'If you don't, I'll kill him.'

Shelly battled with her emotions for a moment, then looked back down at the speech and nodded.

'OK. I'll do it.' She began to speak in a flat tone.

'Mr President, father, as you know by now, I am being held by the Brotherhood of the Martyrs for Truth. With me are Jon Lee from New York and Darcie from England – representatives of the two countries and the UN who have done the most to terrorise the nations of the world. To secure our safe return, you must release the man known as Abu El-Gebel, founder of the Brotherhood, and withdraw all foreign troops from the Middle East by the end of the month.

'If you refuse to do this, or try to rescue us, one of us will be left in the desert to die. It will be a s-slow and painful death – the world shall know that every moment of agony will be your fault. The hands of our abductors will be free of the blood.'

'The Brotherhood sends its condolences to the family of the boy who died yesterday. They want to state for the record that they acted in self-defence.'

Shelly swallowed and looked up at the camera.

'Please, Pop, don't let your daughter die. My life is in your hands. I love you and Mom so much.'

Khaled snatched the speech from her hands.

'We did not write that last part,' he said angrily, shaking her by the shoulder. 'You will say exactly what we tell you.'

Antar made calming noises, intervening between Khaled and Shelly. 'No, no, she did well for us. That was the best part because it was from the heart. Everyone will see that.'

Khaled's rage was replaced by a smile of comprehension. 'You are right, little cousin. You did good.' He patted Shelly on the cheek like a dog that had just performed a new trick. 'Transmit the message, Antar.' He added something in Arabic, looking at his watch.

Darcie kept to her corner, staying as far away from unpredictable Khaled as possible. Antar mentioned that his cousin had been mistreated while in prison. She wondered if that explained his rage, never far from the surface. If anyone was going to give the order to abandon one of them to the desert, it would be Khaled. Preparing for the worst, Darcie ate only half the food given to her, keeping the dried fruit in a pocket of her robe. She made sure Shelly and Jon Lee saw her do so in order that they could follow her example and noticed that they went on to do the same.

At dusk, the group set off on horseback again, heading south. Darcie felt more comfortable now she had been put in front of Antar; Shelly had drawn the short straw and was mounted behind Khaled. Antar did not talk but at least Darcie did not flinch every time he made a sudden move. All around her, the sand glimmered grey in the moonlight. She could see it shifting slightly in the light breeze, trickling from the crest of each dune, down the leeside in a slow-motion wave as it made its way across the desert. The fine grains of grit found entry into her nose, mouth, eyes and ears. Darcie wrapped her scarf across her face, leaving only a small space to see and breathe.

It must have been nearly midnight when there was movement on the brow of the next dune: a camel train was pacing slowly towards them, twelve animals led in a string, saddled and burdened with supplies. Khaled spurred his horse into a gallop and rushed to meet the herdsman at the head of the column. They embraced fervently, leaving Darcie in no doubt that this was another planned rendezvous.

'You go on camel now,' said Antar in a low voice. 'You will like that, Darcie.'

Be careful what you wish for, in case it comes true, Hans had told her once when she had wished to ride camelback under the starts. Darcie tried but could not stop the sobs that tore through her. She felt Antar's grip tighten. His instinct was to comfort her, but what could he say? He was to blame.

'Be good girl and you be all right. We are men of peace,' he said hoarsely.

'But when you don't get what you want, what then?' Darcie asked, tears running down her dust-stained face.

'We will get what we want,' he replied firmly. 'We risk all for our children; the American president will do the same for his daughter or he is not a man.'

Darcie felt so angry. Why did he not understand that they might as well ask for the moon as demand America withdraw all its forces? Even if the president wanted to make concessions, others would surely stop him. She had to explain this to Antar before it was too late.

'But he's also a leader who has to answer for the

lives of others. He can't rule the world just to suit his family.'

Antar said nothing but Darcie sensed she might be getting somewhere and that he entertained his own doubts already.

'You are storing up a terrible revenge for yourself and your people if one of us gets harmed,' she added.

As soon as she said it she knew she had made a false step. Antar's arms turned rigid around her. 'Our people are used to suffering. We are martyrs for the truth – the truth that the soul of Egypt is still proud like the pharaohs. All we need is to be reminded of our greatness.'

'Reminded? How?'

'America must be humbled. We were living in great cities of stone, studying the skies, watering our crops and writing our stories when your people were in mud huts, making a poor living from the forests, with no culture but that of the axe and the bow. The West should remember this and treat us with honour. When I went to your universities, did they value what we had given them? No, we were a forgotten people, ignored.'

Darcie said nothing, but she could tell he wanted to convince her, win her over to his side.

'Your superpower is nothing to what we were then. Even today, America has built nothing to rival our pyramids or our tombs in the Valley of the Kings. You think we have done a bad thing in kidnapping you; but later you will understand. Your passing trouble will make us great again – that is a reward worth suffering for.'

'And Hans? What reward does he get?' Darcie asked bitterly.

'He is with God,' Antar said shortly.

But that wasn't good enough, thought Darcie. Antar was trying to wash his hands of any responsibility for Hans's death, claiming to have acted in self-defence, but what kind of defence was a gun against an unarmed boy? Khaled, Antar and the others, for all their fine words, were thugs, using violence to force people into doing what they wanted.

Before the attack, Darcie might have sympathised with their wish for an Egypt independent of the West; now she just hated them. Her anger boiled over into words.

'If you want to be truly great, you shouldn't kill someone trying to protect his friend, or take children hostage,' said Darcie. Antar dismounted, pretending to ignore what she had said. He held out a hand to help her down, but she did not take it. 'And do you know what else, Antar? You've betrayed my friendship and trust. What kind of man does that make you? The others blame me for not seeing you for what you were. I blame myself.' She slid down unaided. 'You were just like the others, only interested in what I had to say as long as it kept you up to date with what Shelly was doing.'

Antar paused, his hand on the bridle. 'Others?' he asked shrewdly.

Darcie cursed her slip of the tongue. She had meant to keep on Antar's good side, but her desire to lecture him had run away with her and she had almost revealed that she had been used by MI6 to keep an eye on Shelly.

'Oh, just everyone. I suppose you have your reasons for doing all this.' She moved to pat the horse to distract him from her words.

If Antar was suspicious about her sudden change of tone, he did not say. They walked forwards to join the camel driver; the black-robed man was still talking in a low voice to Khaled, using his arms to reinforce his point. Shelly stood to one side, her head hung. Jon Lee approached and put his arm around her, giving her a hug. Darcie felt a pang of envy, wishing she too could have a friend at her side.

Khaled looked round and beckoned Antar over. They began a heated debate. From the looks they cast in the hostages' direction, Darcie had the distinct feeling that the news the camel driver had brought was not good. She sidled over to Shelly and Jon Lee.

'OK, Kiddo?' Shelly asked with an attempt at a friendly smile.

'Not really. I think we should prepare for the worst. Something's happened.'

Jon Lee swore.

'Oh God.' Shelly looked around her in desperation as if looking for somewhere to run. Of course, she could run, her hands and legs were not tied – but there was nowhere to go.

Khaled concluded the discussion with a hail of emphatic gestures, forcing his cousin to back down. He then marched over to his three hostages.

'How have you done it?' he barked at Shelly. He was rubbing angrily at his scarred cheek.

'Done what?' she asked, genuinely bewildered.

'They know we are out here. They did not even bother to track the helicopter. Instead they have sent soldiers to Farafra. How do they know to do that?'

'I don't know,' Shelly replied honestly. She kept her eyes lowered, trying to do nothing to make him angrier than he already was.

'You – they must be punished for breaking our terms.'

'But they haven't!' Shelly protested desperately.

'They've not tried to rescue us, have they?'

'Silence! Troops in Farafra is enough – it shows they are tracking us somehow. Your friend will die for this.' He pointed at Jon Lee. 'We will tell them to take their men out of our land or the other one will die as well. Then they will believe us.'

'No!' cried Shelly.

'I don't want to die!' shrieked Jon Lee. 'No, no, you can't.'

Khaled pushed him away from Shelly. 'The boy first. That is what I have agreed.'

'Look, it's not me you want: it's her!' Jon Lee pointed at Darcie.

A terrible silence descended. Darcie knew what was coming and steeled herself, but her knees would not stop trembling.

Khaled smiled cruelly. 'You are not a brave boy. You would send a girl to die in your place?'

'She's not an ordinary girl. She's a spy.'

Khaled's eyes flashed dangerously. He leaned close to Jon Lee's face. 'How do you know?'

'She t-told us,' Jon Lee stammered.

Khaled turned to Darcie, sweeping his robes around in an imperious gesture.

'Is this true?' he thundered.

'I am not a spy,' said Darcie quietly.

'Turn out your pockets!' ordered Khaled.

They each held out a handful of dried fruit. Khaled knocked them away, scattering the sand with raisins.

'Where are the things we took from them earlier?'

The boy, still wearing Jon Lee's iPod round his neck, brought forward a bag. He drew out Darcie's and Shelly's phones. Khaled took them aside and cracked them open. Shelly's revealed nothing but a sim card and a battery. But as soon as he took the back off Darcie's phone, everyone saw the foreign circuitry, lit by a tiny red light.

'What is that?' Khaled asked Darcie as he ripped it out. The light continued to glow, feeding off some power source independent from the phone.

'I don't know,' she replied honestly, though she

had a sick feeling in her stomach as to what it might be and why it was there.

'That must be how they know where we are,' said Antar. 'It must be sending a signal to the GPS system.' He gave Darcie a look of pure anger as he realised it was she who had betrayed them.

Khaled threw the device on the ground, about to grind it under foot.

'Stop!' shouted Antar. 'It is useful to us. We can send it off in the wrong direction so they have no idea where we really are.'

Khaled nodded and smiled. 'You are right.' Turning to one of his men, Khaled barked out an order. 'Take this to the Ocean of Sand and throw it from the top of the tallest sand dune. We will go past these American troops without problem. They will have another problem by then.'

He turned upon Darcie. She knew her own chances had just run out.

'You are the scorpion among us but you have stung for the last time. It is terrible to use a child as a spy –

even I had not thought the British would go so low.' He gave a sigh and put a heavy hand on her shoulder. 'You know, I pity you. But they must learn that if they send so young a solider into battle, there will be casualties.'

'I am not a spy. They may have been using my phone to spy, but I knew nothing about it,' said Darcie bleakly, though she sensed that nothing she could say now would help.

'That does not matter. They have picked you out and so you will be the one we leave to die. Make your peace with your god – you will have enough time, I think.'

'No!' Shelly was struggling against Jon Lee who was trying to hold her back. 'You can't do this! You don't need to do it!'

Khaled pushed Darcie towards Antar. 'Tie her hands and feet. We leave her here.' He swung round to face Shelly. 'I warned your father and he did not listen. I conclude that he will not take my words seriously unless we offer him proof. And you are going to tell him this. We will record another message and send it into Farafra – that will show that we are not to be messed with.' He waved his arm at the others. 'Get ready to ride.'

'Darcie, I'm sorry!' screamed Shelly as she was hoisted against her will on to a camel's back. Jon Lee was putting up no resistance. He looked as if he was in shock, stumbling as he walked over to his camel. Too despairing to care very much about anything, Darcie couldn't find it in her heart to blame him: he had only been trying to survive. He should never have been in a position where he had to choose between his life and someone else's.

As Jon Lee staggered past, he let something drop at her feet from a fold in his robes. Darcie slumped down to gather it under her skirts. Groping in the sand, she felt the wet seal of a waterskin. Quickly, she hooked it into the belt of her trousers before anyone noticed.

He had given her his water.

Looking up, she met his eyes. She nodded to him.

'Try to survive,' he murmured.

'You too,' she whispered back.

With a whistle and a tap on the rump, the lead camels moved off, taking Shelly and Jon Lee south. The empty-saddled horses trotted along at the rear. The decoy had already galloped off north, eager to rid himself of a device that would pinpoint him for his enemies. Darcie and Antar were left alone at the foot of the dune.

'So, you're going to murder someone for the second time in two days,' said Darcie, now shaking as he tied her hands in front of her. Her only hope rested on his mercy.

'You tricked me,' he said. A bead of sweat ran down his cheek. He brushed it away, his hands trembling.

'No, I'm the one who has been tricked. I knew nothing of that device. I thought . . .' She gave a strangled laugh. '. . . I thought I was going on holiday. Are you going to punish me for that?'

'I am sorry, Darcie, but if I do not do this, Khaled will do it himself and he will not be so kind.' Antar looped the rope around her ankles so her hands and feet were now tightly bound.

'Kind? You mean you can be more cruel than this?'

He knelt at her feet to tie her ankles. 'Don't you care what'll happen when you leave me? Haven't you got a daughter – or a sister – of my age? What would you do if someone did this to them?'

He looked up at her, then stood, brushing sand from his knees. 'I would kill them,' he said matter-of-factly. He took out a knife. Darcie went cold.

'You're right,' she whispered. 'Perhaps it is kinder to kill me now than leave.'

'I am not killing you – I am giving you a chance.' He looked up at the stars and then drew a line in the sand. 'That way is south. If you bear to the south-east, after many miles you will hit the road from Bahariya to Farafra. If you get that far, you may be lucky and some-one may be passing. Keep this hidden until we are out of sight.'

There was the sound of hooves thudding on sand. Antar quickly buried the knife beside her.

Khaled called something in Arabic to his cousin.

'I am coming,' replied Antar in English, getting to his feet.

'You have not gone soft, little cousin, I hope?' demanded Khaled, dismounting and looking at the two people on the ground suspiciously. He tugged on the ropes. 'Remember she is a spy – an enemy. Stake her out. We do not want her hopping after us, do we?' He laughed and threw Antar a mallet and two tent pegs from his saddlebag.

'That is not necessary,' Antar protested.

'No, not necessary, but it is fitting. Do it!'

Silently, Antar knocked the pegs into the ground while Darcie watched him helplessly.

'Please lie down,' he said gently.

With a glance at the watching Khaled, Darcie lay down on her stomach as Antar roped her hands and feet to the pegs. He then crouched over her as if giving her bonds a final check.

'The peg at your feet is loose,' he whispered. 'May God be merciful to you.' He stood up. 'Let us go. The desert will claim her in hours when the sun is up.'

'Good. Farewell, Spy.' Khaled gave her a flourishing salute. 'We have an appointment to keep or I might have stayed to watch your final moments. But your death is nothing to what is to come. When the tomb opens, all the world will tremble.' With that, he rode off, Antar mounted behind him, hurrying to catch up with the slow-moving camel train.

13

05.30, Farafra: Hot, northerly wind, 22°C

Stingo switched off the cranky television in his hostel bedroom. The footage of Shelly's appeal had been on all the world's television stations almost continuously since it had been posted on the web the day before. He couldn't bear to watch the girl's face another moment.

It was now dawn and he felt rough from the lack of sleep and worry. He went to the window and opened the shutters a crack. The white hot orb of the sun was just rising above the horizon, casting long shadows of trees and houses across the beaten earth of the courtyard below his room. He signed and turned away. They were following orders to sit tight and await developments but this was torturing him. By instinct he wanted to rush into the desert, hone in on the kidnappers using the tracking device, and take them out. He played the mission through in his mind: a midday swoop when they would be sleepy, overwhelming force to prevent counter attack, so swift that no one had a chance to hurt one of the hostages. But the Americans had ruled that out while there was still a chance that negotiations would work. No one had yet been hurt, they had argued. The murder of the Austrian boy had not been intentional. There was still a chance it would all end peacefully. What worried Stingo most was how much it would take for the Americans to change their minds. It would be no comfort to the parents of Darcie or Jon Lee if the Yanks only took action after one of them had been killed.

There was a knock and Merlin put his head round the door. 'We've got another message from the kidnappers. It was given to a goat boy out on the north road. You'd better hurry.'

Not bothering to dress, Stingo followed Merlin down to the communications centre in the hostel dining room. The American commanding officer had his hand poised over the keyboard, ready to play the message.

Shelly's familiar face flickered on to the screen, jumping a few frames due to some fault with the machinery. They could see it had been taken at night as her features were torchlit. She was distraught.

'Pop, they know you've sent soldiers after me. To punish you – to prove they're serious – they've left Darcie behind in the desert. They just tied her up and . . . and left her. They say she won't last the day. You must do everything they say or Jon Lee will be next – and then me. Please, please do what they want.'

The footage broke off. The room was eerily silent.

'Do you have the messenger?' barked the American commander.

A junior officer nodded. 'Yes, sir. He is being questioned now.'

'Send this to Cairo. Await further orders.'

'Yes, sir.'

'And that's it, is it?' burst out Midge, speaking for all his team. 'You are going to wait while a girl dies out there?'

The American officer, resplendent in his pristine

desert camouflage, wheeled round. The British contingent looked distinctly shabby beside him and his men.

'Yes, I am. You heard her – any move from us and another one dies.'

'But our girl isn't dead yet!' countered Midge, spitting his words out. 'We can still save her.'

'Just how do you think you can do that?'

'The device – there's a good chance it's still on her.'

'But there's also a good chance they had their phones taken from them when they were captured and her phone will lead right to the kidnappers. If they see you coming, we can say goodbye to the president's daughter and the other kid.'

Midge turned to Knife who was monitoring the phone's signal. 'Where is it now?'

'Moving rapidly north, sir,' responded Knife promptly. 'It could be a decoy.'

'Or the kidnappers,' said the American CO. 'But not your girl – she couldn't be moving so quickly.' He didn't need to add anything because they could all imagine what it was like to walk in the heat of a desert.

'But we can't just sit here and let her die!' protested Midge.

'Those are your orders, captain,' said the CO with finality. 'I trust you will obey them.'

The SAS team huddled in Midge's room trying to decide what to do next. They all knew the consequences of going against their orders – they would be court-martialled, or – worse – endanger the other two hostages. But the seconds were ticking by for Darcie.

'What do you think, men?' asked Midge as he paced up and down in the few feet not occupied by his squad.

'I for one don't remember signing up with the US of A when I joined the army. I don't take my orders from that effing Yank,' said Stingo. His knuckles were white as he gripped his knees. Midge knew that his warrant officer had already decided to go after Darcie on his own if he must – orders or no orders.

Midge didn't want it to come to that.

'But, as you are all well aware, we are under orders to follow their lead,' Midge reasoned.

'We're also under orders from our government to fight Darcie's corner for her, sir,' chipped in Merlin. 'The Yanks aren't going to lift a finger for her – just wring their hands.'

'Neatly put, mate, but where does that leave us?'

'As usual,' said Stingo, 'in the –'

'No,' cut in Merlin. 'It just means we have to be creative.'

A few of the men snorted.

'I don't mean get out our pottery wheels – I mean we should obey our orders and interpret them inventively. I'll bet my pension that we'll soon be ordered to withdraw back to Cairo. My suggestion is we take a little detour.'

Midge scratched his chin. 'How much of a detour?'

'Well, that depends on what we think of the signal the tracking advice is giving out.'

'Heading due north – yeah, that seems bizarre,'

said Stingo. 'There's nothing but the Ocean of Sand up there.'

'They could, of course, be taking our girl in that direction to leave her in that hell hole, but the message said she'd already been abandoned,' continued Merlin.

'Or they could be going that way themselves, but that's one hell of a desert jay-walk: all the way down south and all the way back north,' commented Knife, rubbing his sharp nose thoughtfully.

'Or they worked out the Americans were tracking them somehow and that's when they found out what was in the phone – then that would be why they chose to leave her. It's a punishment.' As soon as Stingo said this, silence fell as they all came to the conclusion that his guess was right.

'So they would've been mad at her. I hope they did nothing worse than leave her behind,' said Midge.

'Oh yeah, leaving her behind's a real picnic – a kid alone in the desert with no food or drink – very mild,' said Stingo bitterly.

'You know what I mean. Khaled is a head case. I

wouldn't put anything past him.' Midge looked round his men. 'I think we all know what we're going to do. Pack your kit: we're going on a manhunt. We'll head for the point where the tracking signal turned back north again: that seems to mark the moment of crisis. It's our best guess as to where she is.'

05.30, Empty Quarter: Clear skies, 26°C

Darcie had waited until she was quite sure that Khaled and Antar had left before trying to work her feet free. She and Antar must have a different definition of the word 'loose', she decided bitterly, as she writhed on the ground, kicking fruitlessly, until she was exhausted. Putting her cheek against the sand, she rested for a while. Lying so close to the earth, she could hear even the smallest sounds: the shifting sand; the scuttle of tiny insects coming out of their burrows to hunt in the cool of the night; the whisper of the breeze. She tried not to think of the bigger creatures that might be attracted to a warm body – Stingo had told her that snakes and scorpions would sometimes visit a bedding roll or curl up in a boot at night to shelter from the cold. Stretched out helpless, her worst fear at the moment was that one of them would slither over her and she would be unable to defend herself. However in a few hours' time her biggest enemy wouldn't be such nightmare imaginings: it would be the heat.

Darcie knew her situation was desperate. Tears welled up in her eyes. She couldn't bear the prospect of such a horrifying death. It would be better just to fall asleep and never wake up. Her mind was full of darkness: why not give in to it and stop struggling to prolong her suffering?

At that moment, the first light dawned. Light glinted on the broken components of her phone inches from her face, giving the illusion that it had just been switched on. The sight reminded her of all the messages it still contained. Desert survival. This was what this was all about. Stingo had said that everyone hit a wall at some time during the survival course he had been on; the ones who got through, were the ones who didn't give up but carried on even without hope.

I can't give up now, Darcie told herself. Antar gave me a chance and I have to take it.

With renewed vigour, Darcie tugged at the ropes lashing her feet to the peg. Her recently mended leg ached horribly but she ignored it. She even gave a sour laugh as she recalled the doctor warning her off any high-impact sports for a few months. He had not anticipated this!

'I . . . can . . . do . . . this!' Darcie panted, giving one last heave. The peg came free like a rocket and shot past her head, the point grazing her scalp. Darcie was momentarily dazed. Blood trickled down her forehead but she did not have the luxury of a free hand to wipe it away. Wriggling into a crouch, she knelt over the other peg and worked the ropes off. Hands still bound, she scrabbled in the sand where Antar had buried the knife and found the bone shaft. With it now sitting securely in her grip, she felt her hope returning. Pausing, she wondered how best to cut herself free. She would have to wedge the handle to use the blade like a saw. That sounded easier than it was in reality. She decided to use the ropes around her ankles as the anchor, her feet to steady the knife handle. Carefully she rubbed the rope up and down against the blade, concentrating so as not to cut her wrists in the process. One by one the fibres of the rope were sliced through and she was able to free her hands. Her feet followed seconds later. Darcie rubbed her calves and arms to restore circulation, allowing herself a little jig of self-congratulation at this first victory.

Back on her feet, she was acutely conscious that her throat was crying out for a celebratory drink. Darcie reached for the waterskin but then stopped. Stingo's words echoed in her mind – *Camels could survive in the desert for up to ten days without drinking, whereas a human will die in two.* She knew the contents of the skin was all that stood between her and death. She had to ration it. From its weight she guessed she had around two litres – that seemed a lot now, but after a day sweating in the sun, it would be barely enough to keep her alive for a couple of days. What is more, she was planning to walk to safety, which would make her lose more sweat from the exercise. She put the waterskin down. Better to wait.

It was, however, time to make a plan. She felt quite calm now she was no longer so powerless. She could take action and this knowledge gave her a focus and reinforced her will to survive. Thinking back to her conversations with Stingo, she remembered that he had told her that in most cases of desert survival the sensible person stayed with their vehicle or in their last known position. Otherwise it was like looking for a needle in a haystack when the searchers came to the rescue. But in her case, she was sure that no one knew where she was and no one would dare to come looking for her. If anything, they would think she was somewhere to the north with that traitorous tracking device, but any rescue team would be too scared of triggering another hostage-killing to come after her.

Darcie gathered the remnants of her shattered phone which had contained so much vital information and cradled them in her lap. The phone was beyond repair: technology was not going to help her now. She gazed up at the fading stars, comparing them to Antar's line on the sand. He had used the stars to find his bearings; she would need to do the same as once she left this place, she could not afford to wander in a circle. She looked behind her: the Pole Star twinkled faintly in the north. If she kept that behind and to her left, she should be heading south-east. The rising and setting of the sun should help keep her on track when the stars weren't out – not that she planned to do any walking by day. That would kill her twice as fast.

So what did she need before she set out? Water she had. Food? Remembering the raisins Khaled had scattered, she sought for the place where he had made them empty their pockets. She found it near where the tent peg had landed. With a fingertip search, she rooted out a couple of handfuls of sandy dried fruit, but she was in no position to be fussy. Though the raisins would not keep her alive for long, they would help stave off hunger pangs. In any case, she knew that the water would run out before she really suffered from the lack of food.

The next thing she needed was shelter. She had to get under cover before the sun got any higher. The dune where she was offered nothing. She had to start walking in the hope that something better would come along before too long.

Finally, before she set off, she should take anything she could to make a signal. The polished screen of the phone might do to reflect light during the day, but what about a fire for night? When she got near the road, she would need to be able to attract attention, particularly if by that stage she could no longer walk any further. Hunting around, Darcie found two wooden tent pegs, a few hanks of rope and some camel dung. When that was dry it should burn – or so she hoped. Making a sling out of her Fresh Start T-shirt and the rope, she gathered the materials for her fire, strapped them to her back and prepared to leave.

Second star to the right and straight on till morning. The phrase from *Peter Pan* drifted into her head as she set her bearing by the Pole Star.

All I need now is fairy dust, Darcie told herself, then this would be easy. I could fly home.

Putting one foot in front of the other, she trudged up the slope of the sand dune.

09.00, Cairo: Stormy, 34°C

A row broke out in the staff dining room at the American Embassy in Cairo. The occasion was the arrival of Christopher Lock interrupting his son and daughter-in-law as they sat over an uneaten breakfast. As soon as Ginnie saw Christopher limp into the room, she was on her feet and dredging up every foul name to fling at him.

'Darcie is out there now, d . . . dying, and it's all your fault, you scheming old goat,' she screamed, her words interspersed with sobs. 'It should be you stranded in the desert. If I had my way, it would be!'

'Ginnie, I implore you to show more self-restraint,' countered Christopher, his face ashen.

'Restraint? What good is restraint now? You're a

heartless vulture. Come to pick over your grand-daughter's bones, have you?' Her fury having reached the stage beyond words, she collapsed into a flood of tears in the nearest chair.

But the barrage had not ended. Michael took over, with an icy control to match his father's.

'You are not wanted here, Father. I suggest you get straight back on a plane and go do whatever it is you do in your office. Keep away from us and out of our lives.'

Christopher turned from Ginnie to Michael.

'You don't understand, Michael: I am not here as family – God knows I haven't earned that right. I am here to help my agent – and I'm possibly the only one who can.'

'Help?' choked Ginnie hysterically. 'Don't you get it, Christopher? You've signed our daughter's death warrant.'

'I very much hope not.' He sat down a table away from Darcie's parents and wearily placed his walking stick on the chair beside him. He was too old to have heart trouble, he thought sadly, but Darcie had awoken something in him and now he felt his heart was breaking. He had resolved to pull out all the stops for her. 'You may not credit it, but it was I who persuaded the prime minister to send that particular team of SAS operatives to Farafra. If I know those men, they will not be content to let Darcie die if they can do anything to prevent it. I'm here to ensure that they have the authorization to do what is necessary.'

'They'll never get it,' said Michael bleakly. 'We're just a sideshow. The show can't get any bigger than the president's daughter – as far as the Americans and the rest of the world is concerned, Darcie is . . . well . . . collateral damage.'

'And you are going to accept that?' asked Christopher, raising an eyebrow in surprise.

'Of course I don't accept it! I've begged, pleaded all morning to be allowed to go and look for her myself, but they have said it's out of the question.'

'Quite right. You'd only end up getting yourself killed. You never made a good scout even as a boy.'

'Father, you can be so –'

'I know, I know. But right now we should be on the same side – Darcie's side – let's leave the family bickering till later. I want you to know that I intend to put my career on the line and order Captain Mahoney and his men to take a covert foray into the desert, hang the consequences.'

'Thanks, that's very noble of you, Father,' Michael said ironically. 'But they are already on their way back to Cairo. They were ordered out as soon as we heard that last message.'

Christopher's face took on a steely expression. 'Well, we'll see about that, won't we?'

09.00, Farafra–Bahariya road: Hot and dry, 39°C

The radio in the borrowed jeep crackled into life. Stingo cast a sideways look at Midge, who was at the wheel, watching the road ripple in the heat haze.

'Shall I answer that?' Stingo enquired.

'Yeah. Best to seem as if everything is normal,' Midge replied.

'Alpha team, do you read me, over?' hissed the voice.

'Yep, we read you,' said Stingo guardedly. It was a British, not an American, voice addressing them. 'Who is that, over?'

The man replied with the correct password.

Stingo grimaced at Midge: 'It's the Firm. I bet this was the one who dropped our girl right in it.'

'What is your position, over?' asked Christopher. He knew full well as the Americans were tracking all vehicle movements on the roads between the oases. Even now the tiny blip that was the SAS team's convoy was travelling north on the screen in front of him.

'We're heading back to Cairo via Bahariya, over.'

Christopher glanced at the American commander sitting at the consol beside him. He could only listen to Christopher's half of the conversation. Christopher tapped his headphones as though he was having trouble hearing them. 'I think you must be experiencing radio problems. Am I right, over?'

'No —' Merlin nudged Stingo in the ribs. 'I mean, yeah, you're right, over.'

'I hope you can hear every word of what I am about to say,' Christopher continued. 'These are your orders. You are *under no circumstances* ordered to go and look for Darcie Lock. Did you get that? I repeat, *under no circumstances* go and look for Darcie Lock, over?'

Back in the jeep Stingo smiled. 'As you say, sir, terrible radio problems. I think we missed a bit in the middle, sir, but we understand you. Over and out.'

Midge was grinning. 'You heard the man: "You are . . . crackle . . . crackle . . . ordered to go and look for Darcie Lock." That's what I heard loud and clear. Didn't you, men?'

'Yes sir!' the others replied.

'Blimey, I never thought I'd meet a man from the Firm with a conscience. Signal to the jeep in the rear. We have new orders. Inform them that their radio is mysteriously caput – see to it, Stingo, when we stop – and that both our vehicles are about to break down spectacularly about a hundred metres up the road. Merlin, I suggest a couple of blow-outs. We'll leave two men with the vehicles and the rest of us will, er, follow our new orders from there.'

'Amazing luck, sir,' said Stingo archly, 'to break down so close to the last known location of the tracking device before it headed north.'

'Isn't it just,' chuckled Midge.

10.00, Cairo: Stormy, 34°C

Airforce One touched down at Cairo Airport bringing the most powerful man in the world to his daughter's rescue.

Right now, President Morris felt anything but powerful. He had spent the past few months believing his rebellious daughter to be the weak point in his campaign for re-election, safe only when far away; now he found her very distance had been his undoing. He should have been more careful, he cursed himself; he should never have let her within a thousand miles of the Middle East. It mattered little to him that his approval ratings had rocketed in the polls, thanks to a mixture of sympathy, outrage on his behalf and admiration for his steadfast refusal so far to deal with terrorists. Inside, he wanted to throw in the towel and agree to everything that was asked of him, if only to get his daughter back; it was the outer man, the shell they called 'Mr President', that kept him from doing that.

Jon Lee's parents had accompanied the president on his sudden departure for Egypt. He stood in the doorway for a moment looking in on them as they sat in the plane's guest lounge holding hands. Mr Vermont was a big man who oozed success from the Rolex watch on his wrist to the Italian shoes on his feet. In normal circumstances, President Morris would have been approaching him as a possible party supporter, the kind of man whose money kept the campaign show on the road. Mrs Vermont reminded him of Oprah Winfrey, beautifully dressed and coiffured, but he understood that this, like his own appearance, was a desperate show to cover the anguish beneath. Neither family had had an easy time with their respective children, but neither had expected the worst pain to be inflicted by complete strangers. He understood their silent misery because he shared it – he almost envied them that they could make no decisions to affect the outcome. He had to be both the anxious parent and the statesman.

'Mr and Mrs Vermont, my aide will be looking after you while you are in Cairo,' he said as the plane taxied to its stand. 'I believe Mr and Mrs Logan are already at the embassy.'

The three parents exchanged a silent look. None of them wished to become acquainted first-hand with the agony that the Logans must be experiencing knowing that their daughter had been left to die a lonely death.

'I will see you later,' said the president.

'Thank you, sir,' said Mr Vermont, rising to take the offered hand.

Patting Mrs Vermont awkwardly on the shoulder, the president thought of his own wife waiting in the White House with the rest of the family around her. He then followed his security agents and stepped out of the plane into the fierce heat of the day. The Egyptians had been told to keep protocol to a minimum – no bands, no guard of honour – but he still had to shake hands with the usual line-up of dignitaries and listen to speeches of regret and sympathy. Once in his limousine, he leaned back and closed his eyes.

'What next, Dean?' he asked his private secretary.

'We're going straight into a briefing at the embassy, then there will be a short meeting with Mr and Mrs Voss, the parents of the boy who –'

'I know who they are, thank you,' he said curtly.

'After that, you'll be introduced to the Locks.'

'Who?'

'The Logans. You may remember that they are now operating under a new name. Ginnie Lock is one of ours – Michael Lock one of theirs.'

'And the girl was working for both of us and didn't know it. Yes, I remember. Poor kid. I should never have allowed it. It seems I can't think straight for matters concerning Shelly.'

Before the president's closed eyes images of his daughter as a little girl flashed by: playing in the pool, making her first daisy chain, coming home with brightly coloured pictures from her first grade class. How had his little girl turned into the tearaway rebel who thought her father satanic? They had barely talked for years – not since his bid for the presidency became serious and took him away from home for weeks at a time. Something had gone wrong then and he had never taken the trouble to find out what it was. Now he might never get that chance.

10.30, Empty Quarter: Hot, 46°C

Darcie had walked till she could go no futher and found no better shade than that offered by a rocky outcrop. She gingerly checked the tumbled stones for snakes or worse, before rigging up her robe as a sunblind. She shook out her bundle, leaving the camel dung to dry in the heat, and put the T-shirt on. This was no time to be repulsed by the smell. Her work complete, she allowed herself a long drink and a few raisins.

Now she was no longer moving, she began to pay attention to her physical condition. The scratch on her head was throbbing. She felt her scalp and found a crust of dried blood in her hair. She knew this was not a good sign as even minor injuries could become major problems if infected, but she had nothing with which to treat it. Pulling off her boots, she was pleased to discover that her feet were in a reasonable condition: no blisters to hamper her on the next march. She left her boots off to air, placing her socks on the rocks beside her. The sand under her toes brought back memories of holidays with her parents.

'What would I give for a long cool dip in the sea now,' she said aloud.

The sound of her voice in the emptiness startled her. She had been lonely before, but now she was experiencing what it was like to be truly alone. It reminded her of the stories of hermits in the books her father had given her. They would retire to the desert for complete solitude, living in a cave and surviving off locusts and wild honey. Their deserts sounded more hospitable than this. Her solitude was unbroken by even a bee or a locust. Only when she looked up in the sky could she see anything of the outside world in the shape of the distant vapour trails of jets on their way from Europe to airports in Africa.

Look down, look down, she wanted to shout. Here I am! But no one could see her.

Or could they? Darcie remembered the satellite imagery she had seen in Kenya – the pictures of houses and vehicles taken from space. She'd taken it for granted then, but now she wondered just how big an object they could spot. At the moment, she would be a tiny dot, but what if she made a bigger sign?

If she was going to do something, she didn't have long. The sun was already climbing in the skies and the sand was baking. Swiftly, she gathered as many rocks as she could and began to lay them out in the sand in a big arrow pointing to her hiding place. The Americans surely must be using their best kit to look for Shelly; perhaps they'd spot her instead?

After half an hour of working in the sun, sweat dripped off her and her calf muscles twinged with cramp. Darcie knew she had to stop. Each attempt she made had to be weighed against the reality of what it took to survive physically out here. She retreated to her shelter and fell asleep.

14

The SAS team had pulled over by the side of the road and made the jeeps appear suitably out of action.

Midge cast a look up to the sky. The sun was near noon – it must be at least forty degrees in the shade.

'Right, men, we are about to break about a hundred rules here. We're not waiting for it to cool down as Darcie will be dead if we do. With no water, I'd not give her more than a day – maybe two at a pinch and only if she can get into shelter. We also have to make this a precision operation – in and out as fast as we can so that we do not alert the kidnappers to our presence.'

'Or the Americans,' chipped in Merlin.

'Or the world's media,' added Knife.

'Them as well. So we are going straight to the coordinates and then, we hope, back here with our girl.'

Packs weighed down with the water they had to carry, the seven men followed Midge in single file.

They were watched enviously by the two left behind with the vehicles: all of them had been up for the rescue mission and to be chosen to stay behind was the least envied role.

Stingo's thoughts were fixed on Darcie as he pushed his body to the limit. As he slid down the side of a dune following Midge's skid marks, he remembered her ridiculous attempt to rollerblade the moment she had been cut out of her plaster. That had led to their conversation about parents. He wished he could tell her that this was the one mission that he was sure his own mother and father would approve. Before he joined up, he had thought the SAS would be all about being a hero, but the reality was often more complicated and ugly. He wasn't proud of many of the things he had done in the line of duty. But his friendship with Darcie and this mad-cap rescue attempt: these were two things about which he could feel good. Darcie seemed to bring out the best in all of them; they'd take risks for her that they'd only make for one of their own squad. After failing to save her in Kenya, Midge's team wanted to settle their debt.

'Halt!' Midge removed his sunglasses briefly to wipe the sweat from their lenses.

'How are we doing?' asked Knife.

'A third of the way. We've covered about ten miles,' said Merlin, who was navigating.

'Take five. Keep drinking. I don't want anyone collapsing on me,' barked Midge. The captain's neck, Stingo noticed, was covered in an angry red rash: prickly heat – no joke in this environment. Everyone was tetchy and exhausted, begrudging even this brief but necessary stop.

'How long's she been out there?' asked the appropriately named Blister as he massaged his feet.

'Our best guess is six hours last night, nine since sunrise,' said Stingo, who had been counting every moment.

'Let's go then,' said Midge, hoisting his pack on to his shoulders again. 'We've no time to lose.'

*

President Morris sat at the head of the conference table gazing dispiritedly at the people who were supposed to be saving his daughter. All of them were conscious that much more than their careers and the life of a teenage girl were at stake: the reputation of America was also riding on the result. The president, who had been raised on a ranch in Texas before embarking on his political journey to the top, found himself wishing that he could saddle up a couple of horses and lead a posse to apprehend the bad guys like they did in the movies. It would be much simpler than all these discussions.

The military chief wound down to the end of his speech.

'So,' the president said sharply, 'what you're really telling me is that you have no idea where the hostages are being taken?'

Colonel Romerez gave an awkward cough. 'No, sir.'

The CIA head of station, a woman from New York by her accent, interrupted. 'What we do know, Mr President, is that this is not about religion. El-Gebel,

279

their leader, is a dream peddler – a kind of mystic who has thought up a grand theory connecting modern Egyptians to the ancient pharaohs. He even claims to be able to trace his lineage from Tutankhamen.'

'Didn't Tutankhamen die as a boy?' snapped President Morris.

'Well, Mr President, El-Gebel isn't too hot on facts, but very potent with his fantasies.'

'So the hostage-takers are all following him on the road to nowhere?'

'Exactly. Their support among ordinary Egyptians is minimal. We're dealing with an isolated band of fervent supporters around one man. Though we can't rule out the possibility that they may gain more followers if they are seen to be succeeding.'

'Thank you, Miss . . .' the president looked down at his briefing papers, 'Mrs Johnson. You've been very enlightening. We're dealing with a bunch of lunatics who we mustn't upset, that much is clear. I think it's also clear that we should plan to bust my daughter out as they're not amenable to reason. I've no doubt you've already been working on that. What's their intelligence capacity? How much about what we are doing could they know?'

Colonel Romerez took the floor again with more confidence now he was on firmer ground. 'We think they have excellent local informers – no doubt this is why they are staying in that area. According to the tracking device signal, they have circled back north again. They spotted our small team of Special Forces in Farafra as soon as they arrived. The area is so sparsely populated that any foreigners stick out a mile.

'Someone in the group also has technical know-how. They are using a sophisticated system to send messages to a website in Libya, concealing the source of the broadcast. They must be using a sat phone, probably piggy-backing on a Libyan military satellite – we're on to Colonel Gadaffi about it now to see if we can do anything about this. The only notable exception to this pattern was the use of a local boy to deliver the most recent video to Farafra in person. We think they did this to make a point, to tell us they knew exactly where we were, and not because they didn't have the capacity to send it by less direct means.'

'So the safest thing is to assume they can see what our people are doing on the ground?' asked the president.

'Yes, sir, that's why I ordered immediate withdrawal –'

A junior officer entered without waiting for permission, whispered in Colonel Romerez's ear and handed him a piece of paper. Romerez glanced at the printout and tugged at his tie. He passed the paper along to Mrs Johnson.

'What do the Brits think they are playing at?' burst out Mrs Johnson as soon as she saw the paper.

'What is going on?' demanded the president.

'The SAS team, sir, they claim to have broken down on the road to Bahariya.'

'So? Send someone to fix their vehicle. Tell them to get the hell out of there.'

'We did, sir. Rather too conveniently for them, their radios were also out of action, so we didn't learn about the breakdown until hours after it happened. Only two of the British team were still with the jeeps. They refused to say where the other men are, claiming their orders were confidential.'

The president felt his anger rise. 'Who's the senior British official here?'

'Technically the ambassador, sir, but –'

'I don't want technical – get me the real commander. I want to know what orders those men are following. If they have put one foot off the road into the desert, I want the heads of all those involved, do you hear me?'

Christopher Lock was not surprised to find himself summoned abruptly to meet the President of the United States. If anything, he was amazed that the Americans had not spotted the vehicles at the side of the road somewhat earlier. He guessed they had been focusing all their effort on the area around the tracking device and not examined other imagery very closely. He took his time preparing for the interview, diving into the bathroom to check his appearance. He wanted his Savile Row suit and gold tiepin to be perfect – a kind of professional armour for the more difficult moments in his long career.

Looking into the mirror over the sink, he nodded at his reflection. 'For Darcie,' he told himself. He no longer cared if they chucked him out of MI6 for what he had done – he was near the end of his career in any case. They could stuff the pension too if it came to that.

'Mr President,' Christopher Lock said smoothly on entering the office.

The president ignored the outstretched hand. 'Are you responsible for this?' He stabbed a finger at the sat photo of two white jeeps on the roadside. 'Who the hell are you anyway?'

'My name is Christopher Lock. I'm Director of Regional Affairs at MI6.'

'Not for much longer, you aren't.'

'I also happen to be Darcie's grandfather.'

The president swore and slumped into his chair. 'I'd forgotten about that. I knew about the parents, but I remember now I was told about you as well.'

'You appear to be labouring under the misapprehension that I ordered the SAS to mount a rescue attempt,' Christopher continued primly. 'Your officers will confirm that I categorically told Captain Mahoney's team that they were not to go looking for Darcie.'

'I wasn't born yesterday, Lock. They told me you suggested some baloney about radio problems. They think now that you planted the idea in the team's head.'

'If my orders were not transmitted correctly, then that is regrettable.'

'Regrettable? You did it on purpose and placed my daughter's life at even greater risk than it already is. By what right do you do that?'

Christopher drew himself up to his full six feet. 'The right of a grandfather, sir.'

'If my daughter is harmed as a result of your flagrant abuse of our trust, you will pay for it. The SAS were only allowed in under strict conditions and only as a mark of the special relationship between Britain and America. Now it seems that you have betrayed our friendship.'

Christopher was not daunted by incurring the

wrath of even the most powerful man on the planet. He'd spent years serving men of his kind; it was time for some frank talking. 'What kind of friendship allows the child of one country to die to save that of the other? Then again, I shouldn't have to remind you that Darcie is half American: she's your responsibility too.'

The president clenched his teeth. 'Put it like that, I would not risk saving one life to put two others in danger, even if one of them is my daughter. Why did you do it?'

'Because if I do nothing, she dies; if I take action, then she stands a fighting chance and so do the Vermont boy and your daughter. At the very least, Darcie's information as to what the kidnappers plan to do next will be very valuable. She is worth the risk, sir. On this, like you, I speak both in my public and private capacity.'

The president felt close to socking the old man one on the jaw but he restrained himself. 'You better hope, Lock, that your men aren't spotted or you will find out what it's like to be at the top of the President of the United States' blacklist. Get out of here.'

'Thank you, sir,'

Christopher left the room as calmly as he had entered, on the whole pleased with the interview. He had been allowed to make his points and had managed to floor the president with the knock-out blow of family kinship. It hadn't occurred to him until he was in the room that Darcie, if and when they found her, might have useful information. Even as he spoke, he began to make plans how to extract the greatest advantage from this. It might just swing the balance back in his favour, turning a potentially damaging episode into a triumph.

17.30, Empty Quarter: Hot, 48°C

A string of exhausted, sweating soldiers stumbled down the last slope to the bottom of the dune.

'Are you sure this is it?' asked Midge.

The sun was setting, casting long shadows on the ground. The baking heat had reduced a fraction but it was still hot enough to fry an egg on a rock.

'Yes, sir,' confirmed Merlin, checking his bearings for the fifth time.

'OK, men, fan out and search the ground. If she was left here, she can't have gone far.'

It didn't take long to find tracks showing that people and animals had recently passed this way, though the sand had already begun to creep back into the footprints, slowly rubbing them away. Stingo paused over some strange marks in the earth, including a long line pointing due south.

'Over here, sir!' he called. 'What do you make of this?'

Keeping the others back so they would not spoil the markings, Midge knelt beside Stingo.

'There are two pits, possibly peg holes, either side of this smooth space here,' explained Stingo, pointing the traces out. He crawled carefully forwards and examined a patch of darker sand. 'And I think . . . I think this is blood.'

'Two peg holes – not enough for a tent,' commented Midge, sitting back on his haunches.

'But enough to stake out a person. Darcie is about five four, five five, I guess.' Stingo lay down on his belly in the same spot Darcie had so recently occupied. 'That works. But why isn't she still here and why the blood? The place is completely clear except for the blood trace.'

'Let's think – what else would there have been? Shall we assume they didn't come back of her?'

Stingo nodded.

'Then she was left pegged out just in the clothes she was standing up in – nothing else.'

'So how did she get free? Where are the ropes and the pegs?'

Midge chewed his bottom lip. 'You know her best: what do you think?'

'She's not here, so she must've freed herself somehow. But she didn't think anyone was coming for her or she would have known to stay here – I'm sure I told her that much about survival. Instead, she's making an attempt to walk to safety. She or someone else gave her a bearing south.' Stingo pointed to the line. 'But does that meant she's heading south? The road's south-east but does she know that?' The question was unanswerable. Midge shrugged wearily. 'Before she left,' continued Stingo, 'she took anything that might come in useful – rope, even the pegs. Good girl. She's got the raw material for a fire. This means she was thinking straight so she can't have been lying out in the sun for long.'

'And the blood?'

'There's not much but I guess she must be injured. If ever I catch up with Crazy Khaled, he'll regret it.'

'Keep your mind on the task, Stingo. We are not going after Khaled, whatever happens out here.'

'Right sir.' Stingo stared southwards for a moment, his eyes following the hoofprints of the camels as they curved up the dune. He then looked to the south-east. Was that a faint trail in the sand or was it just wishful thinking on his part?

'Which way?' pondered Midge. 'If we make a wrong choice now, then we might as well go home. Without water, she won't survive another day.'

Stingo picked up a handful of sand and let it run through his fingers. The grains would not hold the light footprint of a girl for long thanks to the continual breeze shifting the surface. 'She knows a thing or two about survival. Remember the texts I sent her griping about our course? She'll know, even if instinct doesn't tell her, to keep undercover during the day. She would have gone looking for shelter.'

'Come on, Stingo, tell me what you really think: south along this camel trail, north with the tracking device, or south-east towards the road?'

Stingo threw the remaining sand down with a decisive action. 'My gut says that north is just a decoy – south – that's the way the other hostages were taken and Darcie would steer clear of following a trail left by people who had just tried to kill her. No, I think she probably had a little help and decided to head south-east. How long she was able to keep to that bearing, we don't know, but that's my best guess.'

'I'm glad you said that because that's what I think too.' Midge took a swig from his canteen. 'Our biggest problem now is that we might well walk right past her in the dark. We've obviously walked past her once already today if she went the way you think. We could do with some good satellite imagery in case they spot our needle in the haystack, but we can't ask the Americans for anything right now. How far do you think she can go on foot?'

'Without water and injured? A couple of miles at the most.'

Midge gave a wolfish grin – more teeth than humour. 'That means we are getting close. Let's move out.'

'Hang in there, Darcie,' muttered Stingo patting the sand where she had lain. 'We're coming for you.'

Sleeping through the ferocious heat, Darcie woke at dusk to find that her lips were cracked. She could taste blood. Her head was throbbing and she was feeling sick. She had no idea if this was to do with her injury or the effect of the high temperatures in which she had been slowly baking all day. Or both. Whichever was the cause, the result was she felt barely able to walk.

But I can't just sit here and die, she told herself, taking a defiant sip of the water. I must keep going.

Slowly, she packed up her things, pulled on her boots and set off. Above her, the stars seemed to swim in and out of focus. Something was wrong with her eyes. She stumbled and fell to her knees.

I'm not going to make it. I can't walk.

She had only staggered a few hundred metres from her arrow of rocks, but she now didn't have the strength to crawl back. She lay flat, wondering what to do. Her last throw of the dice was to build a fire: she had thought to save it until she reached the road, but now she knew she wasn't going to get that far. Was it worth spending her material on a short-lived signal to shine to an empty desert? How would she light it in any case? She had no matches and her knowledge of fire-lighting was distinctly hazy – only what she had heard from Stingo and seen in films or on TV. Rub sticks together or something – was that what she was supposed to do?

It was very tempting just to give up and not even

try. The stars were so beautiful: a great splash of glitter on a black canvas. What fun it would be to try painting that, she thought; she could almost see herself flicking a giant brush at the sky from where she lay. She began to giggle, waving her arms over her head.

I'm getting delirious, Darcie suddenly realised.

She sat up with a jolt and was promptly sick, retching drily on to the sand. It was so hot she didn't know if she or the earth had a raging temperature.

This is a horrible way to die, she thought as the wave of nausea passed.

Then don't. Build a fire. Her tough side sounded strangely like Stingo as it berated the part of her that had already given in.

Taking Antar's knife in trembling fingers, she shredded her rope into fibres to use as kindling, then made a nest of it in the dried dung. She was sure she'd seen a man do something similar on one of those survival programmes. In any case, it was all she could think of in her state. What she needed now was the spark. She looked at the two tent pegs: they both had a sharp point and a notch near the top to hold a rope. What if she used one to drill down on the other? Would that produce enough heat to light her kindling?

After a few attempts, she found a position where she could twirl the peg between her hands, holding the other peg steady with her foot. It was hard work. Sweat dripped off her nose. Nothing. Her hands felt as if they were burning but she appeared to have made no impact on the wood.

Giving it one more try, she drilled as hard and fast as she could. Then, miraculously, she was rewarded with the slow curl of smoke as one fibre began to char. Cupping it in her hands, she willed the flame on. It ate its way down the rope, spreading to the other threads, flickering into life. All she could do now was wait and hope. She had no idea if the dung would burn – it was as likely to put the flame out as feed it as far as she knew. But at least in the desert everything was bone-dry.

Dry bones, that'll what I'll be soon, she thought, collapsing beside her feeble fire. What did Femi say: a sun-dried mummy? That's me if this doesn't bring any help.

The SAS team were marching south-east at a rapid pace, fanned out in a line, alert for any sign of Darcie.

'What if we march right past her in the dark?' Stingo asked himself this question for the hundredth time. It was all too easy to do so in this broken landscape of rocks and dunes where every other fallen stone could be someone stretched out on the ground.

'Here, Captain, what do you make of this?' Knife beckoned them over to a larger clump of rocks. There, glimmering in the moonlight, were a series of white pebbles laid out in an arrow formation. They pointed north.

Stingo dived at two black objects lying on a flat stone. 'And these!' He held up a pair of socks. 'These must be Darcie's.'

'Why did she leave them? Not as a sign for us, surely?' wondered Midge.

Merlin shook his head. 'My guess is she forgot them. If she didn't notice when she put her boots on, she must be pretty confused.'

'So the arrow means she went that way? That's what I think,' said Midge, seeking a second opinion.

'Seems to,' agreed Merlin.

Stingo shook his head. 'Nah, I think it was a sign to show where she was hiding. It's too big to be for trackers. The clever kid was thinking of sat images.'

'Maybe.' Midge was sceptical. 'But that's pretty nifty thinking for a fourteen-year-old. I think it's more likely just a sign for anyone who might follow her. It looks as if she's confused and lost her sense of direction so we've no other way of knowing which way she wandered off. The ground's too rocky to leave any prints. The arrow's the only guide we've got. We should follow it at least for a little way.'

'No, we must keep heading south-east. I'm sure of it.' Stingo crossed his arms stubbornly.

'I am in command here. The decision is mine.' Midge gave a curt nod to his team. 'We head north.'

Cursing under his breath, Stingo reluctantly trudged after his six companions. He was tempted to follow his instinct, but he knew that it was fatal to try anything on your own in the desert. He'd be no help to Darcie if he just turned up in time to die beside her. But he was sure Midge had underestimated her.

And so had Stingo. She had one more surprise for him. There, not far to his right, a small light twinkled like a fallen star.

Bless you, Darcie, you've done it again, he thought.

'Over there, sir, at four o'clock!' He need say no more. As one, the team changed direction and began to run towards the light. Even as they watched, it flickered and went out, but none of them would forget where it had been.

They found Darcie lying on the ground beside her half-extinguished fire. The rope had burnt well enough but the camel dung had not caught properly and soon fizzled out.

'Is she alive?' panted Stingo as Knife, the medic among them, checked her vital signs.

'Yes, get me some water!' Seven bottles were immediately thrust under his nose. He took one and raised Darcie to rest on his arm. Placing the spout in her mouth, he eased a little down her throat. 'Come on, Darcie, wake up,' he said urgently.

With a cough, Darcie gulped some of the water – and then retched it out over Midge's boots.

'I don't feel that good,' she said hoarsely.

It seemed such an understatement that several of the men laughed in relief.

'No, you're doing fine. You're just dehydrated,' said Knife.

'I think something's wrong with my head,' she whispered.

'Shine a torch someone.' Knife checked the wound. 'Yep, that looks ugly. I'll clean it, put some antiseptic on it, then bind it, OK?'

Darcie nodded. Her brain was just getting round to wondering who these good Samaritans were. They seemed familiar somehow. A second person knelt at her side and took her hand.

'You forgot your socks.'

'Stingo!' She now knew exactly who had come for her. Of course, it could only be Stingo and his mates – no one else would be so daft.

'Midge will lecture you later on the importance of keeping your kit in good order. No socks can ruin a soldier's feet.'

'I wondered why I couldn't walk,' she said weakly. 'I was thinking it was the heat and the head injury – but it was the socks all along.'

Darcie was in no condition to hike any further so the team carried her on the folding stretcher they had had the foresight to bring with them. They all took turns in bearer duty. When not carrying her, Stingo walked at her side, holding her hand, amazed and relieved beyond words to find her alive. She looked pretty terrible: lips blistered, face a mess of dirt, blood and tear-stains, hair matted. He wanted to ask her how she had survived, but that could wait. They had to return to their vehicles before the sun rose – a tall order for men who had already been on the move for twelve hours.

Darcie was trying to say something.

'What's that?' He bent closer.

'Who sent you?'

Stingo gave her a wicked grin. 'No one. We broke down not far from here and decided to stretch our legs. In all the deserts in all the world and we walked into yours.' His Humphrey Bogart impression was rubbish but it made her smile.

'No, I mean really?'

'Let us say, it was a little understanding between us and your grandad. The Americans would prefer to have left you as they're worried about upsetting your captors.'

Darcie grabbed his wrist tightly. 'You haven't, have you? Khaled is insane – he'll do anything.'

'I can't see them anywhere nearby, can you? And to be honest, Darcie, just getting you out alive is all the result I care about. Let the Americans look after their own; we've looked after ours.'

Darcie sank back, too tired to argue. She didn't see it like Stingo: even though they had not got on, she, Jon Lee and Shelly had been in this together. Jon Lee had saved her life with the water. Shelly had tried to be her friend when she hadn't been easy to get along with – so depressed and secretive most of the time. Darcie had to help them if she could.

And as for her grandfather – what did she think about him now? He had tricked her into this trip but then had tried to save her. She didn't know him well enough to understand what he had been thinking. Given the opportunity, she would like a few moments alone with him to ask.

In the dark hours before dawn, the stretcher party stumbled down the last slopes to the road. There was a reception committee waiting for them. Their jeeps had been towed away and were replaced by three Egyptian army vehicles.

Midge whistled. 'They've sent in the local cavalry, boys. Prepare for a bumpy ride.'

Stiffening their backs for the approach, the team marched in good order to the roadside. They were immediately seized by rough hands, handcuffed and bundled unceremoniously into the back of one of the lorries. Four men took over the stretcher and carried it away to a second vehicle.

'Stingo!' cried Darcie in alarm, trying to get up.

The last thing she saw was Stingo's face as he struggled to reach her. He was overpowered and thrown into a lorry. Engine already running, the vehicle pulled out and headed north at high speed. The stretcher was put down on the floor of the second truck and Darcie found herself gazing up into four unfamiliar faces. An older man approached with a medical bag. He said nothing but reached out to take her arm. He held a syringe in his other hand.

'What are you doing?' asked Darcie frantically, trying to pull away from him.

The doctor nodded to two of the soldiers to hold her down.

'No, don't, please!' she begged.

The needle entered her vein and before she could count to ten, she was gone.

15

'Now listen, no one – and I mean absolutely no one –
must know that the girl survived,' the president
instructed Mrs Johnson, the CIA head of station. 'I
don't care what it takes, but you have to prevent
even a suspicion of her rescue reaching my
daughter's captors.'

He walked to the window and looked out on the
green courtyard in the centre of the Embassy compound.
A man dressed in white was sweeping the paths,
watched by four security agents standing in the shadows.

'Of course, sir. The Egyptians are being very
cooperative. A small group of hand-picked men have
dealt with the . . . the evidence. The SAS team have
been taken to a secret location and will be detained
there until we have time to deal with their
insubordination.'

'Where's that old viper?'

'Christopher Lock? He's been summoned by the British ambassador for a dressing down. The British prime minister is personally involved in the reprimand, I understand. He will be kept busy until further notice.'

'So that leaves the parents.' As the president watched, Michael and Ginnie Lock appeared in the courtyard, circling the paths slowly, heads bent in quiet conversation, grieving the daughter they thought dead. 'How is the girl, by the way?'

'In reasonable shape, all things considered. Distressed, obviously. They're keeping her sedated but I think we must talk to her a.s.a.p. – find out what she knows.'

'Who's with her?'

'An Egyptian doctor is keeping an eye on her. Otherwise she's in solitary as you ordered.'

'Man or woman?'

'Pardon, sir?'

'The doctor, for heaven's sake! The kid is only

fourteen – she's just survived abduction and abandonment and now she's whisked off on her own by strangers. No wonder she's distressed. I want to know that she is being shown as much consideration as possible and I thought perhaps a woman, you know, a motherly type, might be preferable.'

Mrs Johnson frowned, remembering the picture of the army doctor from the file – there was nothing maternal about him. 'He's a man, sir.'

'Hmm.' Morris watched the Locks circle the fountain in the centre. Ginnie Lock suddenly sat down and began to sob. Was it right to leave them like this? They were used to dealing with secrets, that was their job, but to trust them with the biggest secret of all – a secret that could put his own daughter at risk, could he do that? 'Tell Mr and Mrs Lock that there is still no word on their girl. Say we'll let them know as soon as we know, but they are not to give up hope. Tell them no news is good news. Yes, tell them that.'

Mrs Johnson grimaced. She and Ginnie knew each other professionally having spent six months on the same training course. 'Are you sure, sir? I believe you can trust Ginnie Lock with this. It is cruel to keep her in the dark.'

Morris flinched at the word. 'It's only for a few days. We may be able to trust Ginnie Lock, but can you answer for her husband? Look what his father just did!'

Mrs Johnson bowed her head. 'Of course, sir, I was forgetting. I'll pass the message on exactly as you say. But what about interviewing the girl?'

The president sized up his CIA head of station. 'Do you have any children, Mrs Johnson?'

'Yes, sir.'

'Good. You go and talk to her. Explain to her why all this is necessary and send her my best wishes for her full recovery. Tell her she'll be reunited with her parents very soon.'

09.00, Egyptian army base, somewhere south of Cairo:
Light haze, 30°C

Darcie woke from her drug-induced sleep to a raging

thirst. Opening her eyes, she found herself in a narrow bed in a cell-like room. It was cool and there were no windows. Was this room underground, she wondered? Fear fluttered in her stomach as she struggled with a sense of claustrophobia. Where were Stingo and the others? Why had they been carried off handcuffed? Where was she?

A jug of water and tumbler stood on the low table beside her. Shakily, she gulped two glassfuls down and then collapsed back on her pillow. The back of her hand was hurting. She raised it and found that it was connected to a drip hanging over her head. Looking towards her toes, she saw that she was dressed in bright orange prison pyjamas far too big for her. Someone had rolled up the bottoms to leave her feet sticking out the end. She had been washed and her cut bandaged. There was no sign of any of her possessions.

Now fully wake, she needed the bathroom. Dragging herself into a sitting position, she spotted a toilet over in the far corner surrounded by pristine white tiles. With a little bit of experimentation, she worked out that the drip moved on a trolley, so she hobbled stiffly over to use the facilities. Feeling more human, she splashed her face in a stainless steel basin. Gingerly she reached up to her hair. No one had tackled that yet: it had been washed, but it still hung in tangles. She wouldn't feel herself properly until she had seen to that, but for the moment, with no comb or brush, she would have to leave it.

It was hard to tell how many hours had passed until the door opened. Darcie curled up into a protective ball on the bed, back against the wall, determined not to be knocked out again if she could prevent it. The doctor she remembered from the lorry came over and held something out to her. It was a thermometer. Silently, she submitted to him placing it under her tongue so he could take the readings. He scribbled something down on a chart, checked the bag of fluids leading to her drip, and then turned to go.

'Where am I?' she asked.

'Safe.' With that one word, he left, closing the door behind him.

When Mrs Johnson arrived at the Egyptian army base south of Cairo, she was shown into the commanding officer's comfortable office with a balcony overlooking the Nile riverbank. In the distance, luxury pleasure ships coasted by, carrying their cargo of tourists upstream to the wonders of Luxor and the Valley of the Kings. The prospect where she stood was less inspiring: a heavily guarded military compound, airstrip and block barracks. The officer came in and shook her hand.

'Mrs Johnson, we are delighted to be of help to our American friends at this terrible time,' he began.

'General Sidrak, thank you but you are already being of great assistance. I take it you have our detainees well hidden?'

He nodded. 'We've put them in the interrogation block which has some useful discreet cells in the basement.'

'And the child?'

'She is there too.'

Mrs Johnson swallowed her exclamation of surprise. 'I thought she would be in your hospital block, not in a cell.'

'Unfortunately we could not ensure complete secrecy in the hospital – there are too many members of staff that we would have to involve. Besides, I understand her physical condition is not serious.'

'And her mental condition?'

'Disorientated and disturbed at first. Quiet now. Come and see.'

He led Mrs Johnson into the adjacent security centre which monitored all parts of the site. Three screens showed the inside of the cells. In two, the SAS team was stretched out in various attitudes of boredom. Only Stingo was pacing restlessly in front of the door. He glanced up briefly at the monitor as if he could feel Mrs Johnson's eyes on him. The third screen showed a room that looked empty until she saw a girl hunched in one corner, head resting on her knees. Mrs Johnson felt a pang of pity for the child and had to remind herself that the girl was an agent with information for her: this was no time for soft-heartedness.

'I'd like to speak to her, if that is possible,' said Mrs Johnson politely.

'Of course. I'll have Dr Ghallab escort you down.'

Darcie raised her head on hearing the door open again. The doctor came in; this time he was accompanied by an unfamiliar woman dressed in a moss-green trouser suit. She looked to be about forty, with well-groomed bobbed hair and nails painted a vibrant pink. There was something about her that reminded Darcie of her own mother. She swallowed the sob that had risen on the thought of her parents. Now was not the time to break down.

'Hello, Darcie,' the woman said. She dismissed the doctor with a nod. 'How are you feeling?'

How was she feeling? Darcie could have laughed.

'You mean apart from being left to die in the desert and then shut up in a windowless cell for I don't know how long? Oh, just wonderful.'

'You can't be too bad if you have the energy to be angry. That's good.'

'Have you come to get me out?'

'I'm afraid not. You see, you have to stay here to protect Shelly and Jon Lee. You do understand, don't you?'

'No, not really. Why can't I see my parents? Why am I being treated like a criminal?' She gestured to her orange pyjamas. 'What have you done with Stingo and the others?'

'Stingo?'

'The men who saved me.'

'They are being detained pending further investigations and, no, you can't see them. They flouted their orders in coming for you – or someone else did in sending them.'

Darcie dropped her gaze to her fingers. 'So you would've preferred me to die?'

Mrs Johnson sat at the far end of the bed and sighed. 'Of course not. Now that risk has been taken and you are alive at the end of it, we are all very pleased.'

'Do my parents know I'm safe?'

Mrs Johnson's expression did not flinch. 'No, but they've been told not to give up hope. As far as the rest of the world is concerned, you are dead.'

'And how long do I have to play dead?'

Mrs Johnson was impressed the girl understood the need to keep out of the public eye.

'As long as it takes, I'm afraid. Shelly and Jon Lee are still out there. The situation has not yet been resolved. That's why I'm here.'

'Oh, I thought you came to offer me a bunch of grapes and sympathy,' said Darcie.

'That too – without the grapes. You've done a good job, Darcie – proved yourself a tough little operator. Few of our agents would have done so well.'

'I am not an agent, can't you people get that?' Darcie's fury roused her into raising her voice. 'Khaled tried to kill me when he found out you'd been using me. Why can't you just leave me alone?'

Mrs Johnson grimaced – the truth was unpalatable

but unavoidable. 'Because you have information that we need.'

'Get me out of here and I'll tell you what I know.'

'I can't do that.'

'Then I'm not saying anything.'

'What about Shelly and Jon Lee? Don't you want to help them?'

Darcie knew her bargaining position was weak. Mrs Johnson was asking for something that Darcie wanted to tell her in any case. But it had been worth a try.

'OK.' She sighed and dropped her voice. 'They're heading south. Khaled said something about keeping an appointment.'

'Not north?'

'No, they found the tracking device and sent it off with one of their men. It's a red herring.'

Mrs Johnson then took Darcie over every moment of her time with Khaled's band, enquiring into the motivations of each member and the state of mind of the other hostages. She was particularly interested to hear how Jon Lee had betrayed her.

'So he's not to be relied on, would you say?'

Darcie shrugged. She still hadn't resolved her feelings about her team-mate. 'He's reliable enough towards Shelly. It was just me, I think.'

'Thank you, Darcie, you've been most helpful. One of us will be back to talk to you again today or tomorrow.' Mrs Johnson stood up. 'Oh, and the president sends his best wishes for your recovery. Do you have any messages for me to take back?'

'Tell my parents I love them.'

'I'm afraid I can't do that.'

'Tell my grandfather that he's a lying –'

'Can't do that either.'

'OK, tell the president that he can stick his best wishes.'

Mrs Johnson smiled. 'I'll do that. Good for you, Darcie.'

Her parting remark left Darcie confused. Then again, she was beginning to learn that people were rarely exactly as they seemed. Mrs Johnson had just revealed that she hated doing her duty of keeping Darcie locked up, but did it nonetheless. Perhaps, thought Darcie, I should resign myself to the inevitable fact that I will be spending a lot of time staring at these walls? But how much time?

16

Darcie's hopes of being left quietly to wait until she could be resurrected were destroyed the next day by a new message from the kidnappers.

'Mr President!' called the reporter from CNN. 'Is it true, as the abductors claim, that the girl they killed was an agent sent by you and the British government to spy on your daughter's inner circle?'

'Did you really sanction the use of a girl of fourteen on such a dangerous mission?' asked the *Guardian* stringer.

Ignoring the questioners, President Morris strode through the ranks of reporters. He was returning from the Egyptian president's palace where he had been 'invited' to give a full and frank explanation as to the true identity of Darcie Logan. He was not feeling pleased. His personal assistant ran beside him and handed him a folder.

'Clippings from the US papers, sir,' he said breathlessly. 'I'm afraid your popularity has nose-dived overnight since the agent allegations.'

The president threw the file back to his assistant and wheeled round to face the cameras.

'You will understand if, at this critical time, I say very little,' he began, giving the nearest camera the benefit of his best grieved-but-firm expression. 'However, I want to scotch once and for all the absurd allegations that the poor child murdered by the kidnappers a few days ago was a government agent. She was only fourteen, for heaven's sake! How could she have been? It just goes to show the minds of the people we are dealing with that they could think up anything so warped to justify what they did to a child. As I've said already, our prayers are with the unfortunate girl's parents and with the two children still being held – including my own daughter. Now if you'll excuse me.'

Once out of sight, the president turned to his assistant again. 'That takes care of the ratings. Get me the CIA head of station.'

Mrs Johnson found the president alone in the ambassador's office looking out of the window at the journalists camped outside the gates. She didn't like it. She preferred discussions to take place in the presence of those who could corroborate the facts afterwards. As it was, her instinct was telling her that her political master was about to ask her to do something that she would not want to do.

'Mrs Johnson,' said the president, 'how long have you been in the CIA?'

'Fifteen years, sir.'

'Career making steady but not spectacular progress?'

'Sir?'

'I know what it's like to be stuck on the middle rungs. I was for a time, you know, Governor of Texas. To get to the top, I realised, you had to take unpleasant decisions and risks.'

Mrs Johnson gritted her teeth.

'You know, of course, that I denied categorically that the girl had anything to do with the security agencies – that I had no knowledge of this?'

'Yes, sir.'

'I had to, of course. Standard procedure.'

'Of course, sir.'

'Then you'll understand that it would be very damaging to all concerned if the person in question was seen again in public.'

'Sir?'

'She must stay dead – very dead. Do you understand?'

The president rocked on his feet, gazing at her intently.

Mrs Johnson stared back in silence. She understood that he thought he wouldn't get re-elected if Darcie Lock had the chance to tell anyone the truth.

'Do you wish her to be relocated – given a new identity?'

The president turned away, his face in shadows with the light behind him. 'I don't want her to get hurt – I don't even wish to know what you do with her, but I never want to hear her name again. In fact, she must be made to forget her own name too.'

'But her parents . . .?'

'They're not to be trusted. I cannot take that chance

now. As far as they are concerned, their daughter was lost in the desert – make sure it stays that way.'

'But, sir –'

'You know what you need to do. How you respond now will show me just what you're made of. Those who prove themselves friends of the president may expect to be rewarded.'

The interview was clearly over. The president turned to leaf through a pile of papers on the desk. Mrs Johnson left the office, anger buzzing inside her. She was an American: she couldn't go round ridding the world of awkward teenagers just to please the president! He can't have been serious. He'd regret it in a few hours – wouldn't he?

But if she didn't do something, he'd find someone else to take care of Darcie, she had no doubt about that. And that person may think relocation and re-education a far too complicated affair – much easier to use a bullet.

'Get me a car,' she barked at her secretary.

*

323

Darcie was pleased to see Mrs Johnson again. The last day had been monumentally boring. She'd begged a comb off the doctor but her request for reading material had been denied. The sight of the American woman bearing grapes and a bundle of magazines was therefore very welcome.

'I also brought you a few things to make you feel a bit more cheerful,' said Mrs Johnson. 'Mascara, eyeshadow, lipstick, perfume – I never feel properly dressed without some make-up.'

'Do you have a shade that goes with orange?' asked Darcie, gesturing to her clothes.

Mrs Johnson gave a nervous laugh. 'Well, that red might clash nicely.'

'OK, thanks, I'll try it.'

Darcie relapsed into silence, expecting the woman to ask more questions, but strangely she said nothing, occupying herself by fiddling with the gifts.

'Any news of Shelly and Jon Lee?' Darcie asked at length.

'There was another message – about you in fact.' Mrs Johnson came to sit beside Darcie. She had a bottle of Chanel and a pad of cotton wool.

'Oh yes? What did they say?'

'They told the world you were a spy.'

'Oh, I see.'

'Yes, not good news for any of us. I thought it was best that it was me who did this.'

'Did what?' Darcie was beginning to feel nervous. The woman was acting friendly but her body language was strangely menacing. She was also sitting too close.

'Do you want to know what the perfume smells like?' Mrs Johnson swigged some of it on to the cotton wool.

'No, I don't think I do,' said Darcie, edging away.

'I'm afraid you must.'

'No!'

Darcie felt the pad clamped on her face. She couldn't breathe. She kicked, struggled, but it was no good: she was dipping out of consciousness again. It went black – then grey. She couldn't be sure, but she thought she heard voices near her. Her eyelids refused to open.

'Your orders are to keep her sedated for her own safety.' That was Mrs Johnson.

'For how long?' asked the doctor.

'Until I tell you otherwise.'

'I'm sorry, but I don't understand.'

'She has become a liability. We can't risk her talking to anyone.'

'But she can't – not here.'

'Still, the risk remains that someone here might betray her presence – a maintenance man or a cleaner – and I'm afraid we think that risk unacceptable.'

'But it's not good for a patient to be kept like this.'

'I am asking you to do this only till after the elections in November. If he is still president after that then, well, we'll have to review the situation.'

'I see.'

'Her old life is over. As far as her parents and friends are concerned, she didn't survive.'

'I should warn you, Mrs Johnson, there are dangers to doing what you ask.'

'Like what?'

'She might slip into a coma; you might not be able to wake her up.'

'That's a chance I'll have to take. The alternative is much worse. In fact, if anyone at the base asks, I suggest you tell them exactly that – she slipped into a coma due to injuries sustained in the desert. It will avoid later – complications.'

Footsteps retreated and a door closed.

Darcie had never experienced real terror until now. The prospect before her was a slow descent into unconsciousness but she couldn't move a muscle to fight it. Her limbs were heavy and unresponsive – she was paralysed. But she had to do something before they hooked her up to a drip again. Once a slow trickle of drugs was entering her veins she couldn't stand a chance. The anaesthetic Mrs Johnson had used had been clumsy and imprecise – that was her only hope. She wanted to scream in fury but even her voice wouldn't obey her.

Keep calm, she told herself.

I can't keep calm. It's like being buried alive!

If you don't use your brains, you're dead.

This blunt realisation acted like a slap in the face. She should use this time for thinking. If the anaesthetic hadn't put her under properly, it was likely that feeling would soon come back to the rest of her body. Her eyelids had already come back under her command. She just needed to lie very still to convince those watching the CCTV that she remained out for the count.

The CCTV. Darcie squinted through her eyelashes at the bag of make-up on the table beside her, past the fake Chanel, to the monitor in the corner of the cell. It was positioned over the toilet to give the inmate some privacy, but kept a constant watch on the rest of the cell. If only she could reach it.

It felt like hours – but was probably only minutes later – when sensation crept back into her arms and legs. She studied her plan through her half-closed eyelids. She had to be swift, banking on the fact that no one would consider it a good use of their time to be constantly watching an image of a sleeping girl.

Now!

Stumbling off the bed, weaving drunkenly for a moment, she grabbed the mascara and dashed to the toilet. Wedging her foot on the pipes behind, she heaved herself up and grabbed the camera bracket. Holding the mascara in her teeth, she one-handedly painted the lens black. Job done, she dropped back to the floor, limped over to the bed, and resumed her original position. A last minute thought prompted her to slosh some more 'perfume' on the cotton wool pad and then she lay down again.

Up in the security centre, the guard on duty turned from his newspaper to check the screens. Two showed the bored SAS team playing cards, the third was black. Cursing, he picked up the phone.

'Maintenance? Fault in camera three in the basement of C block. You want an escort? It's only a girl – she's asleep. Fine, let me know when you've finished.'

Satisfied, the guard put his feet up again and

resumed his reading of the sport pages.

The maintenance man opened the door of the cell and saw the small figure lying on the bed. No problem, he thought, wheeling his equipment trolley into the room as quietly as possible. He'd been told very little about this prisoner – just that everything connected with her was very hush-hush and that it was best not to show any interest if he wanted to keep his job. Trying not to wake her, he got out a step ladder and placed it against the wall by the malfunctioning camera. That was odd: it seemed to be still working but the lens looked dirty.

While the man searched his bag for cleaning fluid, a light-footed girl in orange tiptoed across the room with a cotton wool pad in hand. Suddenly, he felt something clamped to his nose and mouth. He lost his balance and fell heavily backwards, but still the pad was over his face. Before he had time to struggle, he blacked out.

Groaning, Darcie heaved the man off her. She would have big bruises after that fall, but she had no time to worry about that now: she had to get out of here. Fumbling at his belt, she took his keys and security pass, then slipped out of the door. The corridor outside was deserted. She had no idea of the layout of the building, nor how she was going to get past all the guards. The one thing she did know was that she couldn't do this alone. Guessing that Stingo and the others were somewhere close, she searched the corridor. All the cell doors stood open and empty, except two. She sought frantically for the right key. She could hear voices coming down the stairs at the other end of the passageway – she had to get out of sight. Finally, the key turned and she slid inside, shutting the door behind her.

Five men looked up in astonishment as Darcie rushed to stand in the only blind spot under their camera.

'How . . .? What are you doing here?' asked Stingo, rushing towards her.

Darcie frantically waved him away and Merlin grabbed at his shirt. Getting the message, Stingo sat down and yawned, acting as if nothing had happened. They could all hear the echo of voices outside in the corridor coming closer.

'What's going on?' asked Midge, not looking at Darcie but seeming to address Stingo.

'I've escaped,' she whispered.

'Yeah, we can see that. But why? You're safest where you are, aren't you?'

Darcie gave a hollow laugh. 'That was until I became an election liability. The president's decided he wants me to stay dead.'

'You're getting paranoid,' said Stingo, stretching out full length to stare at the ceiling.

'Oh yeah? So why were they going to keep me sedated until after the election and then "review the situation"?'

'How do you know all this?' asked Midge, dealing a deck of cards slowly.

'A woman from the CIA tried to knock me out, but it didn't take properly. I heard her discussing me with the doctor.' Though outwardly calm, Darcie could feel herself shaking. If they found her now, what would they do?

'You must've been hallucinating. They wouldn't do that to a kid,' muttered Stingo, though he didn't sound quite so convinced.

'After the last few days, I've come to realise people will do anything to me if it suits them. I'm not staying around to find out if they want me to live or not – and I want you to help me get out.'

Darcie could tell she'd only got them half-convinced but there was a sudden commotion outside.

'Where has she gone?' That was Mrs Johnson. She must've come back to check on her. She was now shouting at the guards in the corridor.

'The girl cannot have got far,' said Mrs Johnson's Egyptian escort. 'Do not worry – we will find her.'

'She must be stopped at all costs. No one must see her. You understand? Use all necessary means to prevent her leaving the base. All necessary means.'

The SAS men exchanged looks.

'OK, you've got a point,' conceded Midge, still

pretending to play cards. 'Suggestions, men? What did you see as we came in?'

'Two fences, heavily guarded,' said Merlin, throwing down an ace.

'We're near the Nile,' said Stingo, drumming his fingers on the floor.

'How are we going to get out of this basement?' asked Knife, lacing on his boots.

'I've got a pass to all areas,' ventured Darcie.

'What?' Midge half-turned but transformed the gesture into a flourish as he laid out his cards.

'Borrowed it off a maintenance man.'

Stingo chuckled. 'You have to admit she's good.'

'Right then. We'll wait until it's quiet outside, then Merlin – you get the others out. Knife – see to the cameras. We'll split into parties of two and three. Stingo, you're on close protection with Zebra. Your job is to get her out any way you can. The rest of us, our job is to create as much mayhem as possible to give them a chance. If we get beyond the fence, we rendezvous at the British Embassy – at least that'll save us from a summary execution.'

'Guys, I'm so sorry,' Darcie whispered, realising that she was asking them to risk their lives for her, as well as costing them their careers.

'Don't be sorry, Darcie, we're only following orders.' Midge gathered up the cards and stuck them in his breast pocket.

'Orders?'

'To fight your corner. Ready, men?' His colleagues nodded or grunted their agreement. 'Zebra, do what ever Stingo tells you, OK?'

'OK.' She looked very pale, standing huddled under the camera in her ridiculous orange pyjamas.

'And, Zebra?'

'Yes, Midge?'

'Good luck.'

A search team was scouring the army base looking for a small person in prison overalls.

'Any sign?' barked the commander, bending over the battery of screens, Mrs Johnson at his side.

'No, sir,' said the guard. He was having a bad day – he knew that his failure to provide the maintenance man with an escort might cost him his job. Suddenly, the cameras in the cells containing the SAS men went black.

'Sir!'

'Get a team down there now!' barked the commander.

Darcie was crouched behind the door of the cell, Stingo in front of her. He peered out in time to see Midge jump the first man down the stairs. A scrap ensued which resulted in the eight members of the SAS team overpowering the squad and relieving them of their weapons. The soldiers were thrown into an empty cell and locked in.

'Go!' yelled Midge as his men ran up the stairwell in pairs.

Waiting for the sounds of their retreat to die down, Stingo took Darcie's hand and led her out into the corridor. She could feel her heart pumping, her knees were trembling but it was oddly comforting to have her hand held after the terrifying hours she'd spent alone. Stingo squeezed her fingers.

'OK, Darcie. We're going up. The men will have split up and be causing as much trouble as possible. I'll decide our route when we get outside.'

'OK.'

'Are you all right? Can you run?'

'If I have to.'

He put his arm around her. 'You're doing great. Just follow my lead. OK, let's go.'

Stealthily, he led her up the stairs. They could hear noise – plenty of noise – but it seemed to be coming from their left. They emerged at ground level. Through the open doors in front of them, they could see a petrol tanker on fire.

'Ouch! Best keep well away. That might blow,' whispered Stingo.

He pulled Darcie out of the door and immediately to the right. It was dusk. They would have been swallowed up in the shadows had Darcie not been wearing day-glo pyjamas.

'We're going to have to do something about those.'

Stingo stripped off his shirt and passed it to her. 'Try that for size.'

The shirt dangled to just below her knees. Slipping out of the prison gear, she now blended into the background. Stingo used the time to reconnoitre the terrain. He nudged Darcie.

'That's where we're heading.' He pointed out a white car with diplomatic plates.

'Mrs Johnson's, you think?' she asked.

'Yep. And our way out. Stay here until I come back.'

Looking as confident as someone in a camouflage jacket but no shirt could look, Stingo strode out into the open and over to the car. He tapped on the window and began a conversation with the driver resulting in the man getting out and disappearing into the nearest building. As soon as he was gone, Stingo jumped into the car, started the engine and pulled out. Darcie watched as the car slowed near her and the passenger door opened.

'In!' he called.

Darcie bolted across the open ground and dived inside.

'What did you say to him?' she asked as he drove smartly away.

'I said there was a gang of dangerous fugitives on the loose and Mrs Johnson had requested that he go in for his own safety. I was going to park the car somewhere secure for him.'

'That was bare-faced cheek!'

'The best kind. People don't doubt you if you do something so obvious. They assume you must know what you're doing. Now you – you put on the woman's jacket and these sunglasses. Sit in the back and look busy.'

'You're not . . .?'

'Oh yes I am. Mrs Johnson has decided to return to Cairo to report to the president in person.'

'It won't work – this definitely won't work.'

'Just keep your head down and try and look twenty years older.'

'Stingo!'

'Trust me. There's always Plan B if this fails.'

'What's Plan B?'

'Put my foot down and ram the gate.'

'OK. Let's try Plan A first.'

Up in the commander's office, Mrs Johnson had a bird's-eye view of the pandemonium reigning outside. Fires had broken out in three locations. Soldiers were running like ants from a burning nest towards the disturbances. And Darcie was somewhere down there among it all. Mrs Johnson didn't know whether to feel angry or admire the girl's resourcefulness. The main problem was Darcie had put herself beyond the reach of her protection; she could no longer control what happened. She picked up the phone.

'Sir?' The president answered wearily. 'I'm afraid we have a problem – the girl's broken out of her cell.'

She waited for the torrent of abuse to pass. 'Yes, yes, sir, we are doing everything we can to apprehend her. Unfortunately, she managed to free her SAS friends, so I fear that she is not going to come quietly. I would like your explicit permission to use force if necessary.'

There was a pause. Mrs Johnson counted the seconds as the president decided whether or not to make himself personally responsible for the outcome.

'Yes, of course we'll try to apprehend her as discreetly as possible.'

As she spoke, the tanker erupted, sending plumes of black smoke into the air. At the same moment, Mrs Johnson spotted her car heading for the main gate.

'You moron!' she exclaimed. 'No, not you, sir. Sorry, but I've got to go. They're escaping in my car.'

Slamming the phone down on the president, she dashed into the security control room.

'Stop the white car!' she shouted. 'Main gate!'

Stingo had wound down the window and was talking with the guard on duty at the inner perimeter gate; Darcie sat in the back hunched over some papers, trying to look important. The windows were tinted so she hoped the guard would not see her clearly as she had bare feet and nothing on her legs under the coat if he cared to inspect her more closely. The guard stepped back and waved them through, turning his back to answer a call on his radio. Stingo accelerated gently away, keeping the man fixed in his mirror. There came a sudden jerk as Stingo put his foot on the pedal.

'Down!' he bellowed.

Darcie threw herself sideways as a shot cracked the rear window. Fortunately for her, bullet-proof glass was standard in American embassy vehicles. They had passed through one gate but the second was being quickly closed in front, cutting off their escape route.

'Plan B!' shouted Stingo. The car sped towards the narrowing gap; soldiers scattered out of his way. Crunch – both wing mirrors were ripped off as the car squeaked through to the other side.

'Just like my driving test all over again!' crowed Stingo, weaving between the barriers placed to slow vehicles on their approach to the camp.

'Did you pass?' asked Darcie, gripping hold of her seat belt.

'What do you think?'

'Definitely not!'

Glancing behind, Darcie saw the gate was being hauled open again to let out three military jeeps and two motorcyclists.

'We've got company,' she said grimly.

'Yeah, we'll have to dump this car as soon as possible – too recognisable.'

Taking a sudden left, Stingo hurtled down a bumpy track towards the riverbank.

He must be mad, thought Darcie. They were going to get cornered.

'Don't worry,' he said, as if he could hear her thoughts. 'There's method to my madness.'

He stopped the car with a screech of tyres right on the water's edge.

'Out!' he shouted.

Darcie could now hear the throb of a helicopter overhead. The grass around them began to bend in the down-draft, making the water form choppy peaks. Only meters away, gliding calmly down the Nile, undisturbed by the commotion on the bank, pleasure cruisers sailed along the deep channel in the middle.

'Ready for a swim?'

Stingo ran to the bank and splashed into the water, Darcie at his side. The water around them was suddenly pocked with bullets. Darcie dived under the surface, unable to see anything in the muddy waters, relying on her sense of direction to carry her forward. Coming up for air, she saw Stingo's head downstream, searching frantically for her.

'Here!' she gasped.

He pointed to the nearest boat. It was heading upstream, tourists crowded at the side to watch the vehicles disgorging soldiers on to the shore. Darcie prayed that they wouldn't dare shoot them in front of so many witnesses. Swimming to the stern, she battled her way through the choppy wake round to the blind side where Stingo had just disappeared. She could barely keep up and thought for a moment that she was going to be left behind, a sitting duck in the water, but fortunately the captain had slowed to allow his passengers to watch the free show onshore. Using the last of her strength, she struck out to where Stingo was waiting for her, clinging on to a low-slung fender.

'Up you go!' He heaved her out of the water so she could reach the rope and shin up to the deck. Darcie fell on to the floor, exhausted, but this wasn't to be her final resting place. Stingo jumped down beside her, dragged her to her feet and pulled her into the nearest doorway.

'That helicopter might've seen us. Safety lies with people.' Stingo was opening door after door, looking for inspiration. They had ended up in the crew's quarters, far from the plush upper decks. 'They can't do anything for fear of exposing the fact that you're alive. We've got to blend in.'

'Blend in?' Darcie was feeling slightly hysterical as she dripped on the floor dressed only in Stingo's shirt and a designer coat.

'In here.' Stingo picked her up again and towed her into the laundry. 'Perfect. Find yourself something suitable while I see to myself.' He was already yanking clothes off the ironing board – a bright short-sleeved shirt and Bermuda shorts.

Darcie rummaged along a rail and found a halter neck green dress.

'You can't wear that,' Stingo said, when she emerged.

'Not my colour or something?' she asked crossly. She hadn't complained about his appalling taste.

'No, Darcie, you're covered in bruises. Everyone will be staring at you. It's a dead give-away.'

She looked down at herself. It was true – she looked terrible.

'Here.' He threw her a white shirt. 'Put that over the top. Let's mingle.'

Taking her hand again, he led the way back into the corridor. No one was in sight.

'Right, up to the main deck.' Walking purposefully forward, he pushed the door open and climbed the nearest set of steps. At the top, he jumped over the 'Crew Only' sign and slowed. There were people coming down the stairs towards them – Darcie could see their feet on the rungs above. He swung Darcie around, taking her arm in his.

'Good lord!' he exclaimed in a fruity accent. 'Did you see that, my dear?' He pointed over the side at the nearest ship. A crowd formed around them, cameras at the ready. 'Two blighters climbed aboard, cool as a cucumber, and disappeared.'

'Really?' asked an American lady. 'Who do you think they were?'

'No idea, ma'am. Escaped convicts perhaps?'

This rumour began to be spread among the crowd. Soon, everyone was convinced they'd seen two criminals boarding the ship heading downstream.

'Thank goodness they didn't come here!' said the lady. 'I'd've been terrified. Wouldn't you, honey?' She turned to Darcie.

'Oh yes,' Darcie assured her.

'No need for you to worry,' said Stingo bracingly. 'Not when you've got your good old Uncle Ian looking after you. Well, the excitement seems to be over. Fancy a stroll round the deck before dinner?'

'Why not.'

Shouldering through the crowd, Darcie and Stingo made their way up the steps to the upper decks.

'What now?' Darcie muttered out of the side of her mouth. The water around the boat was churning with inflatable crafts searching for the two fugitives in the darkness.

'My guess is they'll come looking onboard soon.'

'And then?'

'Let me buy some drinks at the bar.'

'Stingo!'

'Relax – you have to, otherwise you'll give yourself away.'

Stingo left her at a table and sauntered over to the bar. Slapping a man dressed in a flowery shirt on the back, he got out some money and bought a round. Darcie watched him laugh and joke with his new acquaintance. No one would guess that he was on the run from the Egyptian military – he looked as if he was on holiday.

That was the point, Darcie realised. She tried to

hitch a smile on to her face and played with the flower arrangement on the table. After a long five minutes, Stingo came back bearing a tropical fruit juice for her. She hadn't realised how thirsty she was until she saw the glass misted with ice.

'Our luck's holding,' Stingo told her in a low voice. 'Seems there's a stomach bug going round the ship – that man's wife is struck down with it. He told me that the elderly couple in the cabin next to his had to leave as one of them had become so ill.'

'A stomach bug – that's lucky, is it?'

'Yeah, it means there's an empty cabin. Beds – showers – somewhere to hide.'

'OK, that's lucky.'

'There's a barbecue on deck tonight and a band, so there'll be lots happening, making it more likely that we'll be missed if someone comes looking. First thing we need to do is split up – they'll be searching for a man and girl fitting our descriptions; we need to change that.'

'How?'

'Come on, Darcie, think! It's not hard on a gin-palace like this. You flirt with a few of the lads – dance, giggle, look as if you didn't have a care in the world.'

'I'm hardly in any condition to flirt.'

'Don't put yourself down. You look fit. Anyway, most people here are the wrong side of fifty so I'm sure any young men will be desperate to meet a new face.'

'Thanks.'

'As for me, I'm joining the old boy for a spot of poker in an hour.' Stingo began to chuckle.

'What?'

Stingo bent closer. 'He told me that he had a shirt just like mine – asked me where I bought it. I didn't tell him, but it seems that even before we've started gambling together, I've got the shirt off his back.'

'Stingo!'

'Don't worry, he'll never guess the truth. Now, I'm just going to make a foray back down to the laundry to get the stuff we left behind and pick a shirt for the evening. Anything I can fetch you?'

'No, I'm fine – though I suppose a pair of shoes would be good.'

'Your wish is my command. I'll just break you into your cabin – you take a rest – then we party.'

Darcie lay on her bunk trying to get her head around everything that had happened to her today. Unlike Stingo, who seemed to be thriving on the adventure, she was scared – she felt so powerless. Now the immediate danger had passed, she couldn't stop shivering. What had she done to get into this position? She'd lost count of the number of people who wanted her dead and she still wasn't safe. If only she could somehow make it all right for everyone, but each step she had taken had made things worse.

Three taps on the door and Stingo slid into the cabin. He threw a pair of mules into her lap.

'Courtesy of the lady in cabin 54. She really shouldn't leave her things lying about. I hope I got the size right?'

Darcie didn't answer.

'Are you OK? No, that's a stupid question; of course, you're not OK.' He came and sat beside her on the bunk. 'I think you need a hug and to tell me what happened to you. You've been through hell. I'm surprised you've not gone to pieces.'

Darcie leaned her head against his chest and her shoulders began to heave with sobs. 'I'm sorry.'

'No need to apologise. I'm just pleased that you're still alive.' He checked his watch. 'Tell me all about it. I've got about thirty minutes before I have to meet my new friend. Let's make the most of it.'

Darcie began to tell him about the abduction and what had followed after she'd been rescued. Stingo said nothing, but she could tell he was angry for her from the way his muscles tensed as she reached the most painful parts of the narrative.

'So Khaled was taking them south, was he?' he said when she'd finished talking. 'I wonder why?'

'He said something about an appointment.'

'Well, if he's going to hand the hostages over, I

imagine he'll want to make the exchange somewhere symbolic, bearing in mind his way of thinking.'

'Like where?'

'The pyramids, or a palace, somewhere from Egypt's proud past.'

Darcie stared at the brochure lying on the bedside table advertising the cruise. 'Or the Valley of the Kings. Almost the last thing Khaled said to me was that when the tomb opens, the world would tremble. I thought he meant my death, but now I think he was boasting about what he was going to do.'

'Valley of the Kings? That's Tutankhamen and all that, isn't it?'

'Yeah, and that's where we are heading.' A new and wonderful idea had dropped into her mind – a way of putting everything right.

Stingo looked down at her. 'No, Darcie, don't even think it.'

'But don't you see: it's the only way we can get the team out of the mess I got you into! If we save Shelly and Jon Lee, everyone'll be so thankful they'll forget about that desert expedition – even our attempt to destroy an army base. You'll be heroes.'

Stingo shook his head. 'You're mad. We can't do this on our own.'

'I know.'

'We can't contact the Americans or the Egyptians because they want us silenced for good.'

'True.'

'So what do you think we can do?'

'*We* can ring my parents.'

'Yeah, right.'

'And they can tell any of the team who made it back to the Embassy.'

He scratched his chin. 'That's not a bad idea.'

'We can meet them at Luxor . . .' she leafed through the brochure, checking the timetable, 'the day after tomorrow.'

'Then I hand you over to your parents and the team and I try to save the hostages,' Stingo said approvingly.

'That's the idea. It's better than jail.'

'Yeah,' said Stingo, ruffling her hair, 'a lot better.'

17

Ginnie was packing her case in the hotel room when her phone rang.

'Michael, can you get it? I don't feel like talking to anyone just at the moment,' she said wearily.

Michael put down his glass of whiskey and grabbed the phone.

'Lock here.'

'Hi, Dad, it's me.'

'No, it can't be. Is this a joke?'

Darcie could hear the anger in her father's voice. 'It's not. I'm OK. Alive.'

'Darcie, where are you?'

She could hear her mother's scream in the background, the sob in her father's voice. Tears began to stream down Darcie's cheeks.

'I . . . I'm with Stingo. He and his mates got me out.

The CIA decided to hide me until it was all over.'

'So they've got you in a safe house somewhere? Why didn't they tell us?'

'That's just it, Dad, they weren't going to tell you – they were going to keep me dead – so I decided to make my own plans.' Now was not the moment to tell him about the flying bullets and drugs.

'But where are you?'

She wiped her tears away with the back of her hand. 'Is this phone safe?'

Michael paused. She could picture him working out why his daughter might ask such a question.

'Probably not.'

'Remember that funny book you gave me in Germany?'

Death on the Nile.

'Yes, of course.'

'We're following it up. Meet us the day after tomorrow at the last location of the boy you told me about.' She hoped he'd get it: Tutankhamen, the boy king with the cursed treasure. 'Stingo's friends will be turning up at your country's place soon if they haven't already. Bring them too.'

'All right. But why?'

'I'll explain when you see me. Look, I've got to go. I've only ... er ... borrowed this phone while the owner is otherwise engaged.' Darcie watched Stingo slow-dancing with the plump American lady they had chosen for the honour. 'Tell Mom I love her. I love you both.'

'Darcie?'

'Yes?'

'We are so, so proud of you. We love you just as you are – always have – you know that?'

'Thanks, Dad.'

Darcie ended the call and slipped the phone back into the woman's purse. Just as she was doing so, a party of Egyptian soldiers appeared on the deck, accompanied by the captain. Her heart skipped a beat. Had the Americans traced her call so quickly? Surely not. It must just be the expected search team. Time to mingle.

Darcie spotted a good-looking boy sitting hunched with boredom at his parents' table.

'Excuse me, would you like a dance?' she asked, doing something she would under no normal circumstances dare do.

He looked up and his eyes brightened. 'Sure. But I thought you were with that man there?'

'You mean my uncle?'

'He's your uncle?' The boy looked even happier.

'Yeah. I'm Gina, by the way.'

'I'm Archie. Let's dance.'

Darcie let Archie lead her on to the dance floor and buried her face in his shoulder. If he was surprised by her forwardness, he didn't show it. Indeed, he was soon kissing her neck and holding her tight, doing a very passable imitation of the behaviour expected of a holiday romance. All the while, Darcie had her eyes peeking through her hair at the soldiers who were passing between the tables, stopping to check on the few couples who fitted the age description of her and Stingo.

The song ended.

'Do you want a drink?' asked Archie.

'No thanks,' said Darcie, watching the soldiers at the bar. 'I'd like to keep on dancing if that's OK with you.'

'Yeah, that's fine.' He grinned, taking her by the waist again, nuzzling her forehead.

Darcie tried to act interested, but she could see Stingo leading the American woman over to talk to the soldiers. He was doing his bare-faced cheek thing again. She hoped it didn't backfire.

'Anything the matter?' asked Archie, sensing her thoughts were elsewhere.

'Seems to be something going on,' she said with a shrug at the soldiers.

'They're probably just looking for those escaped convicts. Did you see the fuss on the river a few hours ago?'

'Some of it.'

'People are saying they got on a boat going the other way – lucky escape for us, hey?'

'Yeah, very lucky.'

Feeling the second soldier's eyes roving over the gathered tourists, there was only one thing for it – Darcie suddenly leaned forward and kissed Archie. If he was surprised, he made no protest. He smelt nice – of shower gel and clean clothes. He was also the kind of boy she quite liked: dark-haired, tall, brown eyes. She congratulated herself on her good taste on picking him out. He kissed her back gently as the music started again.

She might be on the run, heading towards yet more danger, but at least this part of the adventure wasn't so bad.

Darcie heard a cough behind her.

'Er, niece, don't you think it's time you went to bed?'

The soldiers had gone, the dancers thinned out, and she and Archie had been smooching for a very long time.

'Oh, OK.' Darcie realised that she was really very tired and had been leaning heavily on her partner. 'See you tomorrow, Archie.'

'You bet, Gina.' He glanced nervously at her stern-faced 'uncle' and kissed her chastely on the cheek. 'Sleep well.'

'You seemed to be enjoying yourself rather too much, niece,' growled Stingo, taking her arm and leading her back to the cabin. 'You didn't tell him anything, I hope?'

'Of course not, I'm not that stupid.'

'Hmm.'

Darcie jabbed him in the ribs. 'Top bunk or bottom?'

'Bottom. I don't want you creeping out without me knowing what's going on.'

'As if. What were you doing with that American woman?'

'I certainly wasn't snogging her, if that's what you mean.'

'You know it wasn't.'

'I was encouraging her to tell the soldiers how she'd seen the two convicts climb on board the other boat. By the time she'd got her story straight, she thought one was slim and boyish, the other about my height, my build and devilishly handsome.'

'Really?' Darcie raised her eyebrows mockingly.

'Well, perhaps not that last bit. She told them the rest though – they were very interested.'

'I bet they were.'

'So I think we've earned ourselves a short breathing space. A day's rest and then the Valley of the Kings.'

'In that case, I know how I'm going to spend tomorrow.'

'Oh, no you're not. Not when I'm on your watch.'

'He's a very cute boy.'

'I was a boy once upon a time – so I don't trust him.'

'Were you cute too?' She curled up under the covers on the top bunk, her eyes already heavy with sleep.

'Very.'

'Don't believe you.'

'Ask my mother.'

'Perhaps I will one day.' She thought of another question that she had been waiting to ask for a long time. 'Stingo?'

'Go to sleep.'

'Stingo?'

'What?'

'Why are you called Stingo?'

'I'll tell you when you're older.'

'I am older.'

'Not old enough for that story. Sweet dreams.'

08.00, Cairo: Sunny, 21°C

Michael Lock had only one contact at the British Embassy that he dare trust – as distasteful as it was to admit it.

'Father, thank you for meeting me.'

The two Locks were sitting in a coffee shop near the bazaar. Michael had chosen it in the knowledge that the noise of shoppers, hawkers and honking cars would be enough to baffle any listening devices that could be trained on them. Ginnie was currently laying a false trail, purchasing airline tickets to Brussels – a red herring for any watchers. Sitting across the table from his companion, Michael tried to forget how much to blame his father was for the situation they were in.

'To what do I owe this honour?' asked Christopher.

He was looking strained: the combination of worry for his granddaughter and a severe reprimand from the prime minister was taking its toll. He was being put on gardening leave until his retirement – in short, been given the old heave-ho.

'Darcie is alive.'

'Is she now?' Christopher allowed himself a little smile. He felt vindicated. 'They did it then.'

'Yes. We've got a lot to thank your team for, it seems. But it's not over yet.'

Christopher stirred three spoonfuls of sugar into his thick dark coffee. 'No, it isn't. I suppose the Americans, for various reasons, are not too happy to have her alive.'

'That's correct. So she broke out of detention and is cruising down the Nile with Warrant Officer Galt.'

Christopher downed his shot of coffee in one and laughed. 'She's magnificent. What is she doing?'

'I think she's trying to sort things out. If I know her, she won't be content in letting things rest where they are at the moment – she'll want a go at putting them right.'

'Can she do it?'

'Not on her own. She wants the SAS team to rendezvous with her tomorrow in the Valley of the Kings – she's convinced that's where the kidnappers are heading. The SAS men that got away will go to the British Embassy. Can you pass a message to them if and when they get there?'

'Of course. What are you going to do?'

'Ginnie and I will slip away later today and meet up with Darcie. We appreciate that she wishes to help the two remaining hostages, but we can't let her anywhere near them, of course.'

Christopher stroked his neat moustache thoughtfully. 'Why not?'

'You must be joking! Of course, we can't. The SAS team is a good idea – hostage situations are their thing – but it's time Darcie stopped risking her life for others.'

Christopher was several steps ahead of his son, having seen the advantages that would spring from a successful operation: exoneration for all and perhaps even promotion. 'You underestimate her. I imagine she has a very good plan. Look how much she's achieved so far. You must at least do her the courtesy of listening and taking her views seriously.'

'Father –'

'Why do you think your relationship with her has been through a difficult patch? What have you and Ginnie been doing but dismissing her opinions and treating her like an infant? She's growing up; you've got to grow up with her.'

Michael swallowed the comment that it was rich to receive parenting advice from his own very dysfunctional father.

'We'll listen. But I doubt she can say anything that will convince us to let her put her life on the line once more, Father.'

'There you go again: making your mind up before you've even heard the child speak.'

Michael felt angry that his father had managed to make him at fault again. 'So she's a child now, is she? You've realised this eventually, have you?'

'I never forgot it for one moment. But what do you

think children are? They are small people – not another species. If I take my granddaughter's wishes seriously, then, by George, you should too as her parents who know her even better than I do. You know what she's made of.'

'Yes, we do.'

'So where shall we meet?'

'We?'

'You don't think I'm leaving you to do this on your own, do you?'

'Father, I think you are the last person who –'

'Rubbish. I've got forty years of experience to offer – dealt with more hostage situations than you've had hot dinners. I speak Arabic. You'll need me.'

'I'm not sure . . .'

'Don't make me pull rank on you, Michael. I want to help.'

'What do you mean, the girl made contact with her parents!' bellowed President Morris.

Mrs Johnson kept calm. One day he would

remember that this wasn't her fault. 'As I said, we'd been listening in to all calls made by the Locks. Darcie telephoned –'

'Don't use her name!'

'The *target* telephoned and left a cryptic message. From something she said, we think she's trying to get to Brussels.'

'Why?'

'The Locks lived there once some years ago. Perhaps she thinks of it as home.'

'Where are the parents now?'

Mrs Johnson coughed. 'They've disappeared.'

'What! Find them – find them now and bring them to me.'

'Sir, may I remind you that both the Locks are trained secret agents widely acknowledged as the best from both organisations? We're not going to find them if they want to stay hidden.'

The president ran his fingers through his hair, spoiling his neatly groomed image that came out so well on the campaign posters.

'What about that grandfather fellow? What's he up to?'

'He's gone too, sir. He left the British Embassy in the company of some SAS men and . . .'

'Disappeared?'

'Yes, sir. He too is a trained agent and the men he was with are special forces – we can't blame them for doing their job.'

'Oh yes, we can. What have the Brits got to say for themselves?'

'The ambassador claimed that Lock and his companions were heading for a military flight home but failed to show up at the airport. He's as angry as you, sir.'

'No he damn well isn't! Nowhere near as angry as me. It's my daughter's life they're gambling with.'

And it's their child's life they're trying to save, thought Mrs Johnson, but she held her tongue.

'Use every means available to look for them. If they foul up this operation then . . .'

The president ran out of words. He couldn't think of

anything that could capture his desire for a wide-reaching and terrible revenge on all those who were making this crisis worse for him.

'We're already doing so, sir. But might it not be wiser if we concentrated our attention on the kidnappers? We need to have something to offer them when they next make contact.'

The president nodded. 'The Egyptians have agreed to release this El-Gebel person. We can arrange an exchange.'

'And if they don't bite?'

'Then I hope to God that our special forces are as good as the Brits in extracting hostages because I'll be sending them in.'

18

As the cruise ship slid up to the pier at Luxor, Darcie's heart sank like a stone to the bottom of the Nile. They thought they had fooled the authorities into believing that they had escaped downstream, but the presence of so many soldiers on land, all looking expectantly towards the newest arrival, could only mean one thing.

'Hmm,' grunted Stingo, leaning on the rail beside her, 'it seems as though they aren't as dim as I'd've liked.'

'So they know we're here?' Darcie began to feel panicky as memories of the doctor, drug-induced paralysis and the bare cell flooded back into her head. She didn't want to be caught – put away where no one would know whether she was dead or alive – waiting for someone to decide her fate by the fortunes of a politician in the polls.

Stingo drummed the rail. 'Not necessarily. They might just be checking every ship that was in that stretch of water when we disappeared – I would if I were them.'

'But still – it's me they're after?'

'Yeah, 'fraid so.' He must have caught sight of her anxious face. A large fist took hers in a tight grip. 'Don't worry – we'll get out of here. What we need is a disguise. We'll have to leave separately.'

'Coo-ee!' Stingo's plump dance partner waved at him from across the deck. 'Coming ashore, Mr Smith?'

'Well, there's yours,' whispered Darcie with a flicker of a smile. 'Mrs Steiner's best buddy. If you play your cards right, you could be her fifth husband.'

Stingo waved back, while saying aside to Darcie, 'No thanks, the mortality rate among her spouses is far too high. A nice safe life in the SAS is all I ask.'

'Would you care to accompany me, Mr Smith?' the widow trilled.

'Yes, indeed. With you in two ticks. Just sorting

out my niece here.' He bent closer to Darcie. 'I'm not sure I can keep this posh geezer stuff going – I'm running out of things to say. Anyway, what about you? That's the real question. I don't suppose they really care about finding me: it's the young European girl with long black hair that they're after.' He tugged her baseball cap borrowed from Archie lower to hide her face.

'What if . . .' began Darcie, 'what if I wasn't a girl when I got off?'

'How'd you manage that?'

'Archie.' They both turned to look at Darcie's new friend. He was staring out at the crowds milling about on the docks but Darcie could tell that he had been watching her until a moment ago.

'Still like football, Darcie?' asked Stingo.

'Uh-huh.'

'I think that would be a nice finishing touch.'

'Yeah, you're right.'

Ten minutes later two teenage boys ran down the gangplank followed by a couple of harassed parents.

The one in front was tall with dark hair, dressed in a Man U shirt; his shorter companion was wearing a baggy England shirt and shorts that looked much too big for him. His hair was hidden under a cap.

'Mind where you're bouncing that ball!' called Archie's father. 'I don't know what's got into him,' he added for the benefit of his wife. 'Only meets her a day ago and already she's borrowing his clothes. I mean, I suppose he must find it flattering, but all the same, you have to draw a line somewhere.'

Archie's new tomboy of a girlfriend commenced a display of impressive ball skills on the dockside, bouncing the ball from knee to knee, much to the amusement of some soldiers waiting at the bottom of the ramp. One nudged his comrade.

'Michael Owen!' he called out, using the only words of English he knew. 'Liverpool.'

Darcie pointed at herself. She could feel her heart pounding but she tried to act natural. 'Chelsea.'

The soldier laughed and shook his head. 'Boy, they no good.'

Archie opened his mouth to correct the assumption that his friend was a boy, only to find a ball hit him in the face.

'Come on, Archie,' called Darcie, 'I thought you said you'd give me a quick game before we went off on one of those deadly boring tours.'

Archie rubbed his bruised nose. 'What did you do that for?'

'Come on!' Darcie began to dribble the ball away, fearing that the bloom had just faded from her brief romance with Archie.

09.30, Cairo: Heat rising, 30°C

The American Embassy received a message from their special forces working with the Egyptian military in the southern reaches of the Nile.

Man answering description of fugitive seen in company of middle-aged woman at Luxor. No sign of girl. Request guidance.

Mrs Johnson sucked the end of her pencil. Luxor? What on earth was Sergeant Galt, aka 'Stingo', doing there? Where was Darcie? Had she drowned when they had tried to escape into the river? She had certainly been seen struggling in the water. Or had Stingo and Darcie gone their separate ways to confuse pursuers? Perhaps he'd already handed her over to her parents and she was now on her way to Brussels? Or maybe she was lying low on the ship?

Decision made, Mrs Johnson sent a reply:

Am coming to Luxor. Search ship. Apprehend man as discreetly as possible. Use force if necessary.

Of course it would be necessary: he was SAS.

If you find the girl, you may use all available means to extract her from the location without drawing attention to her presence.

Her heart felt heavy as she wrote this. She knew she was basically authorising them to use a sniper – a bullet in the back down a dark alley – if that was the only way.

Darcie had to smile when she saw the party arriving at the ticket kiosk at the entrance to the Valley of the Kings. Her grandfather was in the lead, umbrella held aloft, followed by a trail of the beefiest looking tourists she had ever seen. She could hear her grandfather from where she was sitting in a little café, busy with visitors.

'Valley of the Kings, last resting place of the pharaohs. Hidden away up in the hills behind Luxor, the Egyptian kings tried to hide their wealth from robbers in the complex tunnel system burrowed into the rocks.'

Merlin was taking photos on his camera, getting Knife and Blister to pose next to a camel. She could tell he was really recording the terrain to help plan their retreat.

Christopher spotted his granddaughter sitting on the

terrace with a baseball cap hiding her hair; she looked almost boyish. A good disguise, he thought with approval.

'I expect you'll all need a drink before we embark on our tour of the tombs,' he said in clarion tones. He was like Stingo: from the school of the more attention you draw to yourself, the less people notice.

The SAS team crowded into the noisy café. No chance of being overheard here, even if someone was listening.

'Excuse me, but is this seat taken?'

Darcie smiled up at Midge. 'No.'

He sat down and slipped off his jacket. Like everyone else in the team, underneath he was wearing a T-shirt with *Oxford University Rowing Club* emblazoned across the back. He saw her looking.

He winked at her. 'How else could we explain eight blokes hanging out together with that old geezer. Where's Stingo?'

'If he's managed to escape his girlfriend, he'll be up in the hills doing a bit of scouting.'

Midge whistled to two of his men and gave them swift instructions. They took their jackets and left. 'Best not to scout the enemy alone. Why's he gone up there?'

'Because, if I'm right about any of this, we guessed Khaled will approach from the desert and hide out in one of the tombs.'

'Yeah, he could hardly march through Luxor with the hostages in tow. The place is crawling with soldiers. Do you think they know Khaled's heading this way?'

'No idea. We thought they might be looking for me.'

Christopher brought a tray of drinks to the table and sat down. He nodded once to his granddaughter but did not speak.

Darcie carried on with her briefing, acutely aware that the man who had used her so treacherously was sitting at her right hand. 'Khaled said that he wanted to see the kings resurrected. "When the tomb opens, all the world will tremble." I think he really meant it.'

'How soon do you think he can be here?' Christopher asked Midge.

The soldier shrugged. 'He could be here already, but the original message did talk about withdrawal of troops by the end of the month. That's tomorrow.'

'So another message or some kind of gesture would be expected,' nodded Christopher.

'What kind of gesture, do you think?' asked Midge.

'Another sacrifice,' said Darcie, almost in a whisper. Shelly and Jon Lee must have been going through hell since she last saw them. It was hard to imagine how they were coping.

'My granddaughter's right: I would not want to be Jon Lee Vermont tomorrow,' said Christopher in a low voice.

The threesome fell silent as an elderly man pushing a woman in a wheelchair entered the café and took a seat at the table behind Darcie. She shifted her chair to let them pass.

'Abu-Simbel really is splendid, you mustn't miss it,' Christopher said loudly, then stopped with a chuckle. Darcie turned to see what had made him laugh and found herself looking at her father, disguised to look older than his own parent. She felt someone searching for her hand under the table. The woman in the wheelchair clasped her palm tightly.

'How are you, darling?' Ginnie asked.

'I'm fine – really I am.' It was so good just to see them; Darcie wanted to hug them but dare not in case someone was watching.

'Don't you ever do that to us again!' But Ginnie was smiling at her through tear-filled eyes.

'What? You mean, cause a major international incident, upset the most powerful man in the world, and ruin the careers of . . .' Darcie made a quick count. 'Twelve people?'

'Exactly.'

'I'll try not to, Mom.'

Stingo came back into the café and threw a pair of binoculars on the table.

'Ah, niece, I see you've got company.'

'How's she been?' Ginnie asked anxiously, not taking her daughter's own word for it.

'A complete nightmare, if you want the truth.'

Ginnie looked shocked.

'Not the "getting-out-of-the-desert-blasting-apart-an-army-base-almost-drowning-in-the-Nile" bit, no. My role as her moral guardian was stretched to the limit yesterday by a young man called Archie. I'm exhausted.'

Darcie blushed. 'You promised not to tell!'

'But, ma'am,' Stingo carried on, ignoring her, 'I return your daughter to you in one piece, apart from the inevitable broken heart at the end of a holiday romance.'

'I'm glad to hear that she's recovered so quickly to have time for *other things*,' Ginnie said, with a watery smile.

'Hadn't we better make our plans?' said Michael, though he too was smiling. 'Have you seen anything?'

Darcie could tell that Stingo was in a very good mood. 'Yes indeed. Darcie was right. They're heading this way. Thanks to her description, I spotted what I think is their caravan on the horizon. Knife and Blister are monitoring it now; I came down to report.'

'Options?' said Midge, snapping back into action.

'Tell my government we've confirmation,' said Ginnie in a low voice, 'and let them deal with it.'

'Yeah, but that'll mean letting them whisk your daughter away to who knows where so she doesn't spoil the election campaign and throwing the rest of us in the slammer,' said Stingo. 'Besides, they'd never get here in time.'

'Strike while they're still in the open,' suggested Michael.

Christopher shook his head. 'There are too many variables. We don't know what support they've got around them and they will be on their guard. If we take them, it's best to do so when they feel they are secure.'

This seemed the perfect opening for the plan Darcie had had in mind since she first realised where Khaled was going, though it was unnerving to hear that she and her treacherous grandfather might be thinking alike.

'I think we should get on the inside,' she said. 'Some

of us should hide out in the tombs and try and free the hostages tonight without alerting Khaled and his crew. They must be tired after their journey – perhaps even off their guard once they're inside the tomb. If we can slip Shelly and Jon Lee away, we can leave the authorities to deal with the rest of them.'

'Yeah, I could stay behind when the tombs close,' said Stingo. 'But I'd need a diversion – I couldn't tackle all of them on my own. The rest of you will have to draw the kidnappers out.'

'Indeed,' said Christopher. 'You need something non-threatening but plausible. My thought is that Michael and I – and Ginnie, if she wishes – should turn up at the tomb at night, scouting locations for a new production of *Death on the Nile*. I think noisy artistic differences may prove distraction enough.' He shaded his hand and surveyed the terrain beyond the café terrace. 'If Midge's team are positioned along the cliffs, they should be able to deal with those who come out to see what's going on.'

Midge nodded. 'If we take out the terrorists in ones

and twos, it'd make the job of the team on the inside easier.'

'Yeah, with any luck I might be able to finish the job,' agreed Stingo.

'Can we give them a chance to surrender?' asked Darcie, thinking of Antar and not liking the thought of him being picked off by a silent sniper.

'I doubt they'd take it.'

'But still?'

'We'll see. Let's concentrate on getting your friends out. All you need worry about is staying out of sight somewhere safe.'

'Ladies and gentlemen, the tombs will be closing in five minutes!' crackled the loud speaker.

'You're sure they'll choose this tomb?' asked Stingo. 'It's not the most impressive. Not much left in here.'

'No, I'm not sure,' said Christopher, his arm linked with his granddaughter as he pretended to have difficulty walking, slowing the party behind the last visitors, 'but I think Tutankhamen is the most symbolic and that's what they're after – the king who put a curse on his western tomb-raiders after his death. I can see that appealing to Khaled.'

'Yeah, you're right.'

Stingo took photos as the straggling line of tourists retreated down the tunnel to the entrance. Christopher had already decided on the hiding place: a replica sarcophagus in an anti-chamber right at the back of the honeycomb of tunnels. Once everyone was out of sight, they slid the lid aside.

'Damn,' swore Christopher. Inside was a much smaller painted wooden coffin, only big enough to hold a boy. They couldn't move it without alerting the security guards to what they were up to.

'Abort?' whispered Stingo.

'I wonder.' Christopher stroked his chin. His eyes met Darcie's. 'It's our only opportunity. They'll be in here tonight if we've guessed their plan correctly.'

'No way. You're not leaving her here on her own.' Stingo was angry. Darcie could tell he'd like to thump her grandfather for putting her in this situation. Had her grandfather known they'd be faced with this decision all along? After all, he had suggested she accompany them to make their party look less suspicious.

'Darcie?'

'She's not one of your agents!'

Darcie could feel her answer like a weight pressing down on her shoulders. She took a gulp of air. 'No, but I am on Shelly and Jon Lee's team – they're my friends – well, sort of friends.'

'I'm throwing you over my shoulder and carrying you out of here right now!'

Darcie gripped Stingo's forearms, forcing him to face her. 'Please, Stingo. They'll need someone with them when the shooting starts – they might panic. And what if Khaled realises what's happening outside and comes to kill them? They'll be defenceless. If we don't do something tonight, tomorrow Jon Lee might well be dead.'

Stingo groaned and picked her up – not to take her outside but to lift her into the coffin.

'I hope this isn't where you tell me you get claustrophobic,' he said, fumbling in his belt and putting a couple of small, hard packages in her hands. 'Flash bangs – stun grenades. Use these to get out if Khaled comes calling. Throw it in front of you and stay back. They'll temporarily blind and deafen an attacker – hopefully giving you time to slip by.'

'Just try not to shoot us when we do get out,' said Darcie as he replaced the lid, leaving her with a crowbar to lever her way out.

Once they'd left her, it was very quiet in the tombs. Darcie wondered how long she would have to wait. It was hard not to think about the confined space she had squeezed herself into; how in effect she had buried herself alive. She tried to concentrate on the positives: a chink of light still came through the gap in the lid. She had water with her though she daren't drink too much in case she needed the bathroom.

With nothing to distract her, she heard the footsteps of a security guard doing the last rounds as they echoed down the tunnels. The lights went out and a torch flashed. Then the footsteps disappeared into the distance. She had been left in total darkness.

Stingo was standing guard outside the local government office in Luxor while Christopher, Michael and Ginnie talked their way into getting a pass to visit the tombs at night. He suspected that they would not have too much trouble. He'd seen the wad of dollars that Christopher had stashed in his jacket pocket for the purpose of persuading officials. He was feeling restless: he couldn't stop thinking about Darcie lying in the tomb waiting for Khaled's mob to arrive. The girl had some guts. Her parents had been predictably incensed when Stingo and Christopher had returned without her, but by that time there was nothing anyone could do. He hoped he'd made the right choice in letting her stay.

Out of the corner of his eye, Stingo saw a broad-shouldered tourist in a Nike top approaching from the end of the street. Instantly, Stingo's training told him that something was wrong. The man was moving too quickly; his hand was reaching under his shirt to the waistband of his shorts. Stingo swivelled to run for it.

'Not thinking of leaving us so soon, Warrant Officer Galt?'

A woman who, a moment ago, had been admiring a stand of postcards next to him, now had a gun pointing at his ribcage.

Stingo tensed, wondering if he could reach his own weapon before she shot him. No. The man had now reached them. He expertly searched Stingo and relieved him of his Browning.

'Where's the girl?' asked the woman.

'What girl?'

'Don't be clever with me: it won't work. You know exactly who I'm talking about and what happens from here on will depend on your next answer.'

Stingo was thinking quickly. Clearly, this American woman – CIA by the look of her – knew nothing about the hostages. She thought this was just about Darcie and him. What should he do? Let himself be taken off for questioning and leave the others to deal with the stake-out at the tombs or tell her the truth?

The decision was taken out of his hands by new arrivals.

'Drop your weapons.' Christopher Lock was standing at the top of the steps of the government building looking down on the trio, armed only with a stick.

'Mr Lock. You're here too. That really makes my day,' said the woman sourly.

'I'm glad to be of service, Mrs Johnson.'

'And what makes you think I'm going to do what a disgraced official asks me?'

'Because this disgraced official has two guns pointing at you.'

Mrs Johnson glanced over her shoulder.

'Hello, Maria, been a long time,' said Ginnie Lock, digging the barrel of her government issue sidearm into her one-time friend. 'I hear you've been looking after my daughter for me.'

Michael Lock was standing at the shoulder of Mrs Johnson's companion, also armed.

'Now you understand that the balance of power has

shifted in our favour, I suggest you stop threatening our friend and have tea with us,' said Christopher pleasantly.

'Have tea with you?' Mrs Johnson lowered her gun.

'Yes, as you're here, I think you'd better understand exactly what it is you've walked into. When you've heard, then you can decide whether you are going to put us all under arrest or help us.'

Darcie had lost track of the time and was beginning to wonder if their hunch about this particular tomb had been wrong. It had all been a big gamble from the start – perhaps she had lost. Just as she was about to give up and lever her way out of her hiding place, she heard voices echoing down the tunnel. She lay as still as the mummy she was impersonating, a bead of sweat trickling down her brow. A door creaked down the passageway.

'You, in there! Everyone gone. We let you out.'

Feet scuffled. Darcie could hear Shelly complaining about being gagged and tied up in an old service tunnel for the last few hours. Khaled's men, it appeared, knew their way around the tombs and had managed to slip in without alerting anyone to their presence.

'You sleep. Here is your water. Tomorrow last day.'

Darcie heard a thud as something was thrown on the floor. A faint flicker of light came in at the crack in the lid. Someone was walking back up the tunnel, leaving at least two people behind.

'Your turn to be water monitor,' said Shelly in a low voice. 'Start counting.'

Jon Lee slowly counted to ten and Shelly gulped her share.

'Now your go,' she said.

Jon Lee drank as Shelly counted for him.

'Was that fair?' Jon Lee asked, putting the waterskin down.

'Yeah, that's even.'

'I didn't like what Antar said about tomorrow,' said Jon Lee. Darcie could hear him pacing up and down. 'What do you think he means?'

'God knows. Let's hope it's something good. I don't think I can stand any more of this.'

'Yes, you can. You're doing brilliantly, First Daughter of the Empire.'

Darcie now caught the sounds of Shelly sniffing as if trying to hold back tears. Her opinion of Jon Lee soared: he was clearly the one holding them both together.

'No, I'm not. I can't stop thinking about Darcie. It must've been so terrible for her. I hope she didn't suffer much.'

Jon Lee cleared his throat awkwardly. 'Yeah, the kid didn't deserve that. It should've been me.'

'No, no, I didn't mean that,' said Shelly. 'None of us deserve any of this.'

Darcie was suddenly struck by the difficulty of making an entrance from inside a sarcophagus when both of them believed her to be dead. But there seemed to be no other way – they appeared to be alone and she might not get another chance. She tapped on the lid.

'Did you hear that?' said Jon Lee, his voice cracked with fear.

'Yeah, it came from that tomb thing.'

Darcie could hear them scrambling to the far side of the room.

'Hey, guys, it's me, Darcie. Don't panic.'

Shelly gave a scream, which Jon Lee hastily stifled. They all waited in silence to see if the noise would bring anyone to check on them. Darcie counted to twenty, then spoke again.

'Are you on your own?'

'Yeah,' said Jon Lee warily. 'Is that a loudspeaker or something?'

'No, it's me.' Darcie heaved back the lid and sat up. She forgave them their shocked faces. 'I'm alive.'

Jon Lee was the first to move. He rushed to her and held out a hand to help her out.

'Hell, Kiddo, are you mad? What on earth are you doing in here? Do you know what they'll do if they see you?'

'Yeah, they'll try and kill me – again. That's why they mustn't see me.'

Shelly grabbed her to check she really was flesh

and blood, then gave her a hug.

'That's one mean trick. Serves us right, I s'pose, having you rise from the dead in front of us. I hope there's more than pay-back involved in that stunt.'

'I've got a team on the outside. We're getting you out because we think things are going to get nasty from tomorrow.'

'Nasty?' queried Shelly.

Darcie cast a significant look at Jon Lee.

'Oh, I see.'

'My job is to tell you not to panic. Take one of these.' She thrust a stun grenade at each of them. 'The team outside are going to take out as many of the gang as possible, then we use these to get past anyone in the way. Do you know where they are?'

'Yeah, they're holed up in that big chamber by the entrance,' said Jon Lee.

'Good. If we chuck one of these in there, we should be able to get by. All we've got to do now is wait until the diversion has done its job.'

Shelly sat down; her legs were shaking. 'I still can't believe you're alive.'

'Yeah, well, it was a close run thing.'

'Tell us about it – I'm desperate to know what's been going on.'

'You're not going to like some of it.'

'Why not?'

'Some of it involves your father.'

'Nothing you tell me about him will surprise me, believe me.'

Unknown to Darcie, the diversion was delayed by the threat of immediate imprisonment of the rescue team.

Ginnie had to admire her father-in-law: despite his many serious failings, he certainly knew how to fight his corner.

'Mrs Johnson, I struggle to see why you should take such a course of action' – she had threatened to hand them all over to the Egyptian authorities – 'when you so clearly need us. We have the hostage-takers cornered, a plan made, a person on the inside: we're poised to end this crisis. If you take us out of the equation, you just make the situation worse: Darcie will be discovered, the plot revealed and I've no doubt that the abductors will take terrible revenge on our three young people.'

Mrs Johnson was stirring her tea furiously. Ginnie knew how it felt to be out-manoeuvred by Christopher Lock.

'If you combine forces with us, we all stand a decent chance of success. Think how that will look in tomorrow's papers: American and British intelligence services end siege; unique joint operation signals a deepening of the friendship between our two great nations. I can't believe that my prime minister and your president would pass up the opportunity to present this all as one major foreign policy triumph – turning a crisis into a decisive victory.'

Mrs Johnson sighed. She could see what her decision was going to have to be, but she didn't like it. She didn't have enough men in theatre to replace the SAS team who were already here. They should all be locked up in a cell and the key thrown away, but it looked as if she'd have to go along with it.

'All right, all right, but when this is over, there'll still be a reckoning,' she warned.

'No doubt, there will be. I would've thought in the shape of promotions all round, wouldn't you?' Christopher smiled charmingly and sipped his tea.

'Where on earth did he get that pink scarf?' Ginnie asked Michael as they followed their 'director' into the tomb complex. Merlin followed behind carrying an impressive arsenal of weaponry disguised as a camera.

'You know my father – never one for doing things by halves.'

'What do you think, darling?' Christopher drawled, beckoning to Ginnie. 'Do you think Poirot should stand over there with the moon behind him?'

'I don't know. What does our little Belgian detective think?' Ginnie turned to Michael, giving him a nervous smile.

'Absolutely not!' Michael threw his hands in the air

in horror. 'My dramatic talents cannot flourish in a gloomy place like this!'

'What! Do my ears deceive me?' bellowed Christopher, taking them right up to the entrance to Tutankhamen's tomb. 'I bring you to the best location on the planet and you – a mere B-list actor – tell me you cannot perform here! In all my life as a Hollywood director, I've never heard the like!'

Inside the tomb, the chamber nearest the entrance had fallen silent, as the occupants listened intently to the argument outside.

'Check it out,' hissed Khaled to one of his men as he sharpened his dagger on a whetstone. He tested the edge with his thumb – it drew blood. 'Remember, no shooting unless you have to. I want our presence here to be a surprise when the sun rises.'

The man nodded and disappeared outside, gun cocked ready to fire.

Five minutes passed and he hadn't returned. Antar raised his eyebrows at his cousin. Khaled looked round the room. He had three men remaining; the boy was with the camels in Luxor.

'You two, go and see what's happened to Gamal. Antar, go and check on our guests.'

Antar got up and followed the men out. Just beyond the entrance he could see an old man arguing with someone, shouting something about Hollywood. Gamal had probably just stayed to see the show. Antar turned down the corridor and headed towards the captives. He didn't agree with what Khaled planned to do tomorrow, but neither could he see a way out. He knew if he questioned Khaled's wisdom, he'd be killed. Khaled thought that the offer of freeing Abu El-Gebel was a sign that the Americans were cracking; Antar thought it meant the opposite: that it was a last gesture to end this peacefully. It was hopeless. Perhaps Khaled knew this too in his heart of hearts, or why else would he have chosen to bring them to a tomb? In which case, thought Antar fatalistically, perhaps he should make his peace with his maker by helping the two young people. But how?

Shelly and Jon Lee looked suspiciously quiet when Antar came in, sitting too meekly with their backs to the sarcophagus. Normally, if they were on their own with him, they'd try to make conversation, find out where they were going or what was happening. Tonight they said nothing.

'Is everything all right?' Antar asked.

'Yes, thanks,' said Shelly.

Thanks? She'd never thanked him for anything. Antar stood up and sniffed. There was a distinct scent in the air – of soap and shampoo. None of them had had access to such luxuries for days so it couldn't be Shelly or Jon Lee.

'Who's there?' Antar barked into the shadows, raising his gun to his shoulder.

'It's me, Antar.' Darcie walked out with her hands open.

Antar dropped his gun and fell on his knees. 'You're dead?'

'No, I'm no ghost. I've come to offer you the chance to get out alive. If you leave with us, you won't get shot.'

Antar suddenly realised what she meant. He scrabbled on the ground and grabbed for his gun. Seizing Darcie's arm, he stared intently into her face. 'My brothers?'

Darcie gave a helpless shrug, trying to free herself. 'I can't save everyone. I wish I could.'

There was a roar from the tunnel. 'Antar! Antar!' Khaled burst into the room, at first not even noticing that they had a guest. 'We're under attack!' He stopped. His face went white then flushed with rage as he grasped who was there. 'You!'

Antar hurriedly let go of Darcie. 'Leave her, Khaled. It is over. They know we are here.'

'It is not over until I say it is over! And while we have her,' Khaled jerked his head at Shelly, 'we are in control.'

'But what for? We will never get out of this alive. We had a dream – but it has turned into a nightmare. We have to stop now.'

'You think it is finished?' spat Khaled. 'Not before I finish the spy – and the others. Her first, I think.' He lunged for Darcie and grabbed a fistful of her hair, pulling her towards him.

'No!' Antar rushed at Khaled – then staggered back, giving a strangled hiss, a knife in his chest. He dropped to the floor, hands clutching convulsively at the haft.

Khaled gave a hysterical laugh. 'So we are going die like the pharaohs after all – the servants sacrificed around the body of the god-king.' He lunged forward and caught hold of Darcie again. 'You next, girl.'

Knocking Darcie to her knees, he jerked her head back. Shelly reached for the stun grenade but then –

The ear-splitting din of a semi-automatic rifle erupted in the chamber. Khaled was thrown back against the wall. Antar dropped his gun at his side, slumping over it in a pool of blood. Darcie knew they couldn't wait to see if either man had survived.

'Let's go!' Darcie shouted, jumping to her feet and leading the way up the passage. There was no sign of the other terrorists.

The three hostages burst out of the tombs. Suddenly all was confusion – voices, lights, people. Darcie ran into her mother's arms; she saw Shelly and Jon Lee wrapped in foil blankets by American officials and immediately led away.

'Khaled and the other?' asked Stingo.

'Dead – I think,' gasped Darcie as her mother rocked her to and fro.

'Knife, Blister – you're with me!' barked Midge. The SAS team entered the tomb to complete their mission.

'My brave girl,' whispered her mother, kissing Darcie on the head. 'My brave, brave girl. Whatever did we do to get a daughter like you?'

'Whatever you did, Ginnie,' said Christopher Lock, coming to pat his granddaughter awkwardly on the back, 'I'd say you did the right thing.'

19

The president's daughter and her companions were being hosted at Luxor airport out of sight of the world's media until Airforce One arrived to whisk Shelly back to the States. Egyptian officials fussed around the lounge, offering every sort of refreshment they could think of to tempt their guests. Shelly was looking much more her old self: showered, changed and even wearing a little make-up. Jon Lee seemed to have switched right back to how he was before – if a little thinner – baseball cap pulled backwards on his head.

'So, Kiddo,' he said. 'What's next for you?'

Darcie shrugged. Her parents were chatting with Stingo by the door; her grandfather was standing at the window alone. 'I'm not sure. It all depends on how Shelly's father takes what happened last night.'

'How else can he take it but give you a medal!' exclaimed Jon Lee. 'You and your mates saved our lives.'

'Yeah, maybe. But I wonder what it'd do to his popularity if it came out I was involved. I mean, he preferred it when I was dead.'

Shelly scrunched up a plastic cup. 'I dunno, Jon Lee. I think Darcie may be right. Now he doesn't have to worry about me, I think the politician in him may take over once more. The election's only weeks away.'

'We can't let him make her disappear again,' said Jon Lee, sitting up abruptly. 'Who knows where he'll send her?'

'I doubt very much there'll be a Starbucks and a music store, wherever it is,' said Darcie wryly.

The thought of being deprived of such essentials galvanised Jon Lee into action. He stood up. 'We've gotta get her out of here before he arrives.'

Shelly chucked the cup in the bin. 'Yeah, yellow team needs a plan. You give us the nod, Darcie, and we'll swing into action.'

Half an hour later, Airforce One taxied to a standstill outside the airport lounge. Darcie, Shelly and Jon Lee watched the presidential party descend the steps. The president almost ran across the tarmac to rejoin his daughter.

Darcie touched Shelly's arm. 'He's got that doctor with him – the one from the army base.'

Shelly bit her lip. 'Sometimes I hate my father.'

'Don't hate him – he's just . . . just a powerful man. I've got in his way.' Darcie looked over at her grand-father. He met her gaze and nodded a farewell.

'So it's nearly time, then?' asked Shelly.

'Yeah. Goodbye, Shelly. I hope we see each other again.'

'Me too.'

Darcie held her hand out to Jon Lee. 'Bye, Jon Lee.'

'Come here, you crazy girl.' Jon Lee seized her and gave her a hug. 'You're bad, you know that, real bad!'

Darcie laughed. 'Thanks.'

Pulling away from him, she walked over to her parents. 'Mom, Dad?'

'Yes, darling.'

'I think things might get a bit . . .'

'Hairy?' suggested her father.

'Yeah.'

'Stingo, look after our daughter for us – at least for the next couple of weeks,' said Michael.

Stingo gave a sharp nod. 'That does seem to be my mission in life.'

Ginnie stroked her daughter's cheek. 'Just stay alive and out of trouble, won't you?'

'Course, Mom.'

President Morris burst into the lounge and made a bee-line for his daughter. 'Shelly!'

'Hi, Pop.'

The president fell on his daughter and hugged her as if he'd never let go. 'You're really OK?' He ruffled her hair and stared into her face, searching for signs of injury.

'Yeah, fine.'

'In that case, let's get you out of here.' He put his arm around her shoulders to lead her away. 'I've got the engines running.'

'Hadn't you better thank the people who saved me?' prompted Shelly.

He pulled up short, reminded of his duty by his

undutiful daughter. 'Yes, of course. What was I thinking?'

The President of the United States solemnly shook hands with everyone in the lounge, congratulating them on the magnificent joint operation for which he was taking all the credit in the international press.

'Mrs Johnson, I won't forget what you did,' he told the CIA woman. She did not look entirely comforted by this thought.

The president grimaced as he shook Christopher Lock's hand. 'The prime minister spoke very highly of you last night,' he said. 'Seems I judged you too hastily. Your experience proved invaluable. Well done.'

Christopher allowed himself a smug smile, knowing that his gardening leave had just been cut short. 'Thank you, sir. I will always remember this operation as showing the best of intelligence cooperation between our two countries.'

'As if,' Darcie muttered under her breath.

Thanking the SAS team was an easier task for the Texan.

'You're my kinda guys!' beamed the president. 'Real cowboys, riding by the seat of your pants, taking risks, being heroes!'

Midge and his men saluted, having the good grace not to mention that it was on the president's orders they had been incarcerated and shot at.

Last in line was Darcie. The president paused.

'Darcie Lock, isn't it?'

'Yes, sir.'

'I'm glad to see you alive and well.'

No, you're not, thought Darcie.

'Thank you, sir.'

'I'd be grateful if you'd let Dr Ghallab look at you to check you are fit to travel as I have my doubts after what you've been through.' Standing this close, Darcie could see the strain behind his insincere smile. 'I believe Mrs Johnson has made arrangements for your discreet return to Washington.'

I bet she has, Darcie said to herself.

'Sure, whatever you say, sir.'

'Pop, I've just got to go to the bathroom before we

leave,' said Shelly brightly, stepping between Darcie and the president. 'Are you coming, Darcie?'

'Yeah.'

'This Jon has to go to the John,' announced Jon Lee, pointing to his chest. 'How about you, Stingo?'

'Sure.'

The president looked slightly bemused as his daughter marched off to the washroom with the biggest threat to his re-election campaign on her arm.

Christopher Lock appeared at the president's elbow. 'Dodgy tummies,' he explained apologetically. 'Must be the water.'

In the cubicle, Shelly opened the window behind the cistern and helped Darcie up.

'Like old times, hey?' she said, handing Darcie her baseball cap. 'Something to remember me by.'

'Thanks.'

'No worries. You'll be fine. You escaped being abandoned in the desert, remember. This is nothing.'

Darcie smiled, though she didn't feel very calm knowing she was about to take a step into the unknown. 'Yeah, it'll be a breeze.'

'I'll hold them off for you. Get going,' urged Shelly.

Darcie dropped lightly down on the other side to be caught by Stingo. He passed her a package.

'Your grandfather gave me these for you.'

She glanced into the envelope and saw a passport and a wad of dollars.

'Should get us to . . . well, where is it you want to go?' Stingo asked as he took a quick recce of their surroundings.

'Somewhere quiet, preferably with a beach and no reporters,' said Darcie.

'Let's go then.' Stingo's eyes lit on a motorbike abandoned by one of the outriders who had escorted them to the airfield. The keys were in the ignition as the motorcyclist had joined his colleagues to admire the president's plane.

'Ready?' asked Stingo, tensing for the dash.

'As I'll ever be.'

Suddenly, there was an explosion behind them – a flash of light and a deafening percussive boom. They both instinctively covered their heads. Stingo was the first to get up as sirens wailed around the base.

'You didn't . . .?'

'Perhaps it wasn't such a good idea to leave Shelly and Jon Lee with the stun grenades.' Darcie shivered with nervous excitement: this was it.

Stingo grinned, his face hungry for adventure.

'Then let's make the most of your mistake.' He held out his hand.

Darcie took it.

'One, two, three . . . Run!'

Coming Soon...

DEADLOCK

In hiding in Cornwall, Darcie
Lock thinks she's found the perfect safe
haven – that is until UN peace talks arrive
on her doorstep. But peace is the last thing some
delegates have on their minds. Darcie finds herself
catapulted into the middle of an international
crisis in the unwelcome company
of an old enemy . . .

An adventure-thriller starring Darcie Lock

www.egmont.co.uk
www.juliagolding.co.uk

Now in paperback!

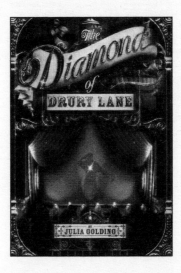

A sparkling mystery set in The Theatre Royal, Covent
Garden, this present day being 1st January 1790.
In which Cat Royal, orphan and ward of the theatre,
stumbles upon a secret . . .
Co-starring Mr Syd Fletcher, leader of the Butcher's Boys.
And Mr Billy 'Boil' Shepherd, evil leader of a rival gang.
And a HIDDEN diamond!

With a new musical interlude by Mr Pedro Hawkins,
late of Africa.

Now in Paperback!

Another thrilling adventure. . . In which Cat must save Pedro from being shipped off to a slave plantation, is obliged to wear the breeches and cap of a boy, and once again comes face to face with her nemesis, the evil *Billy Shepherd*!

Julia Golding

Julia Golding read English at Cambridge then joined the Foreign Office and served in Poland. Her work as a diplomat took her from the high point of town twinning in the Tatra Mountains to the low of inspecting the bottom of a Silesian coal mine.

On leaving Poland, she exchanged diplomacy for academia and took a doctorate in the literature of the English Romantic Period at Oxford. She then joined Oxfam as a lobbyist on conflict issues, campaigning at the UN and with governments to lessen the impact of conflict on civilians living in war zones.

Married with three children, Julia now lives in Oxford. Her first book, *The Diamond of Drury Lane*, won the Nestlé Children's Book Prize and Waterstone's Children's Book Prize, and was shortlisted for the Costa Children's Book Award.

EGMONT PRESS: ETHICAL PUBLISHING

Egmont Press is about turning writers into successful authors and children into passionate readers – producing books that enrich and entertain. As a responsible children's publisher, we go even further, considering the world in which our consumers are growing up.

Safety First
Naturally, all of our books meet legal safety requirements. But we go further than this; every book with play value is tested to the highest standards – if it fails, it's back to the drawing-board.

Made Fairly
We are working to ensure that the workers involved in our supply chain – the people that make our books – are treated with fairness and respect.

Responsible Forestry
We are committed to ensuring all our papers come from environmentally and socially responsible forest sources.

For more information, please visit our website at
www.egmont.co.uk/ethicalpublishing

The Forest Stewardship Council (FSC) is an international, non-governmental organisation dedicated to promoting responsible management of the world's forests. FSC operates a system of forest certification and product labelling that allows consumers to identify wood and wood-based products from well-managed forests.

For more information about the FSC, please visit their website at www.fsc-uk.org